SNAKE EYES

An Abaddon Books™ Publication
www.abaddonbooks.com
abaddon@rebellion.co.uk

First published in 2016 by Abaddon Books™, Rebellion Intellectual
Property Limited, Riverside House, Osney Mead, Oxford, OX2 0ES, UK.

10 9 8 7 6 5 4 3 2 1

Editor-in-Chief: Jonathan Oliver
Commissioning Editor: David Moore
Cover: Clint Langley
Design: Sam Gretton & Oz Osborne
Marketing and PR: Rob Power
Head of Books & Comics: Ben Smith
Creative Director and CEO: Jason Kingsley
Chief Technical Officer: Chris Kingsley

Gods and Monsters™, Abaddon Books and Abaddon Books logo
are trademarks owned or used exclusively by Rebellion Intellectual
Property Limited. The trademarks have been registered or protection
sought in all member states of the European Union and other
countries around the world. All right reserved.

ISBN: 978-1-78108-496-0

Printed in the US

GODS & MONSTERS
SNAKE EYES
HILLARY MONAHAN

ABADDON
BOOKS

*To Mike, who taught me
fun is good and necessary.*

CHAPTER ONE

TANIS HUNTED THE Great White Asshole at Floyd's tavern on the corner of Birch and Promenade. Asshole, also known as Luke Des Moines—like that nice city in Iowa—dressed well: tailored slacks, a button-down shirt. A skinny silver tie and expensive cufflinks with the letters L on his left wrist and DM on his right. His brown hair was slicked back, exposing a pronounced widow's peak and a pair of overly-waxed brows that cast a feminine quality to his slender features.

Tanis would call him handsome if she was into male trade, which she wasn't, and that simplified things because she was going to kill him. Not directly, of course—what would be the point of that?—but she was going to kidnap him, break his legs, and then drag him back to an underground lair so he could be turned into a snake monster and breed with her mother.

No one ever said Tanis Barlas didn't live a complicated life.

TANIS CHEWED ON the end of her cigarette, gazing in at Luke through the front windows of the tavern. The lower panes were dappled with steam in the late Florida spring. She didn't mind the humidity—her snake blood preferred warm climates—but the humans wilted in their sweaty, acrid-smelling meat. Her nostrils flared, besieged by body odor. And smoke. And too-sweet perfume. And the taco stand a block away serving black bean burritos, and the ass-borne catastrophes birthed in their aftermath.

Of all of my mother's gifts. Fuck's sake.

She rubbed her nose like that would do any good.

Luke shifted on his barstool so he could grab a patron's ass as she walked by, a fattish woman in her forties whose red dye job could use a root touchup. She winked at him. He lifted his glass in salute and beckoned her close. A whisper, a caress on her arm, an inviting smile. He'd pocketed his wedding ring, because that was what he did every night between nine and ten.

The behaviors were the same even if the bars changed.

Tanis had watched him for a week, getting to know him and his routines, because that was *her* routine. During the day, Luke was nice as pie to coworkers and clientele at Maverick Motors, an oily prince among men, but the moment his polished shoe crossed the threshold of his two-story Colonial in the suburbs, Ragnarok was unleashed. On his wife. His kids. Punishing words. Punishing blows. After three glasses of cheap scotch, he'd cruise his way to the local bar in search of a pliant woman. If he scored, he'd deliver five disappointing thrusts and a grunt to a fleshy receptacle in the men's room before climbing back into his Lexus with the dealer plates to drive home and sleep it off, spooning the very wife he'd bruised hours ago. Sometimes, if Mrs. Des Moines was really unlucky, he'd flip her on her stomach and have at her, and there wasn't any lube, so she'd wince and bite down on the pillow to stifle her yelps. She knew enough to keep quiet. He'd slap her if she complained.

Tonight looked like one of Luke's lucky nights, the redhead a most-willing rabbit before his slathering, minty-fresh maw. They chatted awhile. He bought her drinks and flirted, his hand creeping along her ample thigh to squeeze and caress and delve. It was eleven when he guided her to the back of the bar, past an ancient cigarette machine that hadn't operated in over a decade so he could kiss her beneath the neon Budweiser sign beside the restrooms.

Tanis lit herself another cigarette and leaned against the streetlamp, idly prying up the edge of the crumbling sidewalk with her alligator-skin cowboy boot. A Rolling Stones T-shirt clung to her sinewy muscle and barely-there curves. Faded jeans hugged an ass that Naree insisted could turn coal into diamonds if Tanis flexed hard enough. Luke would be out in fifteen minutes—twenty if the redhead was lucky. He was a creature of habit.

Unfortunately for him, so was Tanis.

IT STARTED WITH a trip to Walmart of all places, though Tanis could make an argument that a lot of heinous fuckery started and ended in Walmart. The smiling yellow logo invited aggressive bargain-shopping soccer moms *and* meth heads, and nothing good would ever sprout from that combo.

"I'm fucking starving," Naree announced, her hand tugging on the olive green T-shirt with the Army logo across the front. It didn't quite cover her soft belly fat, but Tanis liked the look of Naree's navel tucked between her gentle rolls, so she didn't bother mentioning it. Nor did she mention the way Naree's shorts bit into her pear-shaped ass as she bent over in front of the refrigerator.

For reasons.

"We've got half a jar of Miracle Whip and an eggroll from the Paleolithic age. Let's hit the store."

Tanis tossed aside the leather jacket spread across her knees, a fresh red patch of corduroy sewn onto the elbow. "All right."

"Have we got money?"

Tanis smirked around the unlit cigarette dangling from her bottom lip, reaching into the coat's pocket and producing a man's brown leather wallet. "We've got money."

"That's my girl."

Naree didn't ask questions about the wallet or its previous owner—Nicholas Pope, dead for a month—because she knew she didn't want the answers. That went for a lot of shit in Tanis's stratosphere. Tanis wasn't like other women. That wasn't a coy way of saying she wasn't feminine or didn't adhere to some feminist standard of womanhood; Tanis literally wasn't like other women. Biologically. Naree understood that, had from the first day they met two years ago after a years-long online flirtation. You couldn't apply a human morality to something not human, and while Tanis walked the walk and talked the talk, she was something more. She was *special*. A She-Hulk who could smell a car's exhaust from a mile away. Who could see in the dark, run like a cheetah, and contort her body like she had no bones.

A demigod, just like her hundreds of sisters. And demigods played by their own rules.

"Are we doing full shopping or a snack grab?" Tanis flung the coat onto the green checkered couch. The apartment wasn't much, a four-room affair with a bedroom, a bathroom, an eat-in kitchen, and a living room that doubled as Naree's office, but it was sufficient for their needs. They were in lovely downtown Percy's Pass, in a flat above a small printing press about twenty miles east of the Everglades. The Pass had a whopping population of three thousand, but that was big in comparison to their neighbors. They had a Walmart, a McDonald's, and high-speed internet, and that made them positively urban.

"A little bit of both. I'm not lying. I could eat a horse." Naree slid her feet into a pair of flip-flops, her green sparkle polish glinting in the cheap off-track lighting. "Meet you in the car."

Tanis fished around for her keys and cigarette lighter. Her fingers raked through her hair, trying to flatten it to her head so she looked less like an electrocuted chinchilla. A glance at her reflection in the glass of a picture frame proved it a hopeless venture. She was a light brown girl with crazy black hair and that was the end of it. Fried rodentia was a go.

*   *   *

DOWN THE SQUEALING stairs—especially steps four and eleven on the second flight—through the industrial carpeted foyer, and crunching along the gritty driveway. The car was an old Caddy from the 'eighties, with navy blue paint and leather seats. It wasn't in awful shape, the engine rebuilt from one end to the other, but the dings and scratches on the outside made it look like a shitbox. Tanis didn't mind. The ugliness meant other, more attractive cars ran the risk of being stolen while her breadbox-on-wheels went gleefully unmolested.

She climbed into the driver's side. Naree had already rolled down her window and was using an old copy of *People* magazine to fan her face. Her temples were dotted with sweat, her glossy, black hair tied back in a tight ponytail to keep the weight off her neck. She didn't blend in Percy's Pass. Fat, formerly-Catholic-now-atheist Korean girls with degrees in software engineering from Yale didn't magically appear in Baptist Country, but Naree had been willing to court her family's disdain and give up a great prospective job at IBM to be with Tanis. Tanis told her it wasn't worth it. Naree told her to shut up.

Tanis had shut up mostly because Naree had been kissing her stupid at the time, doing the wiggle wiggle shake that required excessive ass grabbing.

Which is how the two of them had built a life together in Nowhere and were somehow managing to be happy doing it. Even going to Walmart was fun, because Naree was fun. She didn't give much of a damn about what people thought of her queerness, her Korean heritage, her body shape, or her "pinko commie" politics, as she called them. She got looks. She gave looks back. Unfriendlier ones. She was good at putting dissenters in their place. She was better at making Tanis not snap their necks for giving her girlfriend heaps of shit.

"Man. You know those bratwurst with the cheese in the middle? Like, the chemical cheese that tastes like plastic garbage? I want those," Naree announced as the car pulled onto the main drive. The wind rippled through the car, and she threw the magazine in the back seat and reclined, her fingernails raking over the Caddy's felt ceiling. "And lemonade, too."

"Hormonal?" Tanis asked, lighting her cigarette. She was fascinated by the perpetual flux of Naree's body. Her mother's mystical mumbo jumbo had given her hemipenes—just like male snakes. Two functioning cocks instead of one. Tanis was 'blessed' with stacked, double rockets that fired swimless swimmers. And the dicks meant no menstruation. Bleeding from the fun hole looked unfun.

"Yep. I would have skinned a kitten for ice cream last night," Naree said.

"Poor kittens." Tanis pulled the Caddy into the Walmart parking lot and played 'spot the open space' for three rows before Naree pointed out a vacating mini-van, requisite angry mom with four screaming kids scrambling into the cab. Tanis parked and stubbed out her smoke, following Naree toward the double glass doors of the brick building. Naree made straight for the bigger carts, which meant they were going for big game shopping. Good thing Mr. Pope had left them about two-fifty in his wallet. Tanis shoved it at Naree, the crisp bills disappearing into the pocket of her jean cut-offs.

"You've heard that thing: never shop when hungry," Tanis said.

"Never starve your fat girlfriend or she'll eat you," came the sassy reply.

"If I'm lucky."

Naree smirked.

They started in produce, Naree lewdly fondling oranges in her quest for perfect fruit, when a lithe blonde woman turned the corner of the aisle with her cart. She wore a hat and sunglasses above a church revival T-shirt, which wasn't so unusual this close to summer, but when she turned her head, her hair tumbled down her back and away from her face. Tanis caught two things before the woman pulled the heavy curls back over her shoulder and patted them into place. The first was the nasty shiner purpling her left eye, the tender skin swollen, eyeball rimmed red and angry. It was a new hit, not even a day old, with no yellowing along the edges. The second was a cauliflower ear that belonged on a professional boxer, not a woman topping the scales at a hundred and thirty pounds. Not a woman sporting a two carat wedding ring, a Gucci purse, designer sandals and pedicured feet.

She doesn't belong in Walmart. She's hiding here.

Tanis licked her bottom lip and looked away. She didn't want to be caught staring and she was definitely staring. She wished it was something new—a rarity to encounter a woman so fine treated so not-fine—but it was as common as dirt. And every time Tanis heard the story, the last chapter played out the same way.

Monsters for Mother's monstrous appetite.

Monsters for the monster hole!

"Excuse me," the woman said, reaching past Naree for a plastic produce bag, her voice soft, laced with a sugary drawl.

"No problemo." Naree moved aside to let her in next to the bin. Tanis kept glimpsing at the stranger, watching her measured movements, how she flinched away from even the slightest touch with Naree. Her wrist flipped over for a second. Fingerprint bruises on the soft, creamy flesh.

Oh, fuck no.

Tanis reached for a cigarette and remembered where she was. Her fingers twitched. Her eyes slid to Naree. Naree peered at her from beneath a fringe of thick lashes, suddenly solemn with the knowledge that something significant had happened in America's superstore, between the bananas and freshly-misted bunches of kale. Chocolate brown eyes met cold gray ones. Naree nodded once and tied off her bag of oranges before shoving the cart away and into the next aisle, alone.

Tanis hunted.

She maintained a respectable distance throughout the store, not relying on her eyesight to keep tabs on Miss Revival 2015, so much as her sense of smell. The woman wore Chanel #5, washed her clothes in lavender detergent, and was ovulating—all things contributing to her scent. When she pushed her way to the checkout, Tanis slipped into line behind her, a roll of paper towels in hand so she had a reason to be there. She watched the woman pull out her wallet and reach for a shiny silver credit card. That was far less interesting than the license tucked into the top flap, behind a plastic see-through window: Melissa Des Moines, 46 Maple Lane, Percy's Pass. Birthday April 8th.

Tanis abandoned the paper towels and stepped outside for a much-needed smoke. Melissa passed a minute later, bagged goods in hand, beelining for a black Range Rover in the second row. Remembering her license plate wouldn't be hard: it was a vanity plate spelling BR4TTY. She exited the parking lot with an explosive blast of dust and gravel.

Tanis considered the woman and her bruises until she'd smoked her cigarette to the filter. She flicked the butt aside and rejoined Naree in the store, closing in on her just as Naree reached for the economy pack of mac and cheese with the Day-Glo orange sauce packets.

"Verdict?" Naree asked.

"Local," Tanis said.

"Tonight?"

"To start."

And that was all that was said of it. Tanis had a job and that job had to be performed or there'd be hell to pay. One week each month, Tanis traveled around Southern Florida to find what equated to a sacrifice for her mother. At first she'd chosen indiscriminately—drunk college dudebros stumbling back to the dorm, homeless men, anyone stupid enough to pass Tanis by around the third week of the month—but being with Naree so long made it hard not to consider the goodness of the person. The *humanity* of the sacrifice. Naree had quickened the very human-like quality of empathy in Tanis, and while it was a net gain for Tanis as a person, her conscience kicked in after a few hunts. One-night affairs with random snatch-and-grabs were abandoned for due consideration and tactical strikes. Tanis would go to Melissa Des Moines's house and she would learn all she could about Melissa's abuser, and if he was as vile as Tanis suspected, he'd be punished for his crimes.

"Vigilantism," Naree had said once. "Like Batman. Only with more snake."

If that was what got Naree past it, who was Tanis to disagree?

MELISSA 'MISSY' DES MOINES was thirty-four years old with a part-time nanny named Georgette and a fenced-in yard. Affluent neighborhood, a cross on the front lawn lit in such a way that, at night, the Lord rose against the cornflower blue shingles of the house to proclaim His dominion. Ivory columns lined the street-facing façade, supporting a tall black roof with not one but two chimneys, for fires that rarely blazed this far south. Missy's Range Rover occupied the driveway while a navy blue Porsche claimed the left side of the garage. The right was vacant and waiting for Mr. Des Moines's homecoming.

A pool. A hot tub. Three kids enrolled in private school. The veneer was polished, but sooner or later, the rot would manifest, and when it did, Tanis would be watching. She stretched out on her tree branch, a lithe, muscular thing nestled among the green of the giant oak in the front yard of 49 Maple Lane, and then she stilled. Naree called it "reptile-still," when Tanis quieted her body to the point it was hard to tell she was breathing. The only hint of life was the flicker of her eyes, and that came once or twice a minute as the Des Moineses fluttered through their big house with its big furnishings. She was a remarkable predator with a remarkable capacity for patience.

Soon.

Dusk fell. Melissa put away her groceries. The kids sat at the dining room table to do homework and munch on snacks. They seemed happy when it was just the four of them, if a bit muted, but then Luke made his debut, pulling down the street in his sports car with an angry roar of the engine. He didn't bother with the garage, instead stomping his way into the house with a bellowed greeting. The angry shouting started a half-hour later. Night One, there were no strikes, though Luke did throw a dish at the wall when something at dinner wasn't to his liking. He left shortly thereafter and didn't reappear until midnight. Night Two, he grabbed Melissa's hair, yelling at her that she was stupid; when his eldest son tried to intervene, he backhanded him hard enough the kid sprawled out over the back of the couch. Again Luke left for a three-hour block.

The third night, Tanis started following Luke to the bar. She waited in the parked Caddy to see if he'd come, and sure enough, he peeled down the street in his 2016 Lexus Overcompensator at ten. It was easy to slide in behind him and follow him to the Watering Hole. Easy, the next night, to go to Ron & Emma's. Easy the night after that to hit Justine's. She considered snatching him outside of Justine's, especially after the brutal beating he delivered to Melissa before he left for Ron & Emma's and his version of loving sodomy when he returned home, but she gave it one more night to see if there was anything redeemable at all about the son of a bitch. She tailed him to work during the day, searching for a glimmer of goodness, but instead of being swayed by the smiles he levied at coworkers and strangers, she found him all the more repugnant.

When even a snake woman's skin crawls looking at you, something is definitely amiss. Luke Des Moines had written a karmic check his ass was in no way ready to cash.

CHAPTER TWO

HE'S COMING BACK.

Scotch, Luke's fine cologne, latex, and spunk. It wasn't the nicest combination, especially since Tanis couldn't decide if his shoot smelled more like asparagus or bleach. Her own lacked the odor, but his...? Tangy. It was tangy.

I hate the word 'tangy.'

She spit out her dead cigarette, her eyes fixed on the restroom doors inside of the bar. Luke re-emerged ten minutes after his disappearance, the rumpled redhead in tow. She tucked her shirt back into her too-tight jeans, grinning at her lover maybe because she thought the number he gave her was real or maybe because the sink sex had the good grace to be over. Luke murmured to her and made for the bar, grabbing his jacket off the barstool before tossing two twenties onto the counter to cover his tab. The redhead shouted at his back. He didn't turn around.

Tanis oozed from her streetlamp perch to slither up the sidewalk, one boneless, fluid stride bleeding into the next. Floyd's parking lot was up a block from the bar, and unlit;

she could see the silver chrome paint of the Lexus gleaming in the moonlight. She eyed the back left tire, flat thanks to a blade between the rises of the heavy tread, and smiled. She'd expected the alarm to go off when she'd split it hours ago, but no. She'd had to wait around for Luke's skinny ass to do its skinny-ass thing before she could nab him.

Inconvenient, but not insurmountable.

She climbed into the Caddy and pulled out her phone, lifting it to her ear to make it seem like she was talking. Luke may think nothing of the woman in the parking lot six parking spots away, but on the off chance he glanced twice, better to have a plausible cover than not. She turned on the engine and let it idle, her headlights parting the darkness and beckoning an army of moths and mosquitoes. They hovered before her car's massive grill in a roiling cloud of wings, twiggy legs, and furious hissing.

Luke shouldered into his jacket as he approached his car. Ten feet from the back bumper, he spied the damage and stopped. He crouched low, a toady man doing his best toady impression, his handsome looks lost to a bevy of irritation lines.

"Fuck's sake. *Come on.*" He stood, his fingers working the sides of his mouth. He looked between the car's trunk and his cell phone, likely deciding between changing the tire himself or calling roadside assistance at midnight. Tanis would help make the decision for him, because she was a good little Samaritan.

She climbed from the Caddy, one hand resting on her open door, the other waving in front of her mouth to keep the flies away.

"Hey, you need help? I got a jack to change out a spare."

"I... shit. Yeah, alright. Sure."

She popped the trunk to retrieve the metal jack. Her nostrils flared, searching for approaching outsiders, but it was just her and Luke and a vacant parking lot. She kept the trunk open as she neared him, smiling all the while. He searched for a wrench in the Lexus's back so he could loosen the lug nuts. She sidled up beside him, offering the jack. He murmured his thanks.

She struck.

Too fast for him to recoil. Retractable fangs from the roof of her mouth, coursing down, taking him on the side of his neck just below his ear. Curved bone needles stabbed and sliced, splitting his flesh like an overripe peach. Hot copper splashed the insides of her mouth and the white collar of his business shirt before he crumpled to the ground with a yelp, hand smacking at the wound. The venom worked fast. It wasn't like a cobra's venom—it wasn't strong enough to seize his lungs so he'd suffocate—but it did attack his nervous system, his body bucking in the dirt as the poison coursed through his bloodstream, pinging his body's hot spots like a pinball striking the bumpers.

Numbing him. Slowing him.

His heart beat half as fast.

His breaths were shallow gasps.

His pulse thrummed leisurely.

His body went pliant.

Stillness.

Tanis crouched beside him to survey her work. He couldn't roll away even if he wanted to; he was dizzy and nauseated and his eyes swam around in their sockets. The bite on his neck swelled to an egg-sized lump, turning blue near the puncture wounds. If he was allowed to live to the see the morning, he'd recover maybe eighty percent movement. Tanis had seen it before, though not with her own venom. Her sister and friend Bernie—Berenike, actually, but everyone called her Bernie—let one of her tags go once when she discovered he was a father of twelve.

"Guy's got more problems than Ma," she'd said, showing Tanis the roll of school photos in the guy's wallet. "Letting him live is the bigger punishment."

They'd released the man along the side of the road outside of his hometown. He walked slower, reacted more sluggishly, and appeared photosensitive, but he still had his life, which was more than most who were bitten by a lamia ever got.

Tanis never let anyone go.

Luke Des Moines was fucked. He groaned as she closed the trunk of his car, his wrench tucked into the back pocket of her jeans. He gurgled as she looped her hands around his ankles and dragged him to the Caddy. He squeaked as she patted him down, pulling out his wallet and handgun and pocketing his cufflinks and wedding ring. Somehow, through sheer will or dumb fuck luck, he managed to get his eyes to focus on her, mouth opening, a torrent of spittle cascading down his cheek to sully his jacket collar. Tanis grabbed the wrench and flipped it around in her palm.

"Sorry," she said, not sorry.

She brought it down twice on each knee, ignoring the wet cracking sounds and Luke's muted screams.

"You MAY BE asking what you're doing in the trunk of a 1986 Cadillac." Tanis sucked on her cigarette, peering into the depths of the car. She'd parked on a spindly side road, off a dirt road, off another dirt road that was a mile away from an actual paved road that was ten miles away from the nearest street light. Des Moines looked pale, and he'd drooled a whole hell of a lot more during the thirty-minute drive into the Glades. There was a lake of spit beside his head, mucking up his hair, his jacket, her interior. The last wasn't such a big deal—she'd had worse back there. One guy she'd pinched had eaten an entire pizza before she bit him and spewed it all over the place on the bumpy back roads. Luke's saliva farm was no big doings next to a cubic assload of demi-processed tomato and cheese.

"Well, Luke. Can I call you Luke? I'm going to." She reached into the trunk to grab him around the waist and heave him over her shoulder, fireman-style. Every part of him flopped around uselessly, his legs at odd angles thanks to his broken knees, his head a heavy bowling ball atop his spindly neck. His arms were lead weights dangling from his shoulders and struck the backs of her thighs with each step.

Tanis walked a familiar path, her boots snapping twigs and crunching leaves as she crossed the thick, rotting undergrowth.

"We're in Adder's Den. It used to have another name, but no one remembers it anymore. We fled here from Argentina, after most of us were wiped out." Tanis ducked under a thick vine connecting two tall trees that stretched toward the night sky. Her pupils were dilated, the moonlight reflecting yellow off her eyes. Like most snakes, she saw better at night than during the day, an extra lens showing her a spectrum of blue and black shades humans couldn't see. She also had heat vision; the crickets on the blades of grass were ectoplasm-colored green blobs peppering the landscape. "Back in the 'forties and 'fifties, it was a small town, maybe only a few hundred folks, but when it got too hard to keep the Glades out, they abandoned it. Moved to places more people-friendly and less gator-friendly. Can't say I blame them. Gators grow big around here. Ten feet, easy."

Tanis sucked another torrent of smoke into her lungs. "We didn't care much for the above-ground structures, as you'll see. But the pipe system below? Invaluable. We had to hide, Luke. Because we're not like normal people. We're not *people* at all."

She stopped at the edge of town. The dilapidated buildings cut a jagged line against the horizon; caved-in roofs of what had been homes and small stores formed a menacing monolith atop the soggy ground. It had been a circle once, but the swamp had claimed the northern part for itself with shrubs, vines, tall grasses, and shallow water. At the center, an old flagpole stretched for the cloudless sky, the tattered remains of a pair of pants or a shirt or some inane thing that had been tied up there as a joke by one of Tanis's sisters rustling with the breeze. The ground was littered with rusted-out tires and abandoned scraps of metal. A truck worn down to its frame languished between two of the broken buildings, moss creeping over the emaciated carcass of the undercarriage.

It smelled sour, like urine, but there was the sweetness of decay, too, thanks to the pulpy, water-beaten foundations infested with nesting insects.

Tanis adjusted her grip on Luke's waist and pressed onward.

"We're lamias. That might not mean anything to you. It doesn't to most people. They sure as shit remember Medusa with the snakes on her head—and fuck Gorgons forever, the homicidal bitches—but not the woman Hera turned into a snake monster. See, Lamia was one of Zeus's favorite women. Dark hair, golden skin, chocolate eyes. Typical Greek beauty, really. And Hera was the jealous type." Tanis walked toward the last building on the right, with the doors sagging on the hinges. "Finding out Zeus had a family with Lamia, a couple of kids and a love shack, Hera cursed Lamia. Lamia's upper half remained human-ish, but her bottom half? All snake. Hera also cursed her with a huge appetite and the inability to blink. You might not think those two things are related, but they are, because Lamia in her insatiable hunger devoured her own children. She couldn't help it, and because she couldn't blink, she witnessed the whole damned thing. Have you ever seen snakes feed? It's not bloody. It's more 'squeeze 'em 'til they stop kickin' and gulp 'em whole.' Which she did, and then she mourned because she knew eating her kids was wrong but she couldn't help herself.

"Zeus felt sorry for her, for all the good that did." Tanis pulled open the door, the rusted metal screeching its displeasure at being moved. She spit the remnants of her smoke in a bucket placed under a leak in the moldering roof. "He allowed her to take out her eyes when she wanted to. She became like the Fates that way—a prophet when they were outside of her head. She could see all."

Tanis's eyes adjusted as she ventured further into what had, at one time, been a house, but had been repurposed to a sentry shed. It should have collapsed long ago, but the wood was reinforced from the inside with fresh boards to keep it standing, because it was one of the few entrances into the underground tunnels and required preservation. The water pipe system had never been fully fleshed out, the town abandoned long before it came to that, but they'd gotten a good start on it when there'd still been enthusiasm for construction, and what they hadn't finished, they'd furnished supplies for. The townsmen hadn't bothered moving the hulking pipes when they cleared out. When the lamias moved in, they dug the trenches and laid the steel pipes themselves, creating a proper subterranean network.

The boards beneath Tanis's boots squealed as she carried Luke through the house and to the back stairs leading down into the basement. Two figures were seated at a small table with a lantern at the middle, playing cards clasped in their hands. The woman on the left was Sibylla, who everyone called Fi for some reason, and she was such a behemoth no one dared question her about anything. Dark hair worn spiky short, dark tan face, golden eyes cutting through the blackness. She was six feet of straight muscle, thick enough to nearly fill a doorway, and she tended to show off her bulging biceps with simple white tank tops tucked into simpler blue jeans. Like Tanis, she wore cowboy boots. Unlike Tanis, she had brown snake scales over the backs of her arms, and where they'd ended at her elbows, she'd gotten tattoos to continue the pattern up to her shoulders.

The woman on the right was less Everest and more Bunker Hill: Bernie. She tilted her head to smile at Tanis. Lots of teeth, too many teeth, like a piranha, with pale skin, gray hair tugged back into an efficient ponytail that ended just past her shoulders, and eyes that were, in daylight, nearly black. At night, they were as golden as Tanis and Fi's. She was older than Tanis, over sixty and maybe closer to seventy, though she'd never said for sure, with skin so weathered it looked like a topographical map.

Lamia living was hard living.

"Uh-oh. S'breedin' time," Bernie said, slapping her cards on the table. Fi grunted at having to wait to take a turn, but she found solace in the mason jar of moonshine she'd brewed herself. Tanis had made the unfortunate mistake of sampling her milk-bucket booze once and determined, after one sip, that drinking gasoline was not actually part of her repertoire.

Bernie walked around Tanis to inspect the grab, her track pants swishing with each step, her sneakers a Day-Glo pink that matched the print on her black gym T-shirt. She picked up Luke's hand, eyed it, and snorted. "Pretty boy gets his nails done? Really? Ma'll like him." Bernie had a voice like liquid sugar, just enough rasp and music to it you knew if she broke into song, it'd be prettier than a lark.

Tanis had yet to hear her sing. Whenever she asked, Bernie shrugged her off with a strange little smile.

"Yeah, she will."

Luke groaned. A gob of spit took the open-mouthed opportunity to plummet to the floor and spatter.

Bernie biffed him upside the head. "What's his deal?"

"Beating the shit out of his wife and kids. Rape. Being a dickwad. You know, the usual."

"Ooooh. Welp. I'd say you're going to a better place, boyo, but Ma's gonna use you up and send you to Hell." Bernie clapped him on the back with an "Atta boy" before slinging herself back into her rickety chair. "She's in a mood, Tan. Keep your head down, yeah?" She tossed her head, showing off the impressive blue-green scales glimmering along the back of her neck.

"When's she *not* in a mood?"

Fi's answer to that was to grunt, which Tanis took for solidarity. "Good to see you, too, Fi." Tanis lifted the bulkhead door into the tunnels. It was a ten-foot drop to the bottom of the pipe; there was a rusty metal ladder on the left if she wanted it, but carrying Luke, it was easier to jump. She bent her knees and leaped, her boots clanging against metal and kicking up water on impact.

Halogen lamps peppered the main pipeline, strung from the makeshift ceiling with wire and run by generators. It wasn't a lot of light, but it was enough for her to see thirty feet before her, thirty feet behind, and various shorter pipelines jutting off to the sides where the lamia had set up tables, bunks, and in some cases, tents for sleeping. It was an underground village— and evil lair, she'd once told Naree—where the lamia could safely exist.

For a while, Tanis had grown up in the darkness, among the other daughters, toiling while their kind fought for survival.

Lamia wasn't born snake: her transformation was the result of a goddess's curse. As such, making more like herself required effort—magic and human sacrifice, mostly. For reasons no one completely understood, the combination of Lamia and snake-blessed human produced no viable sperm in those daughters with penises, nor had it ever in thousands of years. Hence the kidnappings.

Hence Lamia's disdain of Tanis and all like her.

Lamia played favorites with her three types of children. Her darlings were those she called her "True Daughters." They were considered superior to all other offspring, as they were capable of reproduction. There were only eleven total, eight adults and three juveniles, each of the girls shaped like Lamia herself, with human tops and coils of snake below. While Lamia bred monthly, her brood gestating in three days, the True Daughters only mated once a year, in the spring, and it took them ninety days to lay their eggs. Each breeding was another opportunity for more 'true' lamias, but rarely, if ever, did it work out. True Daughters were present in all clutches, but they didn't thrive. Magically manufactured fathers meant a weaker strain of lamia, and a lot could and did go wrong, babies never breaking from the eggs or dying in their youth due to frailty. Sometimes, though, one would be perfect and, as such, exalted.

They were terribly spoiled, given pretty baubles and luxuries Lamia's other get would never see. Their two birthing chambers, flanking Lamia's own, had lush beds with velvet comforters, silk drapes along the walls, and stacks of pillows. They were given makeup and perfume and all manner of glittery things. Hell, they even had televisions hooked up to generators, kept entertained by video games and DVDs that no one else was allowed to go near, for fear of Lamia's wrath.

The second type of daughter, and by far the most common, were pure serpents. Ten to fourteen feet long, as thick around as Tanis's thigh, constrictors, all female—they didn't do Lamia a whole of a lot of good beyond keeping the cave free of rodents, but Lamia had a soft spot for them all the same.

They thrived even before they were released on the Glades, an unnatural predator in a luckless ecosystem. For a while, their population was kept in check by the gators, but then Florida residents began releasing unwanted pet pythons into the swamp. Lamia's snakes bred with the male pythons, producing an army of mammoth serpents, and now a few types of birds were in danger of extinction and the humans had annual snake hunts to combat the growing threat.

They weren't winning. They had no idea how far the snakes' reach was.

The last of Lamia's get was Tanis's kind: the humanoids. Lamia hated humans and held them responsible for the weakness of her line, so to see her own children look like them didn't make for a happy queen. These daughters were a wide and varied bunch, some sporting buxom, curvy shapes while others were more athletic and narrow. Some had vaginas but they weren't capable of carrying children or eggs to term, for the same reason most True Daughters didn't live: genetic variance between snake and human was too disparate. Others were born with a penis—or, as in Tanis's case, double penises like snakes had—but while many of them could maintain erections and ejaculate, they too were sterile.

The humanoids were far less common than the snake spawn, but far more common than the True Daughters; there were three hundred total, and Lamia loathed them all. It didn't matter that without them, neither Lamia nor her True Daughters would have food, luxuries, or mates. It didn't matter that the humanoids were the soldiers when the Den was in peril. They were, in Lamia's words, "two-legged, pig-fleshed wastes."

If Tanis could muster anything other than weary resignation regarding her mother, it might have hurt her feelings.

Tanis ventured down the pipeline, hopping over juvenile snakes. To her left, a half-dozen biped sisters crouched around a large cooking pot on a fire, weenies on sticks poised over the heat. Some waved to her, some didn't, but she spared them a nod all the same, only knowing some of their names. When an enormous snake rose up from the shallow water to snap at her, rearing toward Luke's head, he managed a moan and a twitch, one of his mangled legs kicking out and birthing a second whimper.

The venom's weakening.

"Don't be overeager, buddy. This doesn't get any easier from here on out."

Past an offshoot that led into one of the two True Daughters' chambers and then to the main birthing chamber. The entrance was twelve feet in diameter, two privacy screens side-by-side demanding a full stop. Kallie, a six-and-a-half-foot-tall humanoid lamia tolerated slightly more than the rest if only because Kallie was better at kissing ass than most, stood guard by the door.

"Yesss?" she asked, tilting her head Tanis's way. She had bulging eyes, snake eyes, in her otherwise human face, her irises tiny slivers in shining green orbs. Her head was covered in spiky blond hair. Her ears were pierced from lobe all the way up to the tippy top of her cartilage with glinting steel barbells.

"Cut the shit, Kallie. You know why I'm here."

"Mmm." Kallie gave Luke a once-over and stepped aside. Tanis pulled Luke from over her shoulder to carry him in front of her body, his head lolling back and making him look like the damsel at the mercy of the horror-movie monster. Tanis was reminded of Dracula with his prey, or maybe that iconic film still of the Creature from the Black Lagoon with the passed-out brunette drizzled across his arms.

"Do you believe in monsters, Luke?" He didn't answer, but she hadn't expected him to—not with a tongue so swollen it made his cheeks bulge. She rolled him forward, angling him so his face pressed into her chest, like an overgrown baby in a freakishly strong mother's arms. Tanis juggled his weight and walked forward, sucking in a deep, deep breath. "'Cause if you didn't before, you're about to."

CHAPTER THREE

TANIS WALKED THE long passage to the main birthing den, as taut as a wire spring. The Den's mingled stench enfolded her: the urine, the wet, watery, mildewy smell, the rot of death. Previous half-devoured feeds added a sickeningly sweet, meaty stench to the place. Feces, the musk of Lamia's terrified paramours, eggs that wouldn't hatch—Lamia was protective of her space and only subjected herself to chamber cleanings twice a month or so. A lot of decay could happen in a few weeks. Tanis had seen the cleaning crew going in before with wheelbarrows, contractor bags, and industrial bleach. Their efforts helped a little, but not a lot.

It seemed they were overdue for a visit.

A few steps more. Tanis cringed, stopping just outside of Lamia's room. The scents pervaded, awful still, but that wasn't what gave her pause. No, it was the pheromones; oh, the pheromones. Lamia's den telegraphed her readiness to breed. It was faint on the air outside of her chamber, faint enough Tanis could handle it without consequence, but the closer she got to the actual room, the stronger it grew. Cloyingly sweet, like cotton candy and Sweet'n Low packets and honey all in one. There was no other smell like it. It was chemical sex that prodded Tanis's reptilian side and coaxed it forth. She didn't want to react, but she couldn't help herself, her cocks thickening inside her pants because, biologically, this was a thing that called to her, calling her to a base function she couldn't actually perform.

Tanis would have rather sawed off her dicks than to ever consider coupling with the mother who'd kicked her out at seventeen because, "Looking at human meat makes me sick."

Fuck's sake. Get a hold of yourself.

From the darkness, "I smell you. What have you brought me?"

Lamia's voice was dry, like gravel scratching over pavement, or two pieces of sandpaper rubbing together. She spoke the old tongue, the home tongue, that Tanis had learned first; she only picked up the English language of the local humans at six or seven, under Barbara, an elder humanoid's, tutelage.

"Your offering, Mother," Tanis replied in kind.

"Bring it."

Tanis gulped air through her mouth, refusing to inhale any more of what, to her human parts, was a rank, disgusting stench, but was to her reptile brain a liquid invitation. It was there, in her head no matter what, but her human blood buffered it enough that breathing through her mouth made it tolerable. She stepped forward. The main chamber was dark near the tunnel entrance, but at the back, forty feet away, two overhead saucer lights were suspended from wires. Centered beneath them were king-size mattresses, four of them, stacked in two layers and covered with rumpled blankets and pillows. Comforters, mostly, to keep the queen warm when it was chilliest, but the cold season was behind them and Lamia would be quite content in the jockstrap humidity of Florida's Deep South spring.

The mattresses were empty.

Tanis walked. Rustling to her left, the sound of hand-sized scales dragging over the floor. The matron's chamber was a dug-out cave, the floor and walls lined with flat slabs of granite, the crevices between patched with cement. If you got close enough, you could see the handprints of the humanoid daughters who'd labored to build this place for their mother despite her disdain. They'd erected a steel beam ceiling, over which they'd laid more stones, exposed to the sun. Above ground, they looked like boulders poking up from too-tall grass, but they acted as a primitive sort of heating system: when the stone warmed, so did the birthing chamber hidden below.

Luke whimpered against Tanis's chest. Either the room's smell or the slithering sounds kicked his terror into high gear, because his bladder let go, piss raining rampant over Tanis's T-shirt and jeans.

"God fucking damn it!" she barked, dropping him to the floor. He landed with a thud and a groan. Tanis paid him little mind, tearing off her shirt and using the dry parts to dash at her pants. The backhand shouldn't have surprised her; Lamia careened at her, closing the gap between them faster than Tanis could blink. Tanis's feet left the floor with the smack, her back striking the wall ten feet away before she crumpled.

The queen snake's strength was unmatched among her daughters. She was nine feet tall and nearly as wide, her upper half a pale, bluish blob of white skin and pulsing veins and rolls upon rolls of grayish fat. She'd been denied sunlight for decades, and her pallor showed it, the skin stretched thin over her breeder-thick corpulence. Her pendulous breasts hung past her waist, where the scales met the human skin, nipples large and brown and pointed at the floor, the ends beaded with a milk no snake child would ever drink, not even the humanoids who could benefit from the nourishment. Her face, once fabled to rival Aphrodite herself, was a pair of yellow eyes and flaring nostrils with a too-wide mouth that reminded Tanis of a guppy. Her hair was a matted tangle of thick, ropey locks that dragged on the floor, each cluster held together by dirt, blood, and other unsanitary bodily fluids.

The rest of her was snake. All snake. Yards of snake, that could raise her three to four extra feet as needed, the thickest part rivaling a tree trunk or, perhaps, two tree trunks. Her scales were rum-colored with gold stripes at the bottom, so brightly yellow they looked like they'd been dipped in twenty-four karat.

Catching a breath wasn't easy. Tanis *oomphed* and held her guts, wheezing, every hard nub of the rock wall imprinted into her back by the force of the collision. Once, when she'd been a teenager, she'd been thrown off a dirt bike and rolled across the sun-scorched Florida pavement, scouring off the top layer of skin on her biceps and hips. The effect of Lamia's blow felt like that.

She'd be bruised in the morning.

"How dare you? He is my darling, my consort, my prince! Useless swine daughter. I should have devoured you."

That Luke Des Moines could be referred to as anything precious after the shit he'd pulled on his wife was reprehensible. That Lamia said it about a human when she had humanish children she abhorred? Vile. But Tanis wasn't brave enough to say it, instead picking herself up off of the floor, her body a throbbing, stinging mess. Lamia collected the heap of man before her, his body dwarfed by her gripping coils. She flipped him about so he faced her monstrousness, looming over him as she inspected his fine features, a taloned finger with swollen blue joints tracing his patrician nose and pretty mouth.

"You've done well, pig. I'll give you that."

Tanis didn't reply; a reply invited attention, and attention was not a thing she wanted, not so soon after upsetting her mother. Lamia slithered across the ground, Luke still in her grasp, the man mewling as he was deposited in the queen's nest of blankets and pillows, all undoubtedly smelling of her mating-time secretions. In a way, Tanis was thankful for her mother's punishment; it'd quelled the straining ardor inside her boxer briefs.

"You will stay," Lamia demanded, looking at Luke but talking to Tanis. Sometimes, Lamia wanted privacy as she 'romanced' her consorts, but there'd been enough incidents of the chosen male dying mid-transformation and Lamia needing a posthaste replacement, that sending Tanis away didn't behoove either of them. If Luke croaked before he could spunk up the snake queen, Tanis would be out hunting again, and as much as she didn't like the old stranger snatch-and-grab, she wasn't above saving her own hide and blind-picking a male sacrifice.

Sorry, Naree. Batman I am not.

Tanis sank back to the floor to become a thing best forgotten, not wanting to behold her mother doing her most-terrible deed, but really having no choice. Besides, Tanis had seen it all before, too many times to count, and she'd become desensitized. This was her job. She was, for better or worse, Lamia's personal hunter. Others served the daughters, others were maintenance or sanitation or food scavengers, but Tanis had drawn the short straw. She was responsible for collecting her mother's playdates.

E-harmony, Match.com, and OkCupid done up lamia-style, in one fine, muscular body.

Tanis slapped at her jeans pockets but remembered too late she'd left her cigarettes in the Caddy. There'd be nothing to distract her from the fucked-up foray going on a couple dozen feet away. Lamia stroked her hands over Luke's body while the man muffle-shrieked, his back bowing as Tanis's weak toxin lost its thrall. Lamia looped one of those razory claws into his belt. She plucked at it, delicate, like it was a harp string, and the thick leather snapped. The pants were next, Lamia cooing as she delicately serrated them at the seams to expose long, furry man legs. Socks and shoes, thrown aside. His shirt, gone, his gray boxer briefs with the black waistband removed because, Tanis knew, they'd tear.

That's what the transformation did. It took two legs and made them one. And then it made no legs at all.

Luke's breaths were rapid gasps and his moans became louder. Lamia didn't care, not as she picked him up and crushed him to her too-warm flesh, his face forced into the side of a basketball-sized breast.

"Don't cry. Don't cry, little thing. I will make you perfect. I'll immortalize you," the queen crooned right before dropping her head, her knotted hair plummeting past his shoulder like the vilest of mantles. She whispered to him, something soft, before plunging her fangs into his shoulder, not very far from the still-swollen mark Tanis herself had made. His body jolted in her grasp, lightning striking twice, the queen's venom surging through his veins. If left unattended, it would kill him, crushing him from the inside as his lungs collapsed, but Lamia had learned a thing or two from her own curse, of how to manipulate the magic that made her existence possible, and with a few uttered words, the venom inside of Luke Des Moines quickened.

Tanis watched. Waited. It was always the same. Luke's nude body went from a slab of meat to a slab of glowing meat, the lamia poison inside of him whizzing through every vein and capillary and glowing green with magic. He was illuminated from the inside, his heart visible inside of his chest, behind his ribs, the strong organ pounding faster and faster as he succumbed. His fingers splayed, his toes stretched out from his feet. All of his muscles flexed at once, his head snapping upright from a lolling, useless weight on his neck, too aware, his eyes bulging from the sockets, his mouth agape with silent screams.

Lamia's hands fell away from him, letting the human drop back onto her blankets. He thrashed atop them, body convulsing and tangling in the queen's soiled sheets. Tanis watched Luke's heart as she knew her mother did, waiting for it to either erupt from the magic building inside of him or to 'swim' inside of his ribcage. Snakes had mobile hearts to make way for large, swallowed prey. Luke would be the same when he was through with his transformation.

If he survived.

It was looking good, by whatever definition of good was at play. Luke's heart slowed and changed position, suggesting that his torso had begun to elongate. It was easier to tell when the men were in their clothes still—seams would rip and burst a la Bruce Banner to the Incredible Hulk—but Lamia'd stripped him raw and so it was harder to gauge where they were at. It'd get much more obvious soon, after...

SNAP. SNAP. SNAP.

That. His bones were breaking. Luke started screaming, real screams that broke through the poison in his system, as his vertebrae pulled apart, his whole body stretched out taffy-like. His legs popped from their joints at his hips, his pelvis cracking to bits that would dissolve inside of the thick flesh forming to fill the new space. His skin rippled like something was trying to claw its way out, but it was the magic, pushing. Kneading. Forcing his body into acquiescence. The skin on his legs grew translucent, the veins inside rewiring themselves to make way for what came next.

The worst part, really, for him.

It started with his penis. Tanis described it to Naree as a banana peel falling off the fruit once, and that was somewhat right, but it was only the first step. His cock glowed red, like an iron left in a blacksmith's fire too long, and then the outside sloughed off, but it didn't exactly fall away. It more coalesced in wait as his midsection, from bellybutton to knees, narrowed. Men usually didn't have much in the way of hips or asses, but the snake had even less, and the fat stores from his buttocks shifted and spread, wrapping around his legs like a meaty blanket.

Still Luke screamed, but, Tanis supposed, she would, too, if her legs were fusing. Luke's bottom half was gone to jelly, his femurs no longer separated as they'd been when he'd walked on two legs, but clumped together and held by burgeoning coils of muscle. The knees did the same, followed by the tibia and fibula. There were more crackling sounds as his foot bones crunched down and tapered, Lamia's rippling magic pulling his body as long as it would go and then forcing it to grow beyond that.

Jelly legs became jelly not-legs. They became yards of translucent snake, still glowing thanks to the green veins inside, still pulsing as the muscles finished forming so they could support his human torso. Six feet of human male had become eight feet of man-snake, the shed skin from his penis finally collecting itself together and forming a second penis, right next to the first one, both glowing red, both turgid with magic and resembling mushrooms on long, pink stems. They weren't inside a cloaca yet, because his body was still forming it, creating a chamber in his new snake tail that would excrete his body's waste and hold his peni inside until it was time to mate.

Tanis watched with disinterest as both cocks sunk into his blob of snake flesh like they'd been sucked under by quicksand.

Luke flopped around on the bed, trying to move, but he was still too fragile, and so the looming queen put her hand on his stomach to hold him while the last effects bore down on him. His lower snake skin cracked, each fissure lit from the inside, before a thousand tiny cuts burst open with sharp, fresh scales, as clear as the rest of his twisting flesh. They'd wear down to smooth curves given time to rub against things, but he'd never get that time. Lamia'd yet to have one of her consorts not go mad with the utter disintegration of his former self, which had to do with the magic and the violence of the snake half's growth, yes, but there was also the chemical onslaught to consider.

The magic worked its way up. This torso was narrower than before, the ribs tapering down to the waist where his scales started, the heart not so much to the left anymore as the right. Shoulders and arms, intact, as was his neck, but his jaw, gaping wide with his shrieking and nonsensical pleading, cracked away from the skull, like an invisible hand had reached into his mouth and jerked it down beyond normal limitations. His tongue divided, left and right side writhing as if they couldn't coexist inside of their shared space without quarrel.

Luke drooled and whimpered, bloody tendrils coursing over his cheeks, neck, and chest. His jaw reattached, but further back, toward his neck, granting him a severe overbite. It allowed for his human canines to tear from their sockets so new fangs—curved ones, delicate ones that would administer poison in times of duress—could erupt from his tender, bleeding gums.

"That's it, darling, that's it. Come to me," Lamia crooned, stroking one of her claws down his cheek. Luke's eyes rolled into his head as the cartilage of his nose cracked and, much like his cocks, receded into his greater self, his nostrils wide, flat vents against his tan skin. His brow hair fell out, followed by his head hair and any other body hair, leaving him smooth all over save for the bumpy texture of his virgin scales. Another crack, and the front of his skull sloped backward, like someone had brought a shovel down on his head, the bones near his now-bald temples disintegrating so he became less rounded on top and more flat and sleek. His brain, once a three-pound mass of human hopes and dreams and cruelties, became three pounds of base, snake instinct.

That was where the madness crept in. Luke the person was all but dead, in the presence of primal urges that could not and would not be denied.

Hunting and fucking, respectively.

Luke, or whatever was left of him, collapsed into the queen's blankets with a sound that was more hiss than scream. The glowing from inside of his body subsided. He was, for all intents and purposes, see-through from the hips down, no color to his scales, though the varying textures and layers made it hard to discern the details.

Like the textured glass on one of those sliding shower doors. You can see the person showering inside, but not get a clear picture.

Fuck, I need a shower. I smell like piss.

And I really wish I had a smoke.

Tanis pushed herself up from her seat on the floor and beat the dust from the ass of her jeans, her back screeching in protest. If she was lucky, it was just scrapes and abrasions that'd go away overnight. If she was unlucky, she had actual cuts that'd need attending and they'd ache for a few days.

"Am I done?"

It was directed at Lamia, but Luke was the one to respond. Sensing something present in the chamber, something beyond what, perhaps, his addled snake brain already accepted as his mate, Luke groaned and growled, flopping around on the mattresses before he rolled onto the hard stone floor. Lamia allowed it, watching curiously. He lifted his head to regard

Tanis across the room, his tongue dangling from his mouth. He hadn't quite figured out the flicking in-and-out trick to tracking, where he ought to bring the tongue back into his mouth to better gather the smells to his new and improved scent glands, and so he let it loll.

Then he crawled, heaving himself along with the power of his arms.

His body wasn't ready for upright movement, his lower half too new and too fresh to support him, nor was his skin ready for the rock he raked against. It shredded at him, prying fragile scales away from more-fragile flesh, but he didn't care. He was too intent on Tanis, his eyes big and bulging, a gurgled half-scream of rage bursting from his throat. He was a mindless thing to his needs, which, in this case, was hunger. She'd become food, the abuse he inflicted upon his fresh-born body secondary to his desire for feeding. Tanis knew, if she didn't serve an immediate purpose to the queen, Lamia would have let him have her, but before he got too far, the queen looped him up into her coils and hauled him back toward the beds.

"Don't harm yourself, love. My love. My sweet thing."

Luke whipped his head around, at first eyeing the much-larger female lamia with hostility that she'd interrupted the least effectual hunt ever, but then she lifted her tail tip to him and ran it over his face. Pheromones, her sexual invitation presented so close to his nose, so immediately, he wouldn't be able to ignore it. Her stench pervaded the Den, yes, but Luke was still addled and adjusting to his monstrousness. So forcibly presented, however, he couldn't ignore it no matter how much his belly pleaded for sustenance.

He bumped his head against one of Lamia's milk-swollen, white udders. She pressed his face in close, rubbing her tail against his tail. Insistence. Distraction. Luke's own tail rose, weak still, but not so weak he couldn't wrap himself around her, writhing against her and growling. His face nuzzled at her, tongue careening over the soiled valleys between the queen snake's rolls of fat. He didn't mind the dirt or the grime; he was there for a singular purpose.

Tanis spied an angry, pink-red presence sliding out of his cloaca.

When there was dick involved, and it wasn't hers, she was out.

Lamia didn't comment on Tanis's escape, instead presenting herself for the mating. Luke would inseminate her once with one cock before going at her with the second. Each crotch rocket had its own seed basket, his testicles 'dividing' to provide sperm to the separate peni. Tanis didn't work the same way—she had a two-for one special when she came—but she and Naree had figured out how to keep it clean.

Cleanish. Unless they didn't want it clean.

Naree.

The idea of a soft, loving woman who didn't smell like Lamia's death-and-fuck prison, who would, at no time ever in her life, be able to unhinge her jaw to swallow Luke Des Moines whole, was nice. Tanis two-timed it from the Den, nearly running her way down the tunnel of the queen's chamber, past Kallie, past her snakier-looking sisters in their hovels, and toward the ladder that'd release her on the Den. Ten minutes. That's how long it would take to get back to the Caddy at a good sprint. That's how long it'd take to get that much-needed smoke.

That's how long it'd take her to get on the road so she could see the one thing in the world she actually loved.

Anywhere but here. ANYWHERE but here.

CHAPTER FOUR

THE DRIVES BACK to Percy's Pass were always thinkfests. Maybe Luke's frailty in the face of her demigod mother afflicted her with existential crisis by proxy. Maybe it was the easy thrum of the Caddy's engine lulling her. Whatever the case, Tanis couldn't escape the tangle of her thoughts. The radio would have been a nice distraction, but station roulette had proved time and time again the only music she'd get in that part of the swamp was the praise-Jesus gospel hour, a few local nutjobs reporting on their UFO sightings, or old time country music. Tanis couldn't abide the first two, but she was fine with the last. George Jones, Loretta Lynn, Conway Twitty. All had a place in her heart, but unfortunately, the reception wasn't good, and white noise ruining "He Stopped Loving Her Today" couldn't be abided.

She took a deep breath. Fresh, above-ground air. Water from the Glades. Pavement, which did have a smell no matter what humans thought; green growth. The ghost of her last cigarette.

So much better than home.

Were the sewers home? Not really. Not anymore, nor had

they been since she was seventeen. Too-human lamias were kicked out of the Den as soon as they were deemed 'old enough' which was an arbitrary, sliding scale based on how quickly the daughters physically matured. In Tanis's case, seventeen. Barbara, the denmother, had given her two hundred dollars and a backpack full of clothes before showing her out on a Tuesday morning.

"I'm sorry," was all she said. She didn't want to see Tanis go—she didn't want to see any of her "babies" go, as she called them—but it was the law of the land. Lamia wouldn't be surrounded by the pink skins anymore than she had to be. Humanoids like Barbara, covered in green scales, with a sloping head and a thin sliver of pupil? Fine. But Tanis, Bernie—Hell, even Fi who had scales on her arms and legs but not on her face—were sent away.

It should have been a freedom; the Den was a hostile, sad place where the bipeds made do with too little food and fewer supplies. But it wasn't, not really. Even if the girls forged better lives elsewhere, they were expected to keep close to the Den wherever they landed. The lamia, not Lamia herself but the people that were lamia, would perish without their cooperation.

Tanis wasn't sure then, or now, that was such a bad thing.

Barbara had prepared Tanis as best she could for their world, instructing her on how money, clothing, language, sex, and everything else worked, but it never felt sufficient, not when Tanis was in the tunnels, and certainly not when she was out in the human towns. "You'll be fine. You're just like any other snake having to adapt to a new habitat after a den's destruction," Barbara had insisted. Except that wasn't really Tanis's circumstance. A den's destruction was predator-born. Tanis's abolishment was because she wasn't what her mother wanted her to be. She'd been rejected by the one person everyone should be able to count on for affection and acceptance.

It hadn't been fair, and it didn't get fair until Tanis walked into Percy's Pass and was taken in by other, ostracized lamia, the denmother a big-hearted, butchy woman with dark skin, dark hair, and dark eyes named Gaia. She was the ringleader of the lesser, the broken, the unimportant; although, Tanis quickly realized under Gaia's tutelage, they were the building blocks of their small society. The Den couldn't operate without them. The humanoid lamias were accepted among the humans, and the lamia could reap the humans for all they needed to survive. Lamia made excellent thieves. Fast, quick, strong—they could get in and get out of tight spaces without detection, stealing what they needed to get by. They made great laborers, too, excelling at factory work that required precision and speed. They took jobs in lumberyards and junkyards because they could haul extra weight. They were great in warehouses and often opted for overnight shifts in security or stocking shelves in stores because they liked night hours. The fewer people to see them and maybe catch a glimpse of scales or a forked tongue or whatever other gifts their snake blood bestowed upon them? The better.

And the lack of a social security number wasn't as big of a problem as most would think. Local businesses didn't mind under-the-table. Less overhead for them, lower pay for the lamia. Gaia hooked Tanis up with a job and a half-dozen more like it after that.

When Tanis was taken in, Percy's Pass had about twenty lamia residents. They'd holed up on the outside of town, their three two-bedroom apartments housing six or seven daughters each. To Tanis, it was heaven; she no longer had to sleep beside a dumpster outside of a McDonald's, there was no mean mother lamia around to make her feel like a mistake of nature, *plus* she'd gotten her own futon mattress, pillow, and soft blanket. Instead of six people huddled inside of her tent in the tunnels, there was only her and two sisters—Alexandra and Adonia— sharing a room. They even had a few luxuries. Her apartment had an old television with a VCR and a mountain of VHS tapes. The apartment next door had a stereo system with tall speakers, and the apartment beside that had what Tanis came to enjoy the most: a computer with stolen wireless internet.

Teenager Tanis found games. The computer was a commodity for all of them, but many of the lamia preferred not to use it, distrustful of technologies they'd never had in the tunnels. Tanis had no such qualms and soon she was addicted to the make-believe worlds beyond her door, so much so that her first major purchase when she'd started working at a local pizza place was a secondhand laptop. The pawn shop had it for a hundred dollars. Tanis saved up for three weeks and, a month later, played *World of Warcraft* for the first time.

Which is where she met Naree.

They were friends for years, killing internet dragons and talking until the late night hours about... well, Naree. About Yale. About her Korean heritage and her parents' expectations. About her atheism and her religious family's disapproval. About computers, her closeted queerness, and what it was like in the cold northeast where the snow stacked to your navel in January. It took Tanis a while to open up, but eventually the small details emerged. That she lived in Florida. That she was tall and athletic and female. Naree asked her if she had a boyfriend and Tanis had to consider, for the first time, whether she liked boys or girls, or if she found humans palatable at all. It's not that she'd never been sexual, it was just that her desires were always chemical based, reacting to the musk of the fertile True Daughters or the queen herself. Some of the humanoid daughters took lovers among their own sisters, but Tanis had always suffered it alone. It was nothing a quick tug and a dirty cloth couldn't fix.

Enjoying a human because of aesthetic, because of *wanting*, didn't occur to her until Naree asked, and after weeks of surveying the humans coming into the pizza shop, Tanis came to a definitive conclusion. Yes, she appreciated them, and in appreciating them, she preferred females, and on the fat side. They looked bouncy.

Bouncy did things to her.

So Tanis admitted it to Naree, and eventually, after another year or so, Naree informed Tanis that they were effectively dating on the internet, which Tanis didn't know was a thing, but she didn't exactly fight it either. She was fond of the girl on the other side of the line who'd convinced Tanis to Skype her every night. They developed a routine; play games for hours and then, at eleven, Tanis would step over or around her sleeping sisters to go into the bathroom and hunker down in the tub. Naree would call and inevitably comment on the ugly pink-beige tile behind Tanis's head. She was round and fresh-faced with glossy black hair and dark brown eyes and everything Tanis admired about the girls who visited the pizza shop.

Only, in this case, she was professing to be Tanis's own. It pleased Tanis in ways she didn't entirely understand.

Through it all, Tanis kept the snake out of their relationship. How did one confess they were a demigod's daughter with magical snake powers without looking like a nutter? She would have been fine to keep it quiet forever, but then spring break of Naree's junior year happened. Naree informed Tanis, three years into their relationship, right after Tanis had gotten a new job as a garbagewoman and made enough money to get her own apartment around the corner from her sisters, that she'd bought a ticket to Florida and was coming to visit. Tanis panicked, giving her a thousand reasons why she shouldn't come. Naree demanded to know what the problem was and Tanis confessed the first of her secrets through gritted teeth.

"I have cocks."

"Oh," Naree had said, looking thoughtful on the computer screen. "So you're trans? That's fine, you know. I don't care."

"No, not trans. I... it's not one cock. It's two."

That had gotten more of a thinky-faced reaction from Naree on the computer screen. She looked surprised, then in awe, and then she had Questions, but she didn't ask any of them, instead shrugging and insisting she still wanted to come down. "Whatever. I love you. I want to see you."

Tanis's last, futile effort at rebuffing her from an in-person meeting was, "I'm not saying this to be melodramatic, but I'm not like other people you know. I can do things they can't. Things you wouldn't believe."

"Let me decide what I can and cannot believe," was Naree's curt reply. Every attempt thereafter to convince her that meeting was a bad idea got argued or outright ignored. She was coming, and Tanis could or could not pick her up at the airport, but abandoning her there meant they were done.

Three weeks later, Tanis drove her new-to-her Caddy to the airport, her hands gripping the steering wheel so tightly she left a dent at the 'two' position. The cat would be out of the bag in short order, and Tanis braced to lose the only person with whom she'd ever really connected. Naree kissing her on the mouth, wrapping her arms around her middle in greeting outside of baggage claim only made the fear worsen. Tanis liked how Naree looked, how she felt against her, and—more than anything else—how she smelled. Sweet, a little sweaty from her time on the plane, a mix of human female, vanilla shampoo, and peanut butter airline snacks.

Naree held her hand as they went to the car. She talked incessantly when they got to the apartment. After take-out Chinese dinner and a scary movie that wasn't all that scary, she climbed in Tanis's lap and kissed her breathless, all the while grinding down at Tanis's straining crotch.

"It's cool, you know," Naree insisted, her hand sliding down Tanis's shoulder to cup a barely-there tit. Tanis had loved it, had settled into the touch with a pebbling nipple, but then she remembered the thing she hadn't admitted aloud yet and she gently pulled Naree away.

"I have to show you what I meant about being different," Tanis insisted. "Before we go any further." Naree'd agreed, albeit reluctantly because she was flushed and smelled eager for sex, and Tanis, not knowing how else to explain herself, took Naree outside, behind the apartment. She found an old hubcap next to the dumpster and showed it to her. "Solid," she said. "Solid metal." Naree examined it, holding it herself.

Tanis took it from her hands and bent it in half.

She did it to three other pieces of random metal around the grounds, all far too strong to be manipulated by a regular human. Naree checked each one, incredulous, trying to bend the metal back into place with her own smaller hands, with their charmingly plump fingers and too many silver rings, and failing.

"How? Are you a fucking superhero or something?" she demanded.

"No. I'm..." Tanis sucked in a breath and braced for the worst. "I'm lamia. That's why I'm strong, and run fast, and smell better than others, and see better than you in the dark. That's why I have two cocks. Lamia daughters can be born with one, or two, or a vagina. We vary, but we're all daughters." She paused. "I'm part human, but I'm also part not human. And I'm not supposed to say this to you, or talk about it, but I am because I care for you. A lot. I won't lie even if it makes you think I'm a lunatic."

Naree stared at the hubcap folded over like a discarded bottle cap. "So that's why you said you're not trans when I asked you. Cause you're lamia. You're your own—okay. Alright. I get it." She said nothing else for a long time. Not as they'd gone back into the apartment, picked at the decimated remains of their dinner, or started a second movie. Tanis didn't dare touch her, sitting down the couch from her to give her space. She felt like she'd ruined everything, that once again, what she was and who she was wasn't good enough for someone. Naree's silence did little to appease it. There should have been a barrage of questions, or more demands of proof, but there'd been none, not until the second movie was over and Naree stood up and looked toward the bathroom.

"Wasn't Lamia a snake lady? In Greek myths?" she said, not looking Tanis's way.

"Yes. She's half snake, bottom half."

"So not the snakes-on-head women."

"No!" Tanis had practically shouted, and Naree flinched. She immediately felt like an ogre, and she reached out a hand, stopping short of actually touching the other woman. "That's a Gorgon. We're enemies. Lamias and Gorgons are enemies. It's a long story, but they're different. We're different. Gorgons hunt our kind for sport."

"Oh, okay." Another pause. "So it's real? The myths? Legends?" Naree asked.

"Yeah. I... yeah. I know that's hard to believe."

Tanis anticipated the accusations to start. She expected Naree to pack her bags and demand Tanis take her home, except instead Naree said, "When I was fifteen, I met someone online. She called herself Amanda. She knew things. Could do things that'd make Anonymous shit their pants. I was joking about a DDoS attack in an IRC chat and a second later—literally a second—Amanda was in my system. My computer went nuts, and when I asked her what she'd done, all she said was, 'Magic.' Which sounded like bullshit, except she turned on my printer that wasn't connected to the electrical socket and printed a hundred papers all reading 'How do you like it?' The laptop in my bag that I hadn't set up to the wireless network at my parents' house? Connected to the IRC chat and I got a wall of, 'How do you like it?' My phone got two hundred text messages. My TV, my DVD player—'How do you like it?' over and over, on the screen and digital window. She was everywhere, and when I freaked out and ran downstairs, she followed me. She was in my parents' phones, computers. The microwave. Even the fucking Roomba came to life and rammed itself against my foot. I couldn't escape it—her—and I didn't until I screamed, 'Stop' and then it did stop, at once, as quickly as it'd started, like she'd heard me. Amanda did things no one should be able to do, and I started to believe that maybe magic was real after all, you know? Cause my microwave shouldn't be warning me off of DDoS attacks. But it did." She paused. "Incidentally, fuck Roombas. I hate those things."

"I don't have a Roomba," Tanis said, for lack of anything smart to say because she had no idea what a DDoS attack was, nor did she understand how any of that other technical stuff could happen. It was all Greek to Tanis.

Or, not Greek. She spoke Greek.

Chinese, maybe.

"No, you wouldn't." Naree'd smiled at her and shrugged.

"So I'm going to get in the shower. You want to come with? Could be fun."

"..."

And that's how they'd started, truly started, from Amanda and Roombas to awkwardly sweet shower sex that extended to 'most of spring break' sex, and beyond. After graduation, instead of moving out west and accepting a top notch programming career, Naree took a contractor job she could do remotely and moved down to Percy's Pass to live with Tanis. Naree rolled with the punches of Tanis's fucked-up snakey life as best she could, discovering fairly quickly that having a preternatural girlfriend had its challenges (like asking her to open stubborn pickle jars meant, more often than not, breaking them by accident), but she muddled through, and when Tanis was summoned back to the Den and assigned her hunting-for-Mother duties, Naree was the one to talk Tanis out of running. The twenty-percent survival ratio wasn't particularly good odds, and neither of them relished the idea of being on the lam the rest of their lives.

Because that's how Tanis thought of Naree—not as a 'for now' or a 'for the foreseeable future,' but forever.

She was the previously unheard-of species of snake who mated for life.

Home. She parked out back, beside the dumpster, and before walking inside in only a bra and her piss-stained jeans, she grabbed a hooded sweatshirt from her backseat. The winding stairs up through the apartment building squealed as she took them two at a time, her finger running over her house key in preparation for putting the night behind her.

"I made lasagna. It's in the fridge. Okay, to be honest, Stouffers made lasagna but I heated it up once already and didn't eat the second half because I figured you'd be hungry," Naree said in greeting. Tanis looked at the clock on the cable box: half past three in the morning. Naree was bundled up in a blanket on the couch looking like a burrito, her bare toes peeking out from the purple fringe along the edge of the afghan. Her hair was in a bun, a few sloppy tendrils framing her face and, on the left side, twisting around her gold-rimmed glasses. The TV blazed. Tanis didn't recognize it, but it was yet another shitty rom-com. Naree had a weird thing for old Meg Ryan movies.

"Missed you," Tanis said, bending over the couch and wrapping her wiry arms around her girlfriend. Naree traced her fingers over the winding snakes tattooed on Tanis's wrists, arms, and up to her neck. She tilted her head back. An awkward, upside-down kiss ensued, but they made it work because that's just what the two of them did: adapt. Tanis sucked on Naree's bottom lip, taking comfort in Naree's gentle squeeze on her wrist.

"Rough night, babe?"

"As per usual." Tanis nuzzled at Naree's head. She smelled like dandruff shampoo and shower gel and... something else. Tanis couldn't place it, but it was there. Something human and female and warm and she wanted to rub herself against it, but that'd be weird, so lasagna it was. She tore herself away and padded toward the kitchen to get food.

It was good she hadn't stuck around the Den any longer than necessary. Watching your mother devour the crazed snake man who'd just inseminated her was a distinct appetite killer.

Two minutes with a microwave and she had a serviceable if not delicious dinner. She flopped down on the couch next to Naree. A soft, squishy body pressed against her, Naree's head propped against her bicep. Meg Ryan did Meg Ryan things on the TV, which included wearing overly large sweaters and looking gassy.

"I don't know how you stomach it," Tanis said between bites.

"What, *Sleepless in Seattle*?"

That, too.

"No, what I do. I can barely stomach it, and I was raised with it."

They'd had the conversation before, numerous times after Tanis's nights out, and just like those other times, Naree answered with, "I understand there are rules that go with you being you. If I dated a human chick, I'd get human rules.

Date a lamia, get lamia rules. Here, gimme a bite. Girlfriend toll." She opened her mouth expectantly, and Tanis shoved a heaping spoonful into her maw. The room now smelled like overly-processed tomatoes and, to a snake nose, chemical preservatives. At least the tomatoes were stronger.

"You coming to bed after dinner? Or are you going online?" Naree asked.

"I'm not tired yet."

"I didn't say anything about sleep. I mean, you could. If you're boring."

"...oh." Tanis paused, swallowing her food. "I need a shower."

"So take a shower. You're really bad at this, babe." Naree leaned in to press a kiss to the corner of Tanis's mouth, her tongue flicking out to capture a wayward gob of sauce. It was just enough to provoke, and then she was gone, sauntering away, her afghan a billowy yarn cloak trailing behind her. Tanis looked from her dinner plate to the hallway Naree had just occupied and started shoveling lasagna. Sure, she'd just seen a pair of lamias doing a twisty, clawy, hate-fucking thing, but what better way to replace the memory than with something hot and wet and...

Shower first. Shower.

She finished her dinner, rinsed the plate, and beelined for the bathroom.

CHAPTER FIVE

NAREE ON HER hands and knees, facing the wall, shoulders pressed into a nest of blankets, ass up and presenting. She grunted every time Tanis's lean hips pounded against her ampleness. It wasn't gentle, but it wasn't supposed to be, either. She'd asked for dirty, and dirty she got. Most times there was one cock in, one capped with a condom to keep it clean when Tanis came, but not this time. This time it was all gripping muscles and the slithery slide of well-lubed orifices.

"Fuck, fuck," Naree panted, reaching between her legs to rub. "I'm close."

Tanis was, too, and she gritted her teeth, enjoying every lewd, wet squish as Naree manipulated her body into orgasm, her yelp strangled as she thrust back at Tanis, forcing Tanis to the hilt in not one contracting recess, but two.

Every muscle in Tanis's body furled as she flooded the girl before her. Pulse after pulse, Tanis's brow furrowed, her heart beating so hard she thought it would explode. Naree went flat on her stomach on the bed, and Tanis collapsed on top of her, buried deep, keeping as much of her weight on her elbows as she could. Naree's hair had come out of its bun halfway through the coupling, and Tanis swept it to the side, over the shoulder with the butterfly tattoo, placing a string of soft kisses across the back of her neck.

"Holy shit, I needed that," Naree gasped.

"Mmmm." Tanis explored soft, human flesh, her hands traveling down Naree's gently rounded sides to stroke over her hips. She brushed her cheek against the back of Naree's head, shifting so she popped free of her body with twin wet slurping sounds. Naree murmured. Tanis nuzzled the side of her neck, tongue sweeping out to capture the salt of her sweat, nostrils flaring at the female scent, so familiar and strange at the same time. It was all Naree, but it was just a little sweeter than usual. A little more sugary.

Anything smells sweet compared to Adder's Den.

Tanis rolled to her side and pulled Naree close, Naree's rump settling into Tanis's front—convex, concave, two shapes perfectly melded, their limbs entwined, their breathing short, the sheets beneath perfumed by sweaty love. Tanis wrapped her arm around her middle, her fingers stroking the underside of a plump breast. Her fingers swept up to graze a nipple and Naree giggle-squirmed.

"I'm a disaster. You do good work."

"I know," Tanis whispered against her ear.

"Smug much? You're smug. I guess you deserve it. I don't think my legs work."

And so Tanis abandoned the warm dent on her side of the mattress to scoop up her girl. If people saw the lithe woman carrying the roundish, wobbly-bitted woman, they'd wonder how she managed, but inside the apartment walls, Tanis could be free with her strength. She cradled her love to her chest and carried her to the bathroom. Naree placed a soft kiss at the base of her throat, her arms looped around Tanis's middle, as they stepped into the tub. A knob turn—three quarters to the right but no more than that—for perfect temperature, the bath faucet spouting out all the cold water on Tanis's feet before she moved the lever over to open the shower. She held Naree close, water pouring over both of them, only relinquishing her hold when Naree insisted on standing.

Naree washed Tanis's hair, her stubby fingernails kneading Tanis's scalp in soothing circles. Tanis attended Naree's back with a marauding loofa. Little kisses and hidden smiles and whispered secrets, the evidence of their tryst swirling down the drain with the suds. Despite soap and gels and water hot enough to turn their skin pink, Tanis could smell herself on Naree when they toweled off and tumbled back into bed. She fell asleep with the comfort of entwined bodies and entwined scents.

It was nice. Until the phone rang at ass o'clock.

Naree growled and burrowed under her mountain of pillows. She'd migrated to the opposite side of the bed over the course of the night and balanced precariously on the edge, a sheet mummifying her from foot to chin. Tanis stretched to snag her jeans from the floor, fumbling around for her cell in the pocket. Luke's piss had sunk into the denim; there were only a few splashes of it here and there, but to Tanis it reeked. Tanis snagged the phone and stumbled down the hallway to throw the jeans into the washing machine.

She thumbed the answer button, barking a barely-tolerant "Yeah" into the receiver.

"Got some bad news, doll."

Bernie. A glance at the hallway clock. Six-thirty. Two whole hours of sleep.

"What's going on?"

"Ariadne's missing."

Ariadne was one of the favored—a True Daughter. She was pretty, with long golden hair, blue eyes, and skin the color of sand despite never seeing the sun. Her body was voluptuous in that pinup way: not too thin, not too fat, with curves for days. She crammed her coconut tits into too-tiny bikini tops, showing off soft, pampered flesh and a belly button ring with a dangling dolphin charm. And though her human half was lovely, it was her snake half that stole the show. Ariadne had some of the prettiest scales in the Den, in iridescent pastel blues, violets, and greens that looked like they belonged on a mermaid. When she slithered around, they gleamed like gossamer fairy wings.

"Any ideas?" Tanis asked.

"*Daphne.*"

"Still?"

"*Oh, yeah,*" Bernie replied.

Daphne was one of Ariadne's guards—not assigned to her specifically, but to her birthing den, the one to the left of Lamia's. She was a big girl, solid like Fi, with dark brown skin and black hair shorn short with silver flecks at her temples. Bright green eyes, a broad nose, a lush mouth. Like a snake she had no ears, and her body from the neck down was completely covered in brown scales. The tips of her fingers had black talons that could peel human flesh off the bone like rind from an orange; Tanis had seen it.

The thing was, she had a secret. Not a particularly good secret, as most anybody with a clue knew about it, but she and Ariadne were lovers. Lamia didn't approve because Lamia approved of very little in general, but that was especially true when it came to her prized breeding daughters. They were hers and hers alone, bearing the burden of her love like canaries trapped in gilded cages. Nothing was supposed to come before the Mother or the People, and so the girls were known to wait for the queen to go into one of her deep slumbers to stage their rebellions. A freshly-inseminated snake queen meant Lamia was at her most tired, the eggs in her belly commanding extravagant resources to mature in their meager, three-day window.

Ariadne and Daphne must have capitalized on it to sneak away.

"Does Lamia know?" Tanis demanded, heading back toward the bedroom.

"*Oh, yes, and she screeched at me to call you. We're on hunting duty. She doesn't want to lose any of the home-based girls in case of breach.*" A breach being the outside world cluing into a den of magical snake women living right beneath their noses. Naree might be alright living amongst lamia, but

Naree wasn't most people, and a regular person spying a pair of giant snake women, one with a long, glimmering snake tail, would incite panic.

Tanis raked her fingers through her hair and dove for the laundry basket with the unsorted-but-still-clean underwear, pulling on a pair of boxer briefs. "Fuck's sake."

She didn't know how or why she'd been picked for the job, but there wasn't much sense in arguing it. What Mama said went, even if Mama was a horrorshow. "Gonna take me a while to get there. She got her eyes out?"

"*You bet. And she's seeing swamp, which is about as helpful as tits on a bull. I'll start sniffing. See you soon, doll.*"

Tanis tossed the phone onto the bed and staggered around the bedroom in search of fresh jeans and a T-shirt, ending up in a gray Marlboro tank top she'd picked up from the secondhand store. A pair of socks without holes near the toes so they wouldn't drive her crazy, alligator boots. She snagged a fresh pack of cigarettes from the bedside table and slipped a smoke between her lips—tired, irritable, and longing for coffee.

"Where you going?" Naree rolled at her, her arms wrapping around Tanis's waist from behind, her cheek pressed to her back.

"The Den. Two of the sisters are missing."

"Oh, shit. Are they okay?"

"I don't know." Tanis turned to press a kiss to Naree's forehead. "You know the drill, yeah?"

"The drill sucks."

"The drill" was that there was forty-five hundred in cash in Tanis's bottom desk drawer along with a gun, in the eventuality Tanis didn't come back from one of her hunts. It wasn't that she feared one of the men getting the drop on her, so much as what if her mother lost her shit one day and snapped Tanis in half? She hadn't courted it, but Lamia was mercurial at best and an absolute shitshow psycho at worst. If Tanis couldn't find her precious Ariadne, someone would pay. It'd be really *swell* if that someone wasn't Tanis or Bernie, but who knew?

"Call if you need anything," Naree whispered.

"I will. Go back to sleep. You're tired."

Naree groaned and sprawled onto her back, her arms and legs stretching for the corners. Tanis shrugged into her leather jacket and made her way to the living room. Halfway there, she heard a jingle, and she remembered she had Luke's personal effects rattling around in her pocket. She left the cufflinks and cash from his wallet on the end table for Naree. His gun would go with Tanis, as would the wallet, so she could throw it out into the swamp en route to the Den. It'd be gator shit within days.

A smoke, a stop at the golden arches for some black tar in a cup, and off she went. Twenty minutes out of the Pass, Bernie called again. Tanis shifted her freshest cigarette over to the left side of her mouth so she could take it.

"Yeah?"

"Good news, bad news. Good news is, Ariadne's in season, so she's easy to scent track. Bad news is, she left the Den altogether. I don't want to follow too far into the swamp without you, plus Ma wants to see us before we leave."

"Greaaat. I'm close."

Tanis pushed the Caddy up to eighty. It was early still; the leather jacket wasn't too hot yet, the sun cresting the treetops on the eastern horizon. She finished the cigarette and the coffee in that order before turning the car onto the dirt road maze leading to the Den. Bernie awaited her outside, leaning against the flagpole with its weather-beaten pants flag. She had on the same fluorescent running shoes from the night before, black leggings, and an oversized white T-shirt. Her hair was up in a bun on top of her head, loose wisps of gray escapee tendrils floating by her face. She squinted against the sunlight, her myriad of wrinkles making her look even more like a gargoyle than usual.

"Morning, doll. Bring enough for the whole class?"

"Eh?" Tanis fell into step beside her as they approached the shed.

"The smokes."

"When we get out. Hedging some bets we'll both need one."

Bernie smirked at her as they passed the newest shift guards, one reading a book in the corner near the open door, the other picking muck from beneath her fingernails with a twig. Tanis muttered a hello and promptly dropped below ground to escape any uncomfortable chatter; they both knew her name, but she hadn't the faintest clue about theirs.

"Where's Fi?" Tanis asked as they trudged through the water, sidestepping a writhing ball of juvenile snakes tumbling their way down the pipeline.

"She's on door duty while Daphne's missing. Volunteered for it before I could. smart bitch." A minute later, Fi came into view, her ass planted on an upended milk crate, playing cards once again clasped in hand. The other guard was likewise positioned. It was something of a known fact that if you spent any time with Fi at all, you'd probably end up playing gin rummy. And losing.

"I'm old. You could have let me take guard duty," Bernie said in greeting, rustling Fi's hair with obvious fondness. Fi swatted her away.

"You're too slow, old woman," Fi replied, deep and low.

"Yeah, yeah. Enjoy sitting on your ass." Bernie looped her arm through Tanis's and walked her toward Lamia's den. The pheromone sex stench tickled at Tanis's nostrils, and she forced herself to breathe through her mouth as they passed a muted Kallie. Kallie was, in general, a smug pain in the ass, so her expression—she looked like she'd just gotten hit with a shovel—boded ill.

So did the echoing, enraged screams.

"*GET DOWN HEEERE!*" Lamia's voice exploded through the pipe and the next pipe and the pipe beyond that, the queen snake's voice big enough to fill every nook and cranny of the Den. Bernie and Tanis pulled away from one another to jog, and then run, their feet splashing in the shallow water below. Upon cresting the lip, they were besieged by a frantic Lamia, holding one eye in each of her puffy, pale hands, fingers delicate around the red-veined orbs, her slitted pupils darting this way and that as she scried. Her empty eye sockets sagged, the puckered orifices thankfully shadowed by the dimness of the birthing chamber.

Tanis looked down, unwilling—perhaps incapable—of peering into those empty voids for too long. It put her mother's swollen, distended middle into focus. Lamia's milky udders rested on a stomach fatter than it had been the day before, bulging more obscenely from the sides, lumps of wrongness disrupting the otherwise gentle swell of her rolls of blue flesh.

Half clutch of eggs. Half undigested Luke Des Moines.

"Ariadne is gone. She's gone. Taken by that loathsome dyke guard. Pig-flesh daughter. I'll rip her apart, feast on her, use her bones as toothpicks. Find her. Find them. Bring them to me." Lamia waved her flickering eyeballs under Tanis and Bernie's noses. "To the west, I see trees, tall trees, and grass."

"Sooo, you see the Glades. The Glades are big, Mother," Bernie said, her voice flat. Lamia roared and whipped around, her trunk-thick tail lashing out to strike Bernie in the side. The older lamia crumpled to the floor, on her knees, gripping her middle, and Lamia struck her in the face with her tail tip. Bernie's mouth exploded crimson, her lips mashing into her teeth and shredding open on the inside. She wheezed at the pain, a long tendril of bloody spittle dripping down to soil her white T-shirt, her left arm pressed to her mouth as if to hold her teeth inside

Tanis wanted to help, but Lamia was there, looming, and a show of sisterly solidarity was a show of rebellion against the Bitchbeast. Two of them bleeding did no one any good. Plus she still sported a tender spot on her shoulder from last night's impromptu cave flight. A matched set didn't appeal.

She dropped a hand onto Bernie's shoulder and squeezed—the only comfort she dared risk.

Bernie grunted.

"Do you think your mother so stupid, Berenike? She that has persevered, has saved our people for thousands of years? Idiot child." Lamia lifted the eyes, hovering both before their respective empty sockets. "There is a house. White with black shutters gone gray beneath sun. A stone fountain before, the basin cracked, with a water bearer who bears no water. Follow the treeline to the south and west; you'll find the scent. Ariadne is ripe for breeding. This one"—Lamia's tail rose from the floor, the delicate, tapered point at odds with the sheer girth of the coils stroking over the crotch of Tanis's jeans, up and down, back and forth—"with her worthless cocks will know best. She'll hunt her sex. She is a slave to it, in her own right." Lamia leaned forward, the black, spidery veins in her cheeks and temples pulsing against the sheaf-like, translucent skin. Her mouth gaped open, unleashing her fetid breath on Tanis's face. Tanis wouldn't breathe it in—refused the chamber's base, reptilian draw—but she was all too familiar with the rankness roiling forth from Mother's maw. It tormented her memory enough that she flinched.

"You are so disappointing to me, but perhaps, this time, you will be less so. Don't fail me, Tanis Barlas, daughter mine, or I will eat your secret."

CHAPTER SIX

"THE FUCK DOES that even mean? 'I'll eat your secret'?" Bernie demanded. She was sour and understandably so; her chin was crusted with dried blood, one of her teeth was loose and probably fated to fall out, and her sneakers had gotten wet in the tunnels, and would never, ever dry in Florida's jockstrap humidity.

Tanis had abandoned the leather jacket in the Caddy before the two of them set off into the unknown with nothing more than a gun, a pack of smokes, and a pair of baseball hats to keep the sun from their eyes. Bernie's was white with red, script lettering that read *Fred's Diner*. Tanis's was a blue *Romney for President* hat she'd gotten for a nickel at a yard sale.

"My girlfriend," she replied flatly. "It's not much of a secret, but she wants me to know she knows about her. She generally doesn't give fuck-all what we do until it suits her purposes, and her purposes this time are to let me know my girlfriend's fucked if I don't find Ariadne."

"How'd we get so lucky, eh? How'd we get so lucky?"

Tanis hoped Bernie meant it to be a rhetorical question, because she was in no mood to answer.

Naree. I'm sorry.

She spit out her cigarette and trudged on, Bernie so close that their hands brushed every few steps. Ariadne's scent was getting stronger further into the Glades. Sour, sweet, enticing. Lamia wasn't wrong about the effect on Tanis. She'd had soft wood for fifteen minutes, and didn't that make an already excruciating walk all the more unpleasant.

Dick chafe. Good times.

A half-hour in, Ariadne's signature was twice as pungent as when they'd first set out and Tanis wanted to dive into any number of the waterways they passed. Sadly, it wasn't one of those things she could will away, or attempt to counter, with unsexy thoughts. She was biologically wired to respond, and respond she did, no matter how much she'd like not to. Her erections had become fucking dowsing rods for Lamia's missing daughter.

"Daphne," Bernie said, tilting her head back and sniffing. Tanis struggled to get past the Ariadne clouding her brain, inhaling deeply. Yes, there were traces of Daphne, though it wasn't a pheromone so much that anything she'd touched or swept past held traces of her. She was on the grass and shrubs; she was an overlay on the vast, verdant green.

"Close," Tanis said.

"Thank God. My face is killing me and my underwear's so far up my ass it's twisted around my tonsils."

Tanis didn't want to smile, but... well. Bernie.

Her lips twitched.

The terrain was terrible, mushy in some parts, covered with brambles in others. Near the Den there'd been hundreds of snakes drizzled over the flora, haphazard and limp like scaly tinsel tossed at Christmas trees, but further out was gator territory. Every once in a while you'd see the lumps in the water that, at first glance, looked like logs, but on second, had eyes, or moved faster than the current. None of them approached the lamia, though some drifted to the edges of their wading pools in case lunch had conveniently presented itself.

It hadn't. In one notable week, Tanis had killed two gators with her bare hands. In her defense, they'd been assholes.

Trying to eat a person was assholish, anyway.

Deeper into the Glades, stepping over and around fallen trees, moldering underbrush, long abandoned hunting camps, and bird nests along the banks. Ariadne and Daphne's scents intensified, which was good. What wasn't as good were the new scents carried in by the wind, equally as present as the lamia, and distinctly... human? Four scents total, beyond Daphne and Ariadne's own. Tanis stopped in her tracks, her eyes narrowing against the blazing sun.

"What's that?" she demanded.

Bernie hunkered down low, her nostrils flaring as she swung her head back and forth. "Wish I could get past the stink of my own blood," she muttered, knees dropping to the damp ground, her hands splaying out before her so she could get right up to the earth and sniff. She crawled forward, veering away from simpler, less-hazardous lakeside terrain and into waist-tall grasses. Tanis followed, honing in on Ariadne's chemical invitation because *how could she not?*

Fuck you, dicks.

"Blood," Bernie rasped. "Forty-five degrees ahead."

Tanis cut in front of her and pulled out the gun; it was a Colt 1911, a big gun, a status gun, typical of a man like Luke Des Moines. Bernie scrambled to her feet. The two of them crept along, silent hunters, and it wasn't long before Tanis recognized something that made the hairs on the back of her neck prickle: decay. Coppery, dank, sour rot. She smelled *death*. On any day that she wasn't bathing in breeding-season lamia secretions, she would have picked up on it much sooner, but better late than never, she supposed, and really, death wasn't something one ever wanted to find.

She advanced.

Blood on the tips of the grass.

Blood splashing the bark of a broken sapling.

Blood pooling on the ground like a sanguine offering.

Tanis spotted the hand first, the foot second. Meaty tendrils dangled from both, the exposed bones slicked red and wrapped in flesh that had, to all appearances, been ripped apart. Someone hadn't taken the time to clean up after themselves. Tanis tiptoed into meatier terrain, viscera painting the Glades wrong. She spotted the torso in a small clearing between two trees, the human man's head twisted so far it'd begun to tear away from his neck. One arm was still intact, but the other lacked a hand, the wrist stub poking out from the remains of a white robe that had been cinched with a forest-green belt beaded with gold.

She only noticed the belt when she spotted the legs. They were fifteen feet away from the torso, the bloodied cloth tangled around his knees, the unsoiled beads glittering.

"Daphne," Bernie said. "She's all over this. I can smell her."

Tanis squatted to survey the damage. The corpse—a pale, bald male with sightless brown eyes that pointed at the sky, who couldn't have weighed more than a hundred and fifty pounds— had been torn asunder. The why wasn't evident, at least, not from the clues left. All they knew was that Ariadne and Daphne had started off alone from Adder's Den, perhaps sneaking away for a tryst. Or perhaps they were sneaking away for good? And then they'd met these people and it turned violent.

Only finding the scent markers leading out would tell how the story ended.

If Daphne ripped one of them apart, it ain't gonna be good.

"This is bad," Bernie said.

"Yep. But we can't go back without an answer."

And if the answer is a body, maybe we shouldn't go back at all.

It wasn't an option, not with Naree out there, not with Lamia's spying eyes, so Tanis forced herself up and away from the messy scene, continuing into the Glades, her nostrils flaring with Ariadne's scent. She kept the gun in her right hand, her left adjusting her crotch. The rot had quelled most of the ardor, but it'd be back soon enough if she didn't do something to stop it.

"You got the scent?" Tanis asked. "Rather not walk into a bad situation packing wood."

"Course I do, doll." Bernie squeezed her shoulder. "You're lucky, in a way. Mia does the tongue flicking thing. Imagine if you did, too?"

"No, thanks."

Bernie smirked at her before taking point, leading them past the arm and foot and torso. They'd just stepped over the legs with the gaping waist and gut confetti when Tanis noticed something about the beading on the blood-saturated belt—it formed a shape. A *distinctive* shape.

"Bernie." She snagged the back of the older woman's T-shirt and reeled her in. "You seeing what I see?" Tanis stooped to pull on the belt, not tearing it away from the corpse but smoothing it out across the grass so the pattern became more distinct. Bernie tilted her head, sussing out the picture. With some beads stained red and some untouched, it was like trying to see the schooner in one of those optical illusion books, but once she picked up on it, her mouth flattened into a grimace.

"Gorgon."

The beading was intricate and hand-done, the features on the face straightforward but elegant. Five snakes from the head, mouths open with forked tongues, the eyes picked out with red beads. Tanis traced a finger along the shape of the leftmost serpent, stopping short of actual contact with the sticky, bloody sash.

She'd never seen a Gorgon—nor had any living lamias save the queen herself—but she'd heard the stories from her mother. Gorgons had hunted lamia for thousands of years, finding them weak and pathetic as a race. Gorgons considered themselves the true snake gods, the lamia a fragile, mortal stain compared to their eternities, and so they chased Lamia and her flock to prove their sovereignty. Their last attack was in Argentina in the early nineteen-fifties, where they killed all but twenty-seven of the six-hundred-plus colony. The genocide forced the lamias to migrate to the States. An injured Lamia was crated and snuck aboard a shipping vessel, her daughters nursing her back to health during the journey across the Atlantic, which probably meant feeding unsuspecting sailors to the monster mama's maw to restore her strength. Lamia was a demigod— hard to kill, but not impossible—and the Gorgons had damned near taken her down. How the few managed to escape wasn't known; Lamia never spoke about it, but what happened to the dead had carried down through the generations, becoming the stuff of child Tanis's nightmares.

All six hundred of them had been turned to stone beneath Stheno and Euryale's deadly stares. Two Gorgons wreaked that much havoc on that many lamia.

There'd been a *History's Mysteries* about the abandoned lamia village southeast of Buenos Aires. It was deemed a secret society, the people living in squalor amidst hundreds of statues of snake women. They'd called it the Latin Roanoke, and Tanis had watched the episode with macabre fascination. Human scholars speculated on cult activity, and old gods, and what might have caused the people to flee and where they'd gone. They were particularly fascinated with the 'sculptors' responsible for the strange masterpieces, and reported that a Berlin museum had paid the Argentinian government exorbitant amounts of money for their treasure trove. And so the statues were packed up and shipped overseas in the early 'sixties. There they were displayed under green spotlights, the exhibit credited to 'Unknown Artist, circa 1954.'

Thousands of people a year unknowingly visited a lamia graveyard.

"They're here?" Bernie's voice was strangled.

"Mother always said they'd come looking for her."

Lamia had one defense against the Gorgons and that was her removable eyes. The scrying, the precognition allowed her to stay one step ahead of the Gorgons—it wasn't foolproof, but it was reliable enough, and if the Gorgons had gotten this close without Lamia cluing in, that meant they hadn't been around for very long. There was still a window of opportunity to escape.

And then what happens when you land wherever you'll land? To you, to Naree?

Tanis cringed.

"We need to tell her," Bernie said. "She'll want to know as soon as possible."

Tanis brushed past Bernie to walk, not back toward Adder's Den, but away from it. "We can't go home empty-handed."

"One True Daughter versus an impending invasion? I think your priorities are a little off, doll."

Tanis paused to glance at Bernie over her shoulder. Bernie had mud on her knees from kneeling, and splatters of blood on her pretty fluorescent shoes, and sweat rivulets streaming from her brow to settle into the deep grooves of her wrinkles. Her face was puckered with worry, her pulse jumping in her throat. "You can go. I got this."

"Like hell you do," Bernie said. "I'm not sending you in there alone. Why don't we go ba—"

"Because she's going to be furious either way. Panicked and furious that the Gorgons are near, and she never got the memo about not killing the messenger," Tanis interrupted. "I'm not giving her an excuse to rip me in half, and not knowing what happened to Ariadne? That's an excuse. So I'll find out what happened to her and Daphne, hopefully not die in the process, and then I'll check in. That's my plan. It's not a good one, but it's the best I got right now. We're hip-deep in shit and sinking fast."

Bernie took off her white hat and fanned her face, gaze skipping between discarded body parts littering the ground like candy from a piñata and the black clouds of flies forming above. "You're right. I know you're right. Just hate that you are."

Tanis pulled out another cigarette and trudged into the hip-tall grasses.

"So do I."

CHAPTER SEVEN

IT TOOK ANOTHER half-hour of awful terrain to find the first statue. Bernie led the way, following the scents so Tanis didn't have to fight a perpetual pants problem while she was, quite likely, walking toward her death.

Getting petrified with hard-ons was an indignity she'd rather spare herself.

The statue was a human male, a hunter by the looks of the tattered camo gear rustling over his stone form. He cowered, crouched low, his hands raised above his head like he was warding off a blow, his face screwed up in terror. Bernie and Tanis circled him, examined him, touched the rock of his skin. Where the sun grazed it, it was warm, and where there was shadow, it was cool.

"That's messed up," Bernie whispered. "You realize that could be us in a little while?"

"Not if I can help it. I have a woman to get home to."

Bernie puffed on her cigarette. "Don't let the girls at home know you're a romantic or they'll ride you for it."

"Fuck them."

She meant it, too. Outside of Bernie, Fi, Gaia in Percy's Pass, and maybe Barbara, Tanis didn't give much of a shit about any of them. She had sympathy for them, even for the True Daughters who seemingly had everything but were prisoners in their own right, but when it came down to it, all her affection was reserved for Naree.

Who will either have to come with me or be left behind, if we uproot.

No, fuck that. She's mine and I'm hers.

We'll figure it out.

Tanis set her jaw.

The second statue was found not too far from the first, the third even closer than that. Soon it was a veritable garden, all humans, all looking like they'd encountered Satan himself moments before their deaths. Tanis's eyes skipped over them, not wanting to see their expressions, knowing that she could end up with her fear forever captured in stone, too. She gripped the gun harder despite its uselessness. The two remaining Gorgons were immortal. Medusa hadn't been, thus Perseus slaying her, but her sisters? Bullets would do nothing other than annoy them a whole hell of a lot.

But I still want it near. Just in case.

"Look," Bernie said, pointing to the left. Nestled behind a line of sycamores, black eaves taller than the trees, was the manor house Lamia described. White paint, the shutters intact but faded gray, it was a jewel of a place, with tall white columns and wraparound porch, hanging fuschia plants and blooming window boxes. Two stories, an attached garage, a water feature of a carved fish squirting water into a stone pool—a house like that didn't belong in the wild with no sign of manicured lawns and domesticity, and yet Tanis couldn't think of a single place that would have suited it better.

It was glorious.

The statue on the front steps, not so much.

It was in mid-step, one leg hiked up, one planted on the ground. An arm reached forward, thick and corded with muscle, fingers extended as if grasping for something. The head was tilted back, an angry, panicked expression preserved on the gray face. No ears, shorn hair, it wasn't hard to identify Daphne. A tank top, tan cargo pants, combat boots. She'd succumbed to her petrification in a less-than-convenient place, and Tanis wondered if they'd bother to move her out with the rest of the bodies or if she'd be left there like a gruesome welcoming mat.

"I'll be damned," Bernie said, her hand going to her heart. "She was alright. Not much of a talker, but she always had a joke when you needed it. Good at puns." She murmured beneath her breath, a prayer or a curse, or maybe a little of both. "She loved that girl, you know. Was sick about her, like you and Naree, but Ma was always down their throats. She's so territorial about the breeders. I used to think they had it all when I was a kid, but now? I know better."

"Yeah," Tanis said, because what else was there to say? Looking at the worry on Daphne's forever-frozen brow, at the desperation in her expression, she saw only Naree. Would she get on alright without Tanis? Would she go back to Connecticut and that clutch of bigoted assholes she called family? Would she head out west and take that tech job she should have taken in the first place? Or would Lamia send someone to clean up Tanis's 'mess' first? Humans weren't supposed to know about lamia. When Tanis took a human lover, she'd promised her mother she accepted responsibility for her discretion, but with her gone...

Don't think like that. Naree knows the plan. Get out fast and go somewhere cold. Snakes hate cold.

Focus.

A slam inside the house, followed by shouting. Tanis and Bernie ducked behind a tree and peeked out around the trunk. A half-dozen people in white robes, all wearing the green sashes with the Gorgon beading, filed from the front door like ants, lining up on the brick path before the steps. Tanis had the poorly-timed thought that they were like the kids in *The Sound of Music*, lining up after Captain von Trapp's boatswain call, to meet their new nanny for the first time, except here, there was no Julie Andrews to sing away their troubles.

One robed individual held back from the rest. She remained in the doorway, a white woman with short blond hair, who wore a red sash over her eyes and carried a folding walking stick in her left hand. She stepped forward, the stick gliding over the deck and tapping against the porch railing. It swung out in a wide arc and struck the statue, tapping along its side from chest to thigh and, at one point, tangling in the pocket of Daphne's cargo pants.

"Move it to the side yard. Stheno won't want to look at it," she snapped, her tone brooking no argument. The group of six moved forward, trying to lift Daphne, but failing that, they pushed her over instead so she plummeted to the ground. The collision of statue and brick walkway resulted in Daphne's head falling off and rolling a few feet from the rest of the body.

Tanis could see her spine. Unlike a statue that would be smooth stone throughout, each of Daphne's body parts had turned to stone; crack the casing, you got a perfect anatomical dummy cast in stone.

The servants rolled the body away from the house and abandoned it on its side in a patch of dense, tall grass beside the driveway. They never said a word. Task accomplished, they followed the blind woman back into the house, the screen door clattering shut behind them. Tanis wouldn't let herself look at her sister, instead surveying the property for good entry points. The windows all had drawn shades, which prevented a quick peek to determine Ariadne's status. There were no patrols walking around, which was good, but with no way to determine how many people were inside or which parts of the house they occupied, the front and back door weren't options. The bulkhead to the basement, however...

Tanis pointed. "We'll go from the bottom up."

"Lucky us," Bernie murmured.

This is insane.

But what choice is there?

None. There is no choice. See what you can see and run. And hope it's enough.

Before she could give into her roiling unease, Tanis sprinted toward the house, a blur of woman, faster than a cheetah with a hundred times the endurance. The bulkhead door wasn't latched—bonus—and it was dark inside the basement—bigger bonus. She snuck down the stairs, gun at the ready, if not for a Gorgon, then for the humans attending them. Priests, maybe, in a cult, if the robes were any indication, but who knew? Lamia was rarely conversational, especially about topics that upset her, and the Gorgons were her biggest upset.

The few snippets she had shared became Tanis's beacons. The Gorgons' strength was predominantly in their magic, physical strength, and resilience. They weren't as fast as lamias. They couldn't smell what lamias could smell, nor could they see as well, especially at night. Gorgons were superior predators, but lamias were the ultimate survivors if the terrain played nice, and for the time being, the terrain was playing nice. It was a big basement with plenty of places to hide, if push came to shove; three closet doors off the main chamber, a big boiler, stacked rubber bins and shelving units for storage. The stairs were at the far end of the room with a nook beneath that could provide cover if circumstances turned dire.

More dire.

Balls.

Tanis's eyes adjusted as Bernie slithered down the steps behind her, pulling the bulkhead closed, slowly, so it wouldn't clang. Bernie tilted her head back and sniffed, pointing first directly above their heads and then at one of the closed doors to their right. People one floor up, people behind the door. A plan wasn't immediately obvious until a loud thud sounded above, like something dropping to the floor, followed by a plaintive wail. Tanis looked up, swinging her head back and forth. There was a break in between the floorboards a few feet above her head. She couldn't see through it from where she stood, and so she handed Bernie the gun and rummaged around the basement until she found an empty milk crate and upended it. Bernie's hand went to support her back as she climbed onto the crate and peeked through the gap, blinking away the dust and debris that rained down into her eye.

Ariadne was above, but not trying to escape, although only two humans held her arms. She was much stronger than them, could have thrown them through the wall if she wanted to, but she stayed put. Tanis swung her head around to see why, but the visibility wasn't good. She heard footsteps above her, a bare foot actually stepping right above her face for a moment before moving away, but still she couldn't discern much.

"You have a choice," a woman's voice said, speaking English but with a thick Greek accent.

Ariadne whimpered and lunged forward, but her body wouldn't *go*, like she was shackled to the floor by invisible bonds. Tanis swept her gaze down. No chains, no rope, but Ariadne's once-brilliant scales looked dull. The iridescent sheen that had made her so lovely was gone, replaced by a sickly gray. She wasn't stone, not like Daphne or any of the other statued people peppering the yard, but she looked... dusty. Antiquated.

She can't break free because she's too weighted down by magic. Her coils can't move.

"I can't. I c-can't. You'll kill me, she'll kill me. I can't," Ariadne sobbed, mascara-stained tears coursing down her pretty face. The tip of her nose was red, her upper lip dewed not with her usual pink gloss but with snot.

A thin arm, the skin the color of brass and gleaming like metal, darted out, clasping Ariadne around the throat. Long, thick fingernails, brown until they tinged green at the pointed ends, dug into her skin, the tips biting hard enough to draw blood. Tanis's eyes followed the arm up to a bare shoulder and a sundress, the fabric yellow with tiny blue flowers. On any other woman, it would have been sweet for the season. On a Gorgon, it looked wrong. *She* was wrong.

Tanis had never seen a Gorgon before, so she wasn't entirely sure what she'd expected, but it wasn't *this*. The Gorgon's body was humanish, curved above and below with a narrow waist between, her skin the color of fresh peaches save for the brass hands. Normal feet, normal legs, no snake coils from the waist down or anything noteworthy beyond toenails as green as her fingernails. The neck up was another story; her face was heart-shaped on a slightly too-big head, her mouth a lipless slash with an overbite of fangs, the ends dripping yellow liquid that crusted her chin and neck in sugary crystals. Her eyes were black marbles in too-round sockets, no irises or pupils to be seen, no lashes fringing top or bottom. In place of a nose she had a flattened bump, like she was hit dead on with a shovel.

Slitted vents replaced nostrils. Ear holes took the place of ears.

Atop her head were snakes; writhing, clay-colored snakes with eyes as black as the Gorgon's own. They weren't nearly as orderly or as matched as the mythology books depicted. Some were thick and long, three or four feet, extending from the Gorgon's scalp to snap at the air in the nearest priest's direction. Some were short and thin and frail, especially the ones closest to her temples, one of them daring to laze across her brow as though napping, oblivious to its cohorts' incessant rustling. It was impossible to say if the size of the snake reflected how long it had grown on the Gorgon's head, or if the variance was perpetual and by design; by the large snake on the back of the head devouring its sister, its throat bulging like it was giving the world's most obscene blowjob, Tanis had to believe that the snakes died off and were replaced with new snakes, much like human hair.

That's fucked up.

Bernie poked Tanis's side. Tanis waved her off, watching the Gorgon's fingers digging further into Ariadne's flesh. The weird grayness around Ariadne's snake-half crept up over her human half, too, her veins blackening beneath the skin and pushing at her flesh, the squiggly, dark worms pulsing in time to the erratic beat of her heart.

"It won't be quick," the Gorgon rasped. "Unless you tell me."

"I can't, I can't, I can't," Ariadne sobbed.

The Gorgon's other hand crept over Ariadne's shoulder, stroking, her gnarled brass fingers plucking at the pink strap of her top. A talon curled around it, the edge as sharp as a razor, cutting the fabric away. A full breast with a pebbled pink nipple fell out.

"I am Euryale," the Gorgon said, her voice low as if she talked to a lover. "I know your mother. I tangled her innards around my fist and pulled, ropes of sausage in my hand. And yet the bitch escaped me."

"Please, no. I... Sh-she fears you," Ariadne managed. "We are all taught to fear you."

"You should. I loathe your kind." Euryale traced the back of her hand over the soft flesh once more before turning the nails inward and spearing the meat. Sanguine stars bloomed where the fingers bit, red rivers drizzling down over Euryale's hand and wrist, over the flat of Ariadne's stomach and onto the gray-tinged scales at her waist. Ariadne shrieked, and then she caterwauled as Euryale's grip tightened. A moment later, the breast came off in the Gorgon's hand, not in a fleshy chunk, but in a single piece of stone, so perfect it could have been pulled from the Venus de Milo itself. Where it had been attached to the chest was a strange wound, a nearly perfect circle of stone, the flesh along the edges curling away like the corners of old paper.

"Piece by piece," the Gorgon crooned, showing the breast to a hysterical Ariadne. "Piece. By. Piece. This is what the lamia deserve for their hand. This is for Medusa."

The hell does Medusa have to do with anything?

"Tanis!" Bernie demanded in a loud whisper.

Tanis tore her gaze from the gap in the floor, queasy, angry, and confused. By the mention of the Gorgon's dead sister, and by the violation she'd seen. Tanis had thought Gorgons did a stone-stare, wham-bam-thank-you-ma'am thing and that was the end of it. Apparently, they'd refined petrification to an art form; something precise and selective. Maybe through a gaze as Tanis had been taught, but it was possible—likely, even, given what she'd witnessed—that it had something to do with the bronze hands or green nails.

Does it really matter, in the end? Euryale is going to break Ariadne down into little stone parts until there's nothing left.

Tanis ran her hand over her face, and Bernie jabbed her in the side again, harder. A part of Tanis wanted to shove her away for being so goddamned insistent, but then she followed the direction of Bernie's gaze and she understood. A sliver of pale light, under the door where Bernie had sensed the other person, that hadn't been there before.

Something stirred.

CHAPTER EIGHT

WE HAVE TO GO.

There was nothing they could do for Ariadne. Even if Tanis and Bernie rushed upstairs like a couple of be-titted Rambos, that would just mean four dead lamia instead of two. Lamia would chastise them for not giving it a suicidal try anyway, but Tanis had other ideas that included living to see the next day. Maybe the warning that the Gorgons were close would distract the Mother Beast from doing what Mother Beasts did best when they were given bad news, which was destroy everything in their path, especially the humanoid daughters unfortunate enough to poison her vicinity.

More shrieking from Ariadne was followed by a loud crash as something heavy hit the floor.

Another body part.

Get me out of this basement.

Tanis tiptoed ahead, avoiding the dim light peeking out from beneath the closed door by hugging the opposite wall, her shoulder skimming a shelf of power tools. Bernie made to follow, but then she stopped and cocked her head to the side, a finger lifted to her lips. Tanis reached for the gun she normally would have tucked into her waistband, remembering too late Bernie still had it. The hand cannon's barrel stretched the tight fabric of Bernie's leggings into an obscene shape against her left ass cheek.

Bernie pointed at the door.

"Hear that?"

Tanis didn't, on account of the screeching upstairs, but once Ariadne quieted for reasons she didn't want to think about, the mad whisper spilled forth. It was raspy and frantic, the person behind the door talking so much they ran out of breath, paused only to gasp, and continued prattling despite too little oxygen. There was a tinny quality to it as well, a faint echo as in a warehouse where the voice bounced off the unyielding walls.

"There's something wrong with that voice," Bernie said. And there was; the inflection and cadence were bizarre, the speaker careening high before dropping to inaudible bass murmurs. The volume was similarly disjointed: loud to soft, soft to loud and back again, making it impossible to understand a single uttered word.

Bernie retreated toward Tanis and the wall. The two were slinking back to the bulkhead door when the voice rang out, much too loud for comfort.

"You. You two. Come. Here, in here. Help me," the stranger said, in the mother tongue. Tanis eyed the road to freedom up the stairs, and then the closed door and its dim light.

"I don't recognize them," Bernie said.

Tanis didn't either, and considering all the fucks had fled the fuck farm about anything other than getting home to Naree, saving a faceless nobody didn't factor into her plans. Too much risk, too little reward.

Until.

"You have one way to save her, Tanis. One way. Through me. It will be hard, yes, but Naree can live. Come to me. Listen. Lissssten."

Tanis stopped dead. "Who the fuck are you?"

"Volume," Bernie cautioned.

Shut up, Bernie.

...although you're not wrong.

Tanis winced and glanced upstairs right as another crash sounded against the floor. This time, there was no accompanying scream.

Maybe Ariadne's dead, and maybe that's a mercy.

"She is your future but not without—come to me. Come, come. Yesss. Free me. I will tell you any and all. But you must free me before the Gorgons do."

Before the Gorgons do?

So not a Gorgon.

"I will tell you what your mother will not," came the singsong reply before she—probably a she?—exploded into piercing, echoing giggles. It was loud enough Tanis took two steps closer to the bulkhead, eyeballing the stairs to the main house in case the clamor called attention, but no one came. Footsteps above, crossing, but they never neared the door

"Probably used to it," Tanis murmured.

Bernie snorted. "Used to nutters nutting? Good times."

Bernie waited on Tanis to make up her mind—to go or not to go. Tanis didn't know. She hedged, her fingertips tapping against the cold, concrete wall. The woman behind the door kept crooning her name. Taunting her? Tempting her? It was hard to tell with the half-pleas, half-demands. "Come to me. Please. I need you, but you need me. Save me, save her. Come, come, come!"

"Fuck it." Tanis reached into Bernie's leggings for the Colt, soothed by its weight against her palm. It'd blow a crater-sized hole in anything, which wouldn't stop either Gorgon sister, but would be a hell of a deterrent for pretty much anything else stupid enough to cross her. She eased over, her hand resting on the knob, the light under the door kissing the toes of her boots. Her pulse was up; temperature, too. She actually sweated, and that wasn't usually a thing with her reptile genes, but she was afraid. She glanced back at Bernie, who lingered closer to the stairs leading out than the ones leading up.

Tanis motioned with the gun. "If it's a trap, get Naree out of Florida. She's got money."

"Promise, doll." Bernie smiled, but it didn't reach her eyes, and in the abysmal lighting of the basement, her teeth looked yellow against her equally sallow skin.

Tanis thrust open the door, pointing the gun in at... well? She wasn't entirely sure, though an iron maiden came to mind, or maybe an old-fashioned dress mannequin. The light was dim inside, but it was enough to show off a metal torso and head piece held up by thick steel rods, the contraption a few inches shy of Tanis's six feet. There were no arms or legs to the thing, only a chrome chest with various wires poking out from the sides like spider legs. One wire led to a saline drip, another to a blood bag, and yet another to a colostomy bag.

On the floor was a lake of stains, none of them all that pleasing to behold.

"Barlasssssss," the thing hissed.

Tanis eyeballed the headpiece. It was a mask, a crude face sculpted in metal, everything uneven and battered like someone had hammered it out with little care for aesthetic. A pair of mismatched round holes revealed big brown eyes, the whites a sickly gold with starbursts of red veins along the edges, the skin surrounding them grayish and puckered like raisin flesh. There were two slits for nostrils mid-mask but no space for a nose. A rectangle, one inch tall by two inches wide and covered in a silvery mesh of wires, formed the mouth. Beneath, Tanis spied two rows of rotting teeth tucked between dry, cracked lips with weeping blisters at the corners.

What in the hell is going on?

"The door, the door, close the door and come to me. Pleeease." Tanis cast a look across the room at Bernie, raising her hand to let her know she was fine, before shutting the door behind her. She was in a supply closet, the shelves crammed with enough dry goods and canned vegetables to survive an apocalypse. The second shelf had been cleared for the medical supplies required to keep the metal-clad Frankenstein going. There was a heart monitor and other monitors—things Tanis didn't know how to read, but which had lots of red and green buttons and white lines on black screens. On the floor to the right was a mini-refrigerator with a first aid sticker. Besides that, a trash bin full of discarded latex gloves.

Tanis dropped the gun, feeling ridiculous pointing it at a suit of armor that, without legs, wasn't coming to get her anytime soon. "What are you?"

"Someone like you, but I am dead but not dead. I am and was Cassandra, they say. Brought back. Here. Here." She groaned and whimpered, smacking her lips behind the mask and slurping in breath with a wet rattle. "Brought here. To life. My heart. My heart, my heart. No, your heart." She wheezed hard. "Nareeee."

Tanis set her jaw.

Don't say her name.

It's profane coming from a thing like you.

"What about her?"

"She is your gift, has your gift. You must flee, but, but, but... you must... take me with you to succeed. To liiive."

"How the hell... I can't," Tanis said. "I can't get you out of here. You'd die on the way out of the swamp if you need all this shit."

"Yesss, die. That. Take my heart, my heart. They will... eat it. As they eat my flesh to see. They want my vision. That is why they brought me here. Back. To see with my sight. Cassandra's eyes see all. Eat the flesh, have the gift. Eating me. Eating me!" She ended on a plaintive wail. Tanis wanted to reach out and clap her hand over the mask's mouth hole, but what good would it do? The voice would just echo out from its metal cage. Her eyes strayed ceiling-ward. Nothing yet, no sign of the priests, but how long would she stay lucky?

"I can't help you if you get me killed. I... wait. Hold up. Cassandra? The prophetess? And what do you mean, 'eating you'?"

And do I even want to know the answer to these fucking questions?

"The ill-fated prophet, brought back with the blood of a

phoenix. To see for the priests. To be used by the priests. To find your queen for their gods and destroy her. They consume, piece by piece. My feet, then my legs. My hands and my arms. Not much left, but if they eat my heart, forever lost, the lamia. They will always see and always find. Potent meat. Most potent." Cassandra burst into laughter that turned quickly to shrieking sobs, made all the worse by the strange, hollow quality granted her by the metal cage. One of her health monitors beeped, a high-pitched, incessant alarm that sent Tanis scrambling. This time, the footsteps above did stop. This time, there was the squeak of floorboards, heading to the door at the top of the stairs.

Tanis abandoned the closet and dove for the shadowed nook under the stairwell, crouching low behind a Rubbermaid trash barrel. She couldn't see Bernie from where she hid, which was a good thing, because if she couldn't see her, neither could anyone else.

Probably.

She hefted the Colt, ready. Ready.

The overhead light snapped on. Through the slats between the stairs, Tanis watched bare feet with blackened heels descend. White robes heralded a priest, not a Gorgon, and a fattish white man with a glossy, bald head rounded the corner, a pair of black-rimmed glasses perched on a wide nose. He was nothing extraordinary or noteworthy, not to look at, and not in demeanor as he entered Cassandra's closet. His hissed "Shut up, you'll wake Stheno" was followed by a clang that sounded like he'd struck the armor holding Cassandra's tortured body.

Cassandra's screams abated to wheezy snivels as the man rummaged around, the hysterical beeping of the heart monitor calming along with the attached patient. The basement was silent, Bernie and Tanis solid ghosts among the dusty miscellanea. Cassandra started to sing as the man doctored her. It was off-key and horrible, with no real melody Tanis could make out. She clued in at the end of the ditty, though, in time to hear the prophetess' garbled, "I see your death, with guts and gore. Your insides spilled across the floor. Goodbye, Karl. Goodbye, goodbye, goodbye!"

Another hard clang sounded from the closet.

"Shut your mouth or we'll take your tongue next."

"It's too late for that, Karl. Too late now. But know your death is a slow crawl awashed in blood. No one will care that you scream."

Karl exited the closet, stripping off his blue latex gloves and tossing them into the trash barrel hiding Tanis from his view. He slammed the door behind him. "At least I won't be eaten, you crazy bitch."

He went back upstairs, oblivious to the lamia in his midst as he snapped off the overhead light and plunged the basement back into darkness. Tanis didn't immediately move from her spot, too busy processing. She knew about gods and monsters and the magical worlds beyond her snake hole from other lamia. She knew about the Usurper, and about the fall from Heaven that made everything much more crowded down here on Earth, a few years before she was born. More recently, she'd heard of the god-killers, and about a new Chronicler. She knew Shit Was Going Down, and the gods were squabbling for power—a fight the Mother was keeping them all the hell out of.

She knew anyone could be more than what they seemed, and that it wasn't power that was good or bad so much as the wielder. But seeing it at play with Cassandra—experiencing something beyond Lamia's fucked-up repopulation tactics—was eye opening at the very least.

"One piece at a time, snakeling. Waste not, want not, so they leave the best for last. Take my heart before they do," came the dulcet call from the closet. "I die so Naree lives."

What am I even doing?

"Tanis."

Bernie. Tanis jerked her gaze over. Her friend was on the other side of the basement, popping up from behind a line of boxes like a prairie dog on its mound. She motioned up toward the bulkhead stairs. "Shit or get off the pot, doll. We gotta go."

They did have to go, and either Tanis went back inside to help that *thing* or she was running and trying to put the memory of the hobbled-together woman behind her, which wasn't likely given the gravity and weird-shit-ness of the moment.

And the fact that she knows Naree.

"Jesus Christ."

Before she could talk herself out of it, before she could regain her damned mind, Tanis pulled herself out from under the stairs and made for the closet.

CHAPTER NINE

"TELL ME A story, Tanis. Tell me a story," Cassandra rasped. Tanis's fingers worked at the sides of the metal casing holding the prophetess together. It was heavy, the cover threatening to snap off the steel support rods and fall to the floor. She didn't like to think how loud that would be.

"Not really in the mood," Tanis replied, placing one of her hands under the front of the case to support it.

"Tell me of Medusa and Perseusss." Tanis sighed, her eyes narrowing as another metal hook got caught on... something. They'd kept the carcass locked up tighter than Alcatraz. She wanted to pry it open like a tuna can, but again, sound factor. She had to work silently or everything would go to Hell.

"Why? Everyone knows the story."

"Tell me," Cassandra crooned. "Tell me a story before I die. Once upon a tiiime..."

"Fine, Christ." Tanis licked her lips, her lungs screaming for a cigarette. "Polydectes was romancing Perseus's mother. Perseus didn't like him, and Polydectes knew it, so to discredit Perseus in his mother's eyes Polydectes held a banquet where all the guests were expected to bring horses as gifts." Tanis shifted her grasp on the breastplate. One more latch and she felt it coming away. "Perseus didn't have a horse, so he said he'd bring anything Polydectes wanted instead. Polydectes asked for Medusa's head."

"Aaand?" Cassandra giggled as Tanis pulled the first piece away... only to reveal a second, thinner metal casing with colored wires threaded through tiny, drilled holes. Tanis ground her teeth. She began poking at it but then paused, hearing movement in the basement behind her.

Bernie?

She dared to breathe through her nose for the first time since the swamp. Yes, Bernie was close. There were other people nearby, too, but far enough she didn't have to worry about them yet. She relaxed a little, but the calm was short-lived when she realized the all-consuming lamia musk was too faint for a live breeder to be nearby. Traces lingered, of course, but it wasn't cock-arrestingly potent.

That, more than anything, told her that Ariadne was dead—she could function without double boners.

The closet door opened and Bernie slipped in. She said nothing, resting a hand on Tanis's shoulder while Tanis worked on Cassandra's manmade carapace. Tanis handed her the first breastplate to get it out of the way. Bernie eyed it, confused, and Tanis raked her hand through her hair, gesturing at the second layer of armor.

"I'm opening her up. I'll explain later."

"Not sure I want you to," Bernie replied, setting the chest piece carefully onto a shelf of canned peaches.

"Keep going, keep going." Cassandra trilled in pleasure as Tanis plucked at the wires, trying to see how they clipped in. If she ripped them all out at once, the monitors would start bleating and she'd have a stampede of Karls to contend with. That'd happen anyway when she took the heart, but if happened any sooner she was humped. She had to go slow, like playing the world's worst game of Operation, except instead of an irritating buzz, it'd be death by Gorgon.

"So Perseus prayed to Athena for help. Athena had a beef with Medusa because Medusa fucked Poseidon inside Athena's temple one time. Turning Medusa and her sisters into snake monsters wasn't good enough, I guess, so Athena decided to help Perseus kill her, too. She gave him a polished shield and sent him off to get other gear. Zeus gave him a sword to cut off her head. The Hesperides gave him a bag to hold Medusa's severed head so he wouldn't get poisoned. Hades gave him an invisibility hat to creep into her den, and Hermes gave him winged sandals so he could travel any terrain to get to her. He went to the cave..."

"No, no, no. That is only half the story. Silly snake. Silly Tanis."

Tanis lifted her eyes to that horrific mask. "There was a journey, but..."

"Journey, yes, and along the journey, Perseus met your mother. Mamaaa." Tanis had been running her hands along the sides of the second plate to see how it connected to the infrastructure, but Cassandra's taunt stopped her. Her mother had never told her anything about meeting Perseus, nor had she gone into any particular history with the Gorgons beyond racial superiority and genocide of the weaker snakes and blah, blah, blah.

The *blah, blah, blah* never involved her directly.

"What's that mean?"

"So ignorant, little snake. So stupid." Cassandra coughed, a wet, hacking thing that ended with sputum propelling from her mouth and mucking up the mesh of wires in front of her face. Tanis winced and went back to work, trying to ignore the smell of sterilized decay perfuming the room. "Perseus was pretty, so pretty. Dark hair with eyes as deep as an ocean. Your mother was alone on her island, her human beauty behind her, human children long in her belly. Eaten, as I am eaten, her first lamia daughters, too. All gone to her appetites. So many appetites, the lamia queen, the worst of her curse, perhaps." Cassandra moaned as Tanis found the lever in the back of the casing that would release the second chest piece. Tanis unclasped it. Bernie's hands came out to hold the sides for her, the older lamia cluing into Tanis's plans without explicit directions.

"She liked human men, wanted them," Cassandra continued. "Loved humans and thought her lamia self hideous."

"Well, that's changed. She hates humankind now." Tanis gently maneuvered the second plate away from Cassandra's body and immediately jerked away from the awfulness. Cassandra was skeletally thin, her skin brown and puckered with sores, her nipples black on shriveled piles of drooping meat. Two thick, metal bands attached her to the metal contraption, one at her shoulders, one at her pelvis. Between them, open wounds oozed, gooey swaths of her body stretching between her chest and the cover in Tanis's hand, thick ropes of pus and other unpleasantness drooping low before splashing onto Tanis's shoes. Wires poked into her chest, her belly, and down, lower, feeding fluids in, taking fluids out. Where her arms and legs had been were a network of sloppy sutures against puckered, dying skin, the wounds cauterized to keep her from bleeding out.

"Holy Jesus," Bernie said.

"Jesus ain't helping no one here." Tanis shivered and looked up at the ceiling, at the naked light bulb, at a pyramid stack of canned carrots. At anything that wasn't the tragic disaster before her. No one deserved that kind of torture. Not even her worst enemy, on his worst day.

Cassandra whimpered and groaned. "Listen. Listen to meee! Time depletes. Time dies."

Tanis maneuvered the plate around, being careful not to pull any of the wires or monitors away from her midsection. "Go on, then."

"Yes. Yesss! Zeus—he did not give his sword directly to Perseus. He threw it from Olympus and it fell upon the shores of Lamia's island. When Perseus came to claim it, Lamia thought to consume him as she'd done so many others, but he was so fair, and she was so hungry. Not for the eating of the flesh, but for the sweaty, grunting lust. To sate the eager wetness inside her coils." Cassandra sniggered, her laughter shaking her emaciated chest and making the pudding parts bounce. "Perseus did not want her, but he wanted the sword, and so he promised the queen he would return, after he took the head of Medusa. They would be lovers, he said. So smitten was Lamia, so full of wanting, she plucked her eye from her head and scried for him. It was Lamia that told the hero where to find the Gorgon. It was Lamia that drew him a map on the sand, and all because she wanted his seed frothing inside of her. Without her sight, Perseus would have sought the Gorgon for years, but with her aid? He killed Medusa *and* avoided detection by her vengeful sisters. Lamia was as much a tool as the shield or sword bestowed upon him by the gods."

"...that's not how Ma tells it," Bernie said. "She never mentioned that."

"Would you?" Tanis countered.

"Well, no, but Lady Babbles-Much could be lying."

Tanis regarded the broken creature before her, the melting flesh and the monster mask, and she shook her head in revulsion. "Wasn't that Cassandra's curse? To speak truth and never be believed? I'm choosing to believe her this time."

"I know all the truths, and the truth is Perseus spoke lies, and your mother waited and longed, and when the vision of his marriage to Andromeda besieged her, Lamia's hatred of humankind was born. Betrayal burns brightest, yes?" Cassandra paused, her tone turning coy. "The Gorgons well know this, too. They wanted revenge upon Lamia for her hand in Medusa's slaying then, and want it still, all this time later, and use me as their weapon. This plague upon you all, Lamia get, was brought upon you by your mother's base desires. By Lamia's insatiable appetites for cock and flesh and flesh and cock."

Delighted with her lewdness, Cassandra hummed beneath her breath, voice loud and soft and everywhere in between. Tanis ignored it, focusing on Cassandra's chest, and most specifically, her heart. The body was so frail, the ribs would probably crack like toothpicks with a single punch, but she couldn't punch too hard or she'd damage the heart with her strike.

Why is that a bad thing?

"Why do I need your heart?"

"If you leave any remnants, the phoenix blood will raise me again. Take me with you; use me for trade. It is currency some cannot ignore. Take it, Barlas. Take it and free me from my prison. Taaake it and save yourself and your love and your legacy. Go home, to your Naree."

Stop saying her damned name.

Just... get the hell out of here. Now. Get out.

"Get to the door and get ready to run." Tanis said to Bernie. "When I pull this thing out, every alarm she's hooked to will go off."

"You can't be serio—"

"Do it, Bernie. Or we're fucked. *More* fucked. Go."

Berenike hesitated, scowling at Tanis, scowling at the half-mad, half-dead woman propped up before them, before abandoning the closet and making her way to the bulkhead. She inhaled deeply, deep enough Tanis could hear it, and grunted. "Clear outside the door. And just for the record, I think you're batshit."

"I probably am." Tanis lifted her eyes to the mask, to the painfully alert brown eyes flickering behind the mismatched eyeholes. "You ready?"

"As the rain. Right as rain. Nothing can be gained without loss, Barlas. Faith. Love. Dawns follow dusks. My heart. Your heart. Strong and true. Follow them. Send me to the Elysian Fields."

Tanis didn't understand, but she wouldn't humor the Mad Hatter any longer than she absolutely had to, either, and so she pulled her hand back, counted to three, and punched forward, into the hot, runny mess of woman. Blood and meat exploded in a spray across Tanis's face, neck and chest. A gob landed on her lashes and she had to blink it away to see. It gushed over her hand as she pushed deeper into Cassandra's torso, toward the strong muscle beating so fast and hard. As she suspected, Cassandra's bones gave way without much pressure. The prophetess didn't react to the pain beyond a pathetic wheeze, not even when Tanis's hand closed around her heart, fingers feeling it pump wet and slimy in her hand. Tanis's forearm was nestled within the cavity, snug as a bug, like Cassandra's body was willing and able to swallow her whole.

Tanis didn't tarry, for her sake or Cassandra's; she adjusted her grip and, with one vicious tug, jerked the heart free. Blood ran in rivers. The monitors exploded with sirens. Tanis released her hold on the second chest piece and let it clang to the floor as she ran from the closet, a blur of woman, toward the bulkhead and the waiting Bernie. Outside, into the midday heat and the brutal spring sun. There were no Gorgons, no priests to greet them. It was only the trees and shrubs of the Everglades. It was only the cold, dead stares of the Gorgons' victims as the lamias sprinted by.

CHAPTER TEN

THE HEART WEPT blood. Tanis pulled off her top, wrapping the organ in a vain attempt to stop it from dripping everywhere. When that didn't work, she took off her baseball hat and dropped it in. What the hell she was supposed to do with the heart of a Chronicler, she didn't know. Trade it, Cassandra said, but to whom? Who'd want it? A bruja or a völva or some other spirit talker? Tanis knew exactly zero of those and she had no intention of eating it herself. She might have all the magical ability of a fart, but she was comfortable with her fartness. Fartiness. Fartishness.

I could feed it to a gator, but when a prophetess says to keep a human heart, you should probably keep a human heart and shut up about it. Besides, better useless to me than in the hands of the Gorgons.

There was no point agonizing over it, and so she concentrated on running. Bernie was the one to veer off into shallow water to help cover their tracks—any dripping blood would land in the marsh instead of on the grass. Boots and sneakers pounded, water flew, their pants drenched from thigh to toes. Soon, they were upon the corpse of the priest Daphne had killed. Soon, they were past it and circling around one of the bigger lakes.

The Gorgons and their priests couldn't scent track like the lamia. They could, however, eat what remained of Cassandra's flesh to gain temporary sight to try to find them. Everything Tanis knew about the sight said it was a fickle gift, often not showing you what you wanted to see so much as what it wanted you to see. Sometimes it could be steered, thus Lamia's somewhat useful vision about Ariadne, but not always. They had to hope it was the Gorgons' day to encounter Murphy and his Law and not the lamias', otherwise they were leading a pair of angry Gorgons and their followers right into the heart of lamia country.

"What are we going to tell Ma?" Bernie panted. They'd sprinted for miles, and only when there were no scent signatures on the wind did they dare rest. Both women leaned against trees, Bernie red-faced with exertion, Tanis's body slick with sweat. Tanis wanted a cigarette but she wasn't sure her screeching lungs could handle it.

Tanis dragged her forearm across her brow, accomplishing nothing more than smearing Cassandra's blood into her hair, too. "Keep it simple. Ariadne, the Gorgons, that's it. Cassandra and the heart, Perseus—that's extra. She doesn't need to know what we know."

"She might know already."

"Depends on what she's seen, sure, but she didn't even know the Gorgons were out here. It's not an exact science. We'll roll with what she throws at us."

Tanis pushed herself away from the tree, swatting flies off of the bloody lump in her hat. She wanted nothing more than to go home, to slough off the sticky meat on her skin and curl up with her best girl and never let go. Or, conversely, to let her go as quickly as possible and get her to safety, if need be. Her mother didn't deal in idle threats.

"Why'd you help her?" Bernie asked, motioning at the hand. "Cassandra. The Naree thing?"

"Pretty much. Well, that and they were torturing her. Let's

get this shit over with," Tanis said, pushing herself away from the tree despite her body's protests. She helped Bernie up and they set off side by side, both smelling like the bottom of a compost heap. Tanis filled Bernie in on what she'd missed in the closet.

"That's pretty fucked up," Bernie said.

"Yep."

"Did she even tell you anything about Naree?"

Tanis shrugged. "Not really. She just said that if I killed her, Naree would live. Maybe Naree would have lived anyway, but it wasn't a risk I was willing to take."

"Fair."

And they walked, and walked, through brush and around saplings and by birds and alligators. By the time the flagpole, with its flapping, rippling shorts, rose against the sky, it was pushing suppertime. Tanis felt heavy all over, the muscles in her legs aching and her back sore. She was sticky and wet and holding a human heart, which was probably not the weirdest thing that had ever happened to her, and didn't that speak to a colorful life.

"I need to hide the heart," she said.

"...wh—right. Yeah. Hell, I'm too old for this."

"Yeah, you are." Tanis ducked into one of the Den's few standing buildings—the half-collapsed post office—and put the heart in the toilet. It was dry and cleanish and the last place anyone would look for anything good in the world, if the heart of a resurrected prophet could be considered 'good.' She put the lid down and walked outside, her sports bra stained rusty red, her midsection still splattered with blood despite sweating gallons. Her underwear glued to her crotch in uncomfortable ways. Her jeans felt like scratchy sausage casings around her thighs and her shoes squished with every step.

I'm disgusting.

"You ready?" Bernie asked.

"I wore my Sunday finest."

The lamias shared a look, then they shared a smoke, and then they headed underground.

* * *

TANIS'S EARS WOULDN'T stop ringing. A high-pitched, incessant screech stabbed at her brain no matter how many times she shook her head. Her vision swam, too, like she was drunk on a tilt-a-whirl. When Lamia struck, she struck hard, and Lamia was in the process of pummeling both of them, potentially to death in Bernie's case. Her heavy tail lifted and crashed down again on Bernie's huddled form, punishing her ribs and lower back with each strike.

At least Tanis was mostly deaf to the verbal diarrhea spewing from her mouth.

"Worthless!"

"You should have died instead!"

"I hate you!"

Feeling's mutual, you psychotic bitch.

"MOTHER!" Tanis was shouting, though she still couldn't hear herself. "THE GORGONS ARE COMING. WHO'D HAVE WARNED YOU IF WE'D DIED?"

Lamia had grabbed Bernie by the hair to pull her up off of the floor. She looked like she wanted to snap her in half, but Tanis's proclamation, ill-advised as it was, stopped her. She settled for smacking Bernie across the face and sending her sailing instead. Bernie hit the floor and curled into a pill bug shape, her shoulders trembling as she sniveled in pain.

The old girl needs help. I have to get her out of here.

Lamia whirled around, her coils circling Tanis's waist. So much muscle beneath those scales, squeezing, constricting, but not so much they'd crush Tanis to death. It was just enough to make it hard to breathe. Just enough to make her feel like her spine was pressed against all her guts and her hips were about to dislocate from the sockets.

"What do you know?" Lamia demanded.

"Ariadne wouldn't tell them your location; they tortured her to death for it. They're still looking for you. There's time to get away."

"Yes. Yes, she is a good daughter. *Was.* Oh, *oh!* Ariadne! My beautiful girl." Lamia bellowed, her lament filling the cavern and echoing out, beyond, down the pipe and into the main expanse where the unloved daughters toiled, waiting for news. Lamia's hands covered her face while she sobbed. Her swollen midsection rubbed against Tanis's back; Tanis could feel the shapes there, the oval eggs already formed and pushing at Mother's flesh, demanding their birth.

Don't be so eager, girls. It's not so good on the outside.

Lamia wiped away tears and snot with a wad of her matted hair before thrusting Tanis away. "Get me Sibylla. Yes. She will look for a new den. We must plan our escape. Soon, but not in haste. Errors are made in haste. Like Argentina." She slithered back to her pile of mattresses and sprawled on her back to stare at the stone roof of her den, her mountain of skim milk flesh quivering with upset. Again she burst into sobs. Tanis didn't care. Ariadne and Daphne were a loss, yes, but a small, twisted part of Tanis relished her mother's suffering too much to grieve for them.

It was petty. Sometimes, petty was okay.

"Take Berenike with you," Lamia said. "She soils my floor with her blood. You too. You're disgusting."

"Yes, Mother."

Before Lamia's mercurial mood landed either of them in traction, Tanis collected Bernie from the floor and threw her over her shoulders, fireman's carry style, and jogged from the Den. Bernie groaned with every step.

"How bad are you hurt?" Tanis asked.

"I'll live," Bernie rasped. "Have I mentioned I'm too old for this shit?"

"What?"

"I SAID I'M TOO OLD FOR THIS SHIT."

"I'm sorry."

She meant it. Lamias could take a lot of punishment, but there was a limit. Bernie's face was bloodied again, and the tooth that had threatened to come out after Mother's first tantrum had been knocked out during the second, leaving a gap in her front bottom row. Her nose was swollen, her left eye puffed up and nearly closed and fated to turn ugly shades of yellow and purple. Four shallow gashes crossed her shoulder and chest from a slap that had landed at a bad angle. Bernie's middle was nearly as bloodied as Tanis's, and Tanis had ripped a human heart out an hour ago.

Tanis juggled Bernie's weight so it fell more naturally against her neck. "Where am I taking you?"

"Barbara. She'll get me."

Bernie had to repeat it three times thanks to the ringing in Tanis's ears. They trudged through the main pipe, getting looks from their sisters—some curious, some afraid, some disdainful. The last came from the loyalists, the few humanoid daughters who thought the answer to pleasing their mother was copious amounts of ass-kissing. It bought them some indulgence sometimes, but Lamia was just as quick to abuse them if they displeased her. They were, just like every other human daughter, tools to be used and discarded.

They probably think Lamia's tears are my fault.

Well, fuck you, too.

Tanis stopped mid-nest, where the population was thickest, midway down the passage from Mother's chamber to the end of the pipe. A fluorescent light hung overhead, granting her a spotlight in all the shadowed dankness.

"LAMIAS!" Tanis's voice boomed, echoing through the vast expanse. She was too deaf to gauge her volume, but by Bernie's wince and the collective swivel of heads, she had their attention. "Ariadne and Daphne are dead. May they rest in the Elysian Fields together, strong."

There were some gasps and some groans followed by whispers and tears. A few of the true daughters emerged from their silken prison for news, and when it was relayed, they keened, feeling the loss of one of their own. They clung to one another, arms and tails entangled, moaning their sadness. Tanis looked none of them in the eye as she resumed hauling Bernie toward Barbara's hovel.

One delivery, one message to relay to Fi, one heart to collect from a shitter, and she could go home to the only person she wanted to see.

She licked arid lips.
Get me the hell out of here.

"HOLY CRAP, BABE. You look like shit. Are you okay?"

Naree was on the couch in front of the TV in her dinosaur print pajama pants and a blue T-shirt with a tech logo printed across the chest. In one hand she had the remote; in the other, a box of crackers. Her feet were propped on the ottoman, one of those silly foam things separating her toes to keep her blue sparkle pedicure fresh. Her hair was in a ponytail, her contacts off and her glasses on. A box fan was propped on an Amazon carton by her feet to keep her in the direct blast zone of more tolerable air.

"Long day. I'll explain in a bit. How are you?"

"Kinda gross," Naree confessed. "I'm bloated. Like, *Hindenberg* bloated. If I explode you can have all my cool stuff."

"Don't explode. I'd miss you."

Naree grinned. "Okay, but you're missing out; my stuff is really cool. I have a Nintendo 64, you know, and a copy of *Paper Boy*. That shit's like nerd gold."

"Tempting! But no."

Tanis wanted to bury her face in Naree's hair and breathe her in, to stroke her face and kiss her, but didn't want to get any of the grossness on her, so she slunk off to the shower, stripping out of her clothes and dropping them in the trash bin, the Colt left in the sink until she could put it with the six or seven or ten she already had in the closet. The heart was in the trunk of the Caddy; it wasn't an ideal place for it, considering the Florida heat, but it was a whole hell of a lot better than bringing it in and stuffing it in the freezer.

Wasn't it?

She wasn't going to worry about that for a while.

The water circling the drain went from crimson to pink to clear quicker than she anticipated. She brutalized the soap, cramming it into places no soap was meant to be crammed, scrubbing her skin raw to eradicate any last traces of viscera from her hair, her ear. Her hearing was better—not great, but better—and the weird gob of people that had gotten stuck behind her ear washed off, so all in all she was feeling better.

Hungry, but better.

She toweled off and slipped on a pair of boxer briefs and the first clean T-shirt in the laundry basket, which happened to be one of Naree's that read, *All I Hear is Noise, Noise, Noise*. The Colt was put on the top shelf of the closet along with its cousins. A trip to the kitchen reminded her that they'd grocery shopped the day before, and she threw together a couple of sandwiches before heading over to the couch and gingerly sitting down. The right cushion had a spring that could get stabby if you weren't careful, which each of them had found out the hard way before.

Tanis tucked into the sandwich, content to be home with her familiar smells. Dust, a little bit of mold in the walls, the ghost of cigarettes past, and Naree, who was... she smelled good. Freshly showered, covered in that vanilla-scented glitter lotion she liked to buy from Walmart. And hormones. She'd smelled sweet still, sweeter than usual, though that was probably due to Tanis's poor nose being stuffed full of death, lamia pheromones, and heart blood all day.

"I have a heart in the trunk," Tanis said in opening. "I'd like to put it in the freezer if you don't mind."

Naree side-eyed her.

"...okaaay. Why?"

And so Tanis filled her in on everything, start to finish. Naree looked properly horrified, asking questions Tanis didn't know the answer to, mostly about Cassandra's resurrection and how they'd found her body in the first place. She did, eventually, ask the question Tanis feared about the encroaching Gorgons, though, and that wasn't a feel-good maker.

"So what's this mean for us?"

Tanis crammed bologna and cheese into her mouth, condiment free, because mayonnaise and mustard both just smelled like vinegar to her. "If I think you're in danger, you'll have to head home to Connecticut or far north, like Alaska, where it's cold."

Naree frowned. "But you're coming, right?"

"...I don't know."

Naree stared at her for a long minute before chucking her box of crackers at her. Tanis winced as it smacked against her forehead and tumbled to the floor. "Bullshit. You're coming."

"It's not that simple. I would, you know I would, but my mother..."

"Oh, fuck your mother."

No thanks.

Naree jabbed Tanis in the side with a pointy fingernail. "Seriously, why can't we just go? You hate her, she hates you. Should be end of story."

Tanis sighed and crammed the last half of Sandwich One into her mouth, washing it down with a stolen guzzle from Naree's water bottle. "I had a sister. Name was Agnetha. She got tired of my mother's shit, I guess, because she took off. My mother spent two months straight scrying for her, and when she finally tracked her to Arizona, sent three of my other sisters to drag her home. She assembled all of us in her den and made us watch as she ate her, alive. I remember my mother's jaw dislocating and her throat bulging and Agnetha's muffled screams as she was swallowed. She suffocated before Mom got her halfway down, but it... I was six. It happened again when I was eleven, and again when I was fifteen. You don't forget that. It's awful, and my mother's so goddamned petty, I don't trust her not to send an army after me. Us. And you can't outrun a lamia nose. You just can't."

Naree frowned, but her hand came out to capture Tanis's, lifting it to her mouth and pressing soft kisses to her knuckles. "We'll figure it out, babe. We're smart. We got the tools. Go to Europe or, I don't know, the mother country. I know like six words in Korean and one of them is 'bathroom' and another's 'umbrella.' We got this."

Tanis didn't want to smile, but she couldn't help it. That's what Naree did to her—make her laugh when all she wanted to do was watch the world burn. "Maybe." She pulled Naree close, avoiding the murder spring in the couch as she tucked her best girl's head against her shoulder. Her cheek pressed to the glossy black hair, her arms held her tight, and for a few minutes, she enjoyed the simple comfort of a warm body pressed against hers.

CHAPTER ELEVEN

"THAT'S LOVE, YOU know," Naree said, watching Tanis slip the heart into the freezer. "Giving you the good Tupperware so you can store some dead chick's heart in it."

Tanis grinned, closing the freezer and pulling Naree close to drop her chin on top of her head. Her arms wrapped around Naree's waist. Naree's hands settled on Tanis's ass, fingers digging into the taut muscle.

"Man, if I didn't feel like dirt, I'd be all over this right now," Naree said, giving a few firm squeezes. "It's like two hams."

"Hams. Having a ham ass is good?"

"Oh, yeah. Firm. Juicy. Not really pink, though. So like... light brown ham. Beigey-brownish ham."

Tanis grinned and snuffled at her, looking for sickness or anything off in her body chemistry that could be responsible for her malaise, but all she got was that surge of hormones, that concentrated sweetness that happened before Naree bled. "I don't smell any sickness."

"Oh, you probably wouldn't. It's probably the cheese in a can I ate."

Tanis pulled back to look her in the face. "You actually ate that garbage?"

"Why not? Easy Cheese is bomb. I was putting it in Bugles and making mini-ice cream cones while I watched *The Avengers*, but then I decided the corn delivery system was secondary to cheese whippets. I have regrets now. Huge ones. I probably won't poop for, like, a year."

Tanis smirked and pressed a kiss to Naree's forehead, her atrocious day further behind her because Naree was there, being Naree, and that was the best thing in her world. "I honestly have no idea what to say to you right now."

Naree grinned despite the horrific gurgle shrieks going on in her mid-section. "YOLO?"

"Sure. I guess."

Naree slapped her on the ass before tromping through the apartment toward their bedroom. Tanis checked the locks, checked the lights, checked the everything so she could rest somewhat easy. Naree had moved the box fan from the living room into their bedroom so she wouldn't melt to death, and was busy mummifying herself in a sheet when Tanis came in to flip off the switch.

"They're like flashlights," Naree said.

Tanis went to the closet for a gun. Nothing vulgar like the Colt, but something more respectable: the Glock 19. It was smaller than the other pistols, but it still held fifteen rounds of Fuck Off. She put it in her nightstand drawer and climbed into bed. "What, my eyes?"

"Yeah. If the light catches them at all, it's like two laser beams. Zshoooooooo."

Zshoooooo was apparently what laser beams sounded like in Naree Land. Tanis chuckled and pulled her close. Her head dropped to Tanis's shoulder. Within minutes Tanis was out cold, the day's events draining her enough that she didn't dream, or if she did, she'd have no recollection of it upon waking.

Which was at nine in the morning.

Because Naree was puking out her brains in the bathroom.

It was rare for anything to get past Tanis—she woke at every cat's fart—but the Gorgon thing and the Cassandra thing and the brutal beating she'd taken at the end of it all had wiped her out to the point Naree was able to sneak past her—not good in the event of an emergency. She rolled out of bed and headed for the bathroom, squinting against the too-bright sun polluting the hall.

"Are you okay?"

Naree spit into the toilet. She was on the floor on her knees, one hand braced against the gold-tiled wall, the other flat against the side of the sink cabinet. Her eyes watered, her cheeks were red from strain. The room reeked of bile. Tanis crouched beside her to rub her lower back, her free hand going to her hair and holding it so she didn't get vomit in it if she retched again. *When* she retched again; Naree's shoulders heaved, her abdominal muscles contracted, and she spewed liquid nothing into the toilet water.

"I feel gross," Naree managed, voice raw.

"I'm sorry. Do you want some water?"

"Yes. Please."

Tanis headed for the kitchen to grab one of the plastic bottles beside the sink. The tap water was always too chlorinated for her nose, and so they tended to buy cases of a local spring instead. She brought it back to the bathroom and put it next to Naree's knee, on the pink shag rug with the funny hole cut out in the middle for the toilet base.

Naree retched twice more before going slack, her forehead resting against the cool porcelain. Tanis pressed a kiss to her shoulder, running the ball of her hand along Naree's spine.

"What do you need?"

"I'm late," Naree said.

"What?"

Naree rotated her head to look Tanis in the eye, her face still resting against the toilet. Her hand reached up to fumble with the lever to flush her sick away. "I did the math. I'm late. Two weeks. Didn't really think about it. So this is either canned cheese from Hell or something really messed up is going on."

"Messed up."

Pregnant. She's saying she might be pregnant.

But... Mother said.

Oh, fuuuck.

Tanis sat up straighter. She wasn't awake enough for this shit. Or, hell, she wouldn't be awake enough for it *ever*. Ever since she'd been small, her mother had told her how useless the humanoid daughters packing cock were; "all that potential, wasted." She'd never outright said it, but the implication was that she'd tried to breed with her own get to produce purer-blooded lamia in the past, and it hadn't gone anywhere, ever, in thousands of years.

What if she was wrong?

Or what if I'm different.

"I didn't cheat on you," Naree slumped, eyes closed. "I swear."

"I know you didn't." It wasn't just that she trusted Naree, although she did. Tanis's nose would have smelled someone else on her, especially semen. It had a distinct odor, and even post-washing, it lingered too far inside the vaginal canal to get it all out, even with a douche. Tanis could smell herself on Naree for a full day after they coupled. There was no way she would have gotten a lover by the boards, not that she would have thought it of her in the first place; the nose was never wrong.

She has that stronger scent. The sweetness...

"Hell." Tanis stood up and padded back toward the bedroom to get dressed. She pulled on fresh boxers, jeans, and a T-shirt, not bothering with a bra because she didn't have much tit anyway and no one would know the difference. The boots were still wet, and so she went for an old pair of olive-green Chucks that she didn't bother to lace.

"Where are you going? Are you okay?" Naree called.

"I should be asking you that. I'm fine. I'm just going to run to the store and get you a test. Better to know for sure."

"Maybe it's the Easy Cheese," Naree offered, her voice a little stronger. "That shit's toxic sludge in a can."

"It's not Easy Cheese."

"Yeah, I know it's not, but you could humor me a little. Just once."

She said she's bloated. Mother gestates quickly. Shit, shit, shit.

"Okay, so maybe it's the Easy Cheese," Tanis said, opening a fresh pack of Marlboros and slipping one between her lips. She smiled around it, trying to look a lot calmer than she felt, and went back to the bathroom to stroke Naree's head. She smelled like puked-up Skittles, which wasn't nearly as charming as pukeless Skittles. "You okay for me to go now?"

"Yeah, just hurry back."

"Eat some crackers."

"You're not my real mom."

"Okay, don't eat crackers."

"Fine! I'll just sit here and puke instead."

"You do that."

Tanis grabbed her wallet and keys and jogged down the apartment building's steps. She climbed into the Caddy spied her cell phone on the passenger's seat, tossed there at some point during her drive back from Adder's Den the night before. The light at the top flashed with a message. She called her voicemail, because borrowing problems about Schrödinger's Baby did nothing for her equilibrium; though, to be fair, neither did Bernie's voice when it hit her ear.

"Hey, doll. It's me. Do yourself a favor and avoid the Den today. Ma's on a tear. We're fortifying in case of attack. I'm laid up bad, but feeling a little better. Toothless, but better. Talk soon. Text me if you need anything."

Tanis had no inclination to go to the Den on a normal day, never mind a day after she got smacked so hard she saw stars like one of those *Looney Tunes* cartoons. She slipped the phone into her pants pocket and put her hands back on the wheel, trying to focus on the smoke blackening her lungs and not the panic stewing in her belly.

If Ma finds out, she'll never let me go. Ever. I'd be her fuck puppet forever. She'd hurt Naree. And the baby. Shit, she's already threatened Naree. And if we run... fuck. What if she sees it? Scries it out and sees a fat swollen belly or a baby? And what if it's a fucking snake? Would Naree ever forgive me? I wouldn't. I'd hate me.

Fuck, fuck, fuck.

By the time she parked the Caddy at Walmart, her heart beat fast and a long string of obscenities paraded through her head on repeat. She practically ran to the Family Planning aisle, blindly fumbling for a box and making her way to the ten items or less checkout. The old man behind the counter in his too-chipper blue vest eyed the test and then her left hand. Seeing no ring, his lips flattened into a disapproving grimace. Tanis practically tossed the twenty-dollar bill at him, hoping the old fart was stupid enough to say something about her unwedded bliss. It was better to scream at a judgmental clerk than to let Naree know she was fast approaching a breakdown about their kid.

Maybe kid.

But I'm pretty sure it's a kid. Shit.

She drove home, stopping at the golden arches to score breakfast on the off chance Naree found an appetite after her spewfest. Into the driveway, up the stairs, through the front door. Naree had migrated, now sprawled on the couch, a metal bowl by her head, the empty water bottle clutched to her chest. Her eyes were closed, her coloring better than it had been before Tanis left.

"I brought coffee and a bacon, egg and cheese."

"Cool. Let's pretend food's not gross and put it on the coffee table."

Tanis did as she asked, dropping off the bag and moving down to her feet. She lifted them up and sat, rubbing Naree's toes, her eyes skimming up her legs to her stomach and lingering there. It was swollen. Her girl was 'fluffy'—Naree's word for her chub—so a few extra pounds wasn't something that would have called attention right away. But now that she was looking, really looking, she couldn't help but notice that the stomach looked different from usual. Her midsection was less gentle sloping rolls of soft girl fat and more a mound with the rolls portioned out to the sides.

Mom's clutches gestate in three days. She could be a day along, or two days, or months. I have no idea.

"Do you have to pee?" Tanis asked. "It said on the box to do it in the morning."

Naree groaned. "No, but I'll find some in me. Help me up."

Tanis did, walking her to the bathroom by the elbow. Naree shook her off, frowning as she jerked the Walmart bag from her grasp and closed the bathroom door. Tanis stuffed another cigarette into her mouth because she was absolutely positive the next three minutes would be the longest three minutes of her life. She let herself out of their living room and onto their 'veranda'—a shitty little walkway with only enough room for a rusted-out folding chair and an empty flower pot—and smoked her butt to the filter far faster than she should have.

A little while later, she heard the bathroom door opening, feet shuffling. She glanced behind her. Naree appeared in the hallway, her hands in her hair, her cheeks red.

"Well. Congrats? I guess?"

Tanis ground out the cigarette on the metal railing and tossed the dead soldier into the flower pot by her feet. Her brow was furrowed, she could feel it, and she evened it out so she looked as calm as possible when she went back inside, pulling the screen door into place in case a breeze wanted to usher out the humidity.

"We need to talk."

"I... yeah. Okay." Naree sat down again, her eyes fixed on the blank TV screen, her arms wrapped over her stomach. Tanis sank in beside her, her hand going to her knee and squeezing. Naree's hand slid over to rest atop of hers, her fingers light against Tanis's darker ones. There were no words, only silent comfort and shared terror. Tanis's brain swam with a million what-ifs, but she wanted to give Naree time to adjust to the first bomb before she dropped any more.

"So maybe this is years of being cunt-punted by the Catholic church, but I don't think I can get rid of it," Naree said eventually. "I don't feel good about that possibility."

"Okay."

"I've got insurance still. Blue Cross through my parents for at least another six months. I should call a doctor." Tanis nodded. Naree sucked in a breath. "Probably an OB/GYN." Tanis nodded again and pulled out her phone, finding the insurance website and plugging in their zip code for offices nearby. There was an OB/GYN not ten miles away, in the next town over, that'd take their insurance, according to the internet.

But.

"Hon." Tanis handed the phone over so Naree could call and swept a lock of thick black hair behind Naree's ear. A strand got caught on her topmost piercing, a little gold hoop, and she gently disentangled it. "You realize it's quarter-lamia. I'm sorry."

"Sorry for what? It's on me, too. I could have gone on the pill and I didn't." Naree put the phone down to balance on the meatiest part of her thigh.

"You didn't because I told you I was sterile. I'm supposed to be. All the other lamias are. I just... maybe we're evolving? Nature finds a way or some bullshit."

"Or maybe you're special," Naree said, smiling faintly. "Well, you are special, but now we know you're super-special." She eyed the McDonald's bag and pulled away from Tanis to dig into her breakfast, the nausea clearly replaced by something that looked vaguely feral as she crammed McMuffin into her face. Tanis watched her, her gaze drifting down to the midsection poking out the T-shirt at the waist. That was her son or daughter in there. It was, if they were lucky, a healthy little boy or girl and not some fucked-up half-snake-monster with four dicks and venom spit.

"I'm afraid of what its snake blood could mean for it," Tanis admitted quietly.

Naree nodded and eyed her, her cheeks stuffed full like a squirrel. "I get that."

"No, I don't think you do. My mother has snakes—like actual snakes—sometimes. Or daughters like me or—some of the other daughters have human shapes but are covered in scales or have retractable fangs and venom. Sometimes the genes aren't compatible at all and it'll hatch—right. Hatching. So it could be an egg. My mother has eggs, and they hatch, and the babies sometimes can't sustain themselves. And sometimes, rarely, really rarely, it's human up top and snake at the bottom. They die a lot when they're kids, the True Daughters. Naree. If we go in to see a doctor, and it's wrong on the ultrasound..."

"We'll terminate," Naree said. "If it's wrong. I... an egg? Wait, you're saying I could lay an egg?"

"Maybe," Tanis confessed. Naree looked nonplussed as she grabbed her hash brown and bit into it. Tanis shifted on the couch. "...it'll also probably gestate faster than a human baby. My mother's clutches gestate in three days."

Naree's eyes got real big, her chewing stopped, and she looked down at the phone. One minute later, she was hash-brown-free and calling the doctor.

CHAPTER TWELVE

"I CAN'T FIND my insurance card."

A cancellation at the doctor's office meant they could sneak in at four, which the secretary assured Naree was super-lucky because they were usually booked out, and with Naree not knowing how far along she was but actually showing, it was imperative that she see someone as quickly as possible.

Tanis waited by the door, holding Naree's *My Little Pony* pocketbook while Naree tore through the house. She wasn't the most organized girl; her personal stuff was sorted into neat stacks, yes, but neat stacks of *everything*: junk mail, important documents, video game discs. Her diploma was in there next to a print-out from the internet of a guy in a unicorn costume next to pizza delivery coupons.

"Ha! Got it. Okay, cool."

Naree flourished it like it should have been gilded. Tanis offered her the purse and held the door. It was raining out, one of those sky-piss ordeals in Florida that lasted a half-hour and went away without touching the humidity, and so they ran to the car. Along the way to the doctor's office, they stopped for iced teas from a drive-through, both of them quiet. Naree looked out the window, stroking the straw in her plastic cup with a faraway expression on her face. Tanis watched the road and stewed. She and Naree had never discussed kids because kids were, as far as they both knew, off the table. Now she was not only looking down the barrel of being a parent, but there was the distinct possibility she'd implanted a monster in the woman she loved.

Stop borrowing problems.

Even if they're totally reasonable fears to have about a baby that's a quarter snake.

"We don't have to," Naree blurted. "Have it, if you don't want."

Tanis opened her mouth to respond, but nothing came out. No sound. No witticism or assurance. What the hell was she supposed to say? "It'd be easier if we didn't"? Sure, it'd be easier, but would Naree regret it? For that matter, would Tanis? It was something they'd made together, possibly a once-in-a-lifetime thing. Who knew if it was the single sperm that could? If they couldn't do it again later, when maybe they wanted to, would they look back at their haste and mourn?

"I support you, whatever you want to do," Tanis managed instead, taking a turn.

Naree frowned. "If it's fine—normal—I still want to keep it, I think. You just look so miserable."

Do I?

"I'm sorry." Tanis licked her lips. "I'm worried about you. Not just the physical stuff. We'll find out if that's a thing soon enough, but my mother. She hates humans. I've told you that." She could see Naree nodding from the corner of her eye. "Right, so if she finds out that one of her half-lamias can knock her up, giving her purer snake children, I'm afraid of what she'd do. To me. To you. You'd be carrying her line and it'd be... she'd see it as weak. Lesser."

Tanis thought that's all she had to say, but more came spilling out, like once she'd uncorked the keg, the spigot wouldn't stop. "I worry that you're saddling yourself with me, or some part of me, forever. I've watched my mother kill people. I've kidnapped for her so she *can* kill people. I've lied, cheated, and stolen. Shit, I have a body part in my freezer. I'm grateful that you put up with it, that you can see that I'm not all bad, but I'm not good either. I worry that this is another way to tie you to a really fucked-up situation. A fucked-up person."

"It is, but." Naree reached over for Tanis's hand, pulling it away from the steering wheel and locking their fingers. "I picked you. I love you."

"I know you do. I'm just not sure *why*."

Naree snorted. "Heard a saying once from my neighbor back in Connecticut. 'Love's where you find it, even if it's up a pig's ass.' It doesn't matter why I love you. I do. Every part of me. You're mine, I'm yours. Your mother isn't going to take that away from either of us."

Maybe not. But she'll try.

"You can tell by looking at the genital tubercle," Dr. Patel said. He was an older man, in his mid-to-late-sixties, with black hair fringed with salt, brown skin, and a birthmark on his temple shaped like Kansas. His pens were neatly lined up in his pocket, his lab coat was pristine white. His silvery mustache was the stuff of Tom Selleck dreams. "It's parallel to the spine, so I'm comfortable saying it's a girl. Ninety percent comfortable. Leave a little room for error."

Tanis stared at the screen.

It's a human baby. No egg. No weird snake tail. No deformities. It's a girl. A daughter. I have a daughter.

Dr. Patel lifted the wand from Naree's stomach to squirt more cold gel onto the side. She squirmed and squeezed Tanis's fingers, her eyes affixed to the monitor. She looked amazed at the small person growing inside of her. Also horrified, because he'd said during her initial exam, "You're around four months," and insisted they take a look with imaging, but she'd bled last month and the month before that, so the gestation was clearly very rapid. Sure, it was possible she'd been pregnant and bleeding at the same time, but Tanis had only honed in on her sweeter-than-normal scent for a day or two. She'd have caught onto it sooner otherwise.

Always trust the nose.

"Things are looking good. Let me print that up for you, and you'll start on the supplements, like I said." Dr. Patel hit a button on the keyboard and removed the wand. He used a soft cloth to de-goop Naree's roundish middle. "The lab is down the hall to the right for your blood screens. I'll follow up with you in a day or two. Make sure you stop by the front desk to schedule your next appointment."

"I'll have to call you," Naree said. "I don't have my calendar with me."

"That's fine."

Dr. Patel offered his hand. "Nice to meet you, Miss Kwon. Miss Barlas." He never batted an eye at either of them as he shook, standing from his short stool with its wheeled feet and excusing himself from the exam room. The picture of the *in utero* baby sat on the printer tray. Tanis picked it up, tracing her finger over the weird little alien with the too-big head and barely-there nose.

"I'm not going to make it to another appointment, am I?" Naree whispered.

"...probably not."

Naree looked resigned. She looped her arm around Tanis's waist and the two of them drifted down the hall together. Tanis started to turn toward the lab, but Naree shook her head and walked on, past the receptionist and out the double doors of the brick building and into the parking lot. The squall was already over, puddles amassing in the cracks and dips in the uneven pavement. With the humidity, they'd probably be there for another six years.

"I'll have to lie," Naree said. "To the hospital. I'll say I didn't know I was pregnant. How great is that? Graduated *magna cum laude* from Yale and I have to pretend I'm one of those teenagers on a reality show who mistakes an in-utero human for too many burritos."

"I'm sorry," Tanis said, because she was sorry, and while a healthy baby was a good thing, it was also an immediate thing that they weren't even a little bit prepared for.

We need to baby proof. And we need a crib and a high chair and diapers and formula and those weird bras that help leaky tits and a bazooka to keep my mother away and...

Naree ran her hand over her middle. "It's just my pride. I'll get over it. Man, I am... I have no idea what to think of any of this. My parents are going to shit themselves."

"We need stuff," Tanis announced, easing the car back onto the road. "Lots of stuff. Baby stuff. And a plan. Because when this gets out—"

"*If* it gets out. You're not sure yet," Naree interrupted.

"No, I suppose that's true, but we should have a contingency plan ready. Like, an actual place for you to go, that kind of thing." Tanis slipped a cigarette between her lips and promptly stopped herself from lighting it because not three feet away from her was the woman carrying her child. Second-hand smoke was bad for both her and the baby, and open windows would only do so much.

Everything has to change. Everything.

She put the cigarette back into the pack, slurping on the last vestiges of her iced tea instead, which was really just sun-warmed brown water after an hour in the car.

"I'll make a list," Naree said. "Of stuff. Some of it we can get from secondhand. Like, clothes and maybe the furniture. But we'll need diapers and formula. Jesus Christ, this is really real. Likely really, really real."

"Yeah it is," Tanis said.

And isn't that swell.

Naree was hungry, so they stopped to get her a burger, and then she was tired because pregnancy apparently made you tired according to Google, and she wanted a nap. When they got home, Tanis tried three times to talk to Naree about the aforementioned contingency plan, but every attempt was met with resistance. Naree would talk over it or outright ignore it to continue making a shopping list of baby supplies.

"Why don't you hit Goodwill and see what they have while I'm asleep? You know how random it is. I'd hate to miss out on a crib if there's one on the cheap."

"I don't like leaving you alone," Tanis said.

Naree looked annoyed as she got up from the couch to pad down the hall to their bedroom. "I get it, Tanis, but, like, I need you to lay off, please? This is stressful enough. If they're going to come, there will be groups of them, like you said about that chick that ran off to Arizona. Not a whole hell of a lot you're going to do against four people who are as strong as you."

"I'm worried," Tanis said, following her down the hall.

"So am I, but I'm not leaving you no matter what you say, and you're not going to hover over me for the rest of my life and the life of our kid. That's not how this is going to work."

Naree shut the door and turned on the fan, probably as much to drown out Tanis's objections as to get the bedroom cooler.

"What would you like to do about it?" Tanis said through the door. "Because 'nothing' isn't an acceptable answer to me. I love you, and I'll probably love our kid, so I'd like to know that we'll get through this."

"You'll *probably* love our kid? Good times. That's reassuring. If you're that freaked out, maybe we should take the risk and move, but I'm not talking about it right now. I'm tired."

That tone suggested that the conversation was over unless Tanis wanted to find herself in the middle of screaming match, which wasn't really a two-sided thing so much as Naree losing her temper, yelling a lot, and Tanis staying unflappably calm and making Naree angrier. It never went well, and with Naree being pregnant, riling her was a bad idea in every possible way. It was annoying, though, and Tanis gritted her teeth and strode through the apartment, locking both locks on the door like that would do any good keeping angry lamias away from her girlfriend.

Family. My family.

"Jesus Christ."

She slid a cigarette between her lips and leaned forward, staring at the odometer in the dash as she reconciled all that had happened, all that could happen, and all that certainly would be.

It was only a little terrifying.

GOODWILL HAD A high chair and one of those baby sling wraps you used to tie your kid to your chest so you weren't stuck carrying the little goblin around all the time. It also had a stroller and a single nursing bra in her size. There were cribs, too, but looking at them, Tanis couldn't decide what Naree would want, so she waited. It wasn't like they were going to run out anytime soon; they had a dozen on display. Cribs were one of those things that were used for a couple of years and quickly not needed anymore. Everyone wanted to get rid of them.

She was about to pack her loot into the trunk of the car when she realized she was being watched from inside the store, near the window. She raised her head, narrowing her eyes. There was a woman there she'd never seen before, small and dark-haired and dark-eyed, staring at her, a cell phone attached to her ear. Tanis frowned at her, but the woman kept right on looking despite Tanis's unspoken challenge.

It could be coincidence.

She sucked in air through her nose.

Not a familiar scent.

She climbed into the car and backed out of her parking spot. As she eased onto the curb, the woman trotted from the store, craning her head like she might be trying to read Tanis's rear license plate. Florida only required the one, so the front of the Caddy had the name of the dealership where she'd bought the thing still attached. That, she could change out. The rear plate, not so easy.

Not today, Satan.

Tanis checked the rearview. Seeing no cars, she backed up along the empty road, not into the lot next door, but the one after that, Mitsy's Diner, her wheels screeching and kicking up dust as she swung the car around as fast as the big ol' boat would go. Instead of going home the way she came and potentially driving past the woman, she took off in the opposite direction from Percy's Pass, away from Naree, to see if someone followed. The Glock was with her, tucked into the glove box, and she reached for it, sliding it beneath the bag of baby clothes so it was nearby in case of emergency.

No cars behind her. No cars in front of her. She was alone on the street.

She took a turn off onto a side road that would take her to a parallel route to the one she'd been on. It added some minutes to her drive, but she couldn't be too careful, not with two different species of snake women potentially spying on her with psychic powers. Not with her girlfriend at home sleeping off the trauma of finding out that she was impossibly pregnant and on an impossibly short timeline to give birth.

Naree's right. This isn't sustainable, and I need to take care of her instead of saddling her with my paranoia.

She smoked another cigarette as the adrenaline drained from her body.

Only for it to rise right back up again at the four-stop intersection at the center of Percy's Pass. It was a man, this time, on the fat side, with fair hair; he wore a blue T-shirt, a baseball hat, and a pair of jeans. The moment she stopped at the light, she glanced over at him and his pasty, unremarkable face. He promptly lifted his phone, aimed it right at her, and snapped a picture.

Oh, hell no.

CHAPTER THIRTEEN

TANIS DIDN'T EVEN shut off the engine. She grabbed the gun and climbed from the car, leaving the Caddy idling at the four-way stop.

"Who are you?" she demanded. The blond man's eyes widened beneath his hat brim, and then he took off. With that long a start, he should have been able to outrun most people, but not a lamia; Tanis closed the distance easily, her arm looping around his waist. She yanking him between two brick buildings, an empty store front with a *For Rent* sign and a dry cleaner with laundry lining the windows.

She threw him against the wall, the gun against his temple, her forearm pressed against an Adam's apple big enough to double as a baseball.

"Drop the phone," she snarled.

His eyes, cold and blue, showed no fear. She saw his jaw working, which didn't seem particularly strange until she heard a cracking sound. He swallowed, and the air—which had smelled of garbage and cat piss—had a new scent, a pungent, powdery suggestion of bleach. A smile spread across the stranger's as she figured out what he'd done. She grabbed his jaw and pulled down. Debris littered his tongue—white powder that could have been salt or sugar, but wasn't either. He convulsed once, there was a clatter as his phone dropped to the ground, and he bucked against her like they were fucking. His eyes rolled up, his lids fluttered, a trace of spittle flowed from the corner of his mouth.

"No. No, you fuck. *Who are you?*"

She shook him and pounded his shoulders back against the brick, but it did no good. Ten seconds was all it took for whatever he'd ingested to hit his blood stream, then his brain, and finally his heart. He slumped against her, dribbling down the wall, a fleshy sack of useless that spilled out over her olive-green sneakers. Tanis kicked his corpse in frustration, and was about to do it a second time, when his phone beeped. She picked it up and swiped her thumb across the screen, grateful that he didn't password protect.

It was a text message from a random number, no name accompanying it.

Visual confirmation?

Tanis desperately wanted to text back *FUCK YOU* but that'd alert whomever—maybe the goodwill store bitch—that something had gone awry sooner than necessary. She scrolled through the phone, to blond guy's pictures, deleting the one he just took and looking to see if he'd somehow managed to send it while he ran from her. No messages, no emails, no nothing. The phone was practically empty, other than the apps the phone company always installs when you sign up. It was new to him, issued perhaps hours ago for him to do his reconnaissance on her.

With nothing on it to identify him, she tossed the phone aside and slipped her arms around his middle, dragging him away from the scene, her nose on alert for approaching problems. Twenty feet down the concrete alley, over broken beer bottles and crumpled cellophane, and she swung left, behind the vacant business. She propped up the body and patted him down, looking for cash or guns or anything that'd make him useful to her. While there was nothing material, she did discover something quasi-noteworthy—a mark on his shoulder, a tattoo. It hadn't been done long ago, if the saturation of the ink was any indication: a circle with what looked like a menorah attached to the top. If she used her imagination, it formed a crude Gorgon head, leading her to believe that her suicidal friend may have been in the habit of wearing white robes and a green belt in his spare time.

Tanis snagged her own phone from her pocket and took a picture of it. She headed back up the alley after that, leaving the mystery man to rot behind the business for however long it'd take for someone to find him. Considering the building was vacant and the dry cleaner had their own alley on the other side, he'd cook a while in the humidity.

They'll smell him before they'll see 'im.

She jogged back to the car, more intent than ever to get home. An elderly man had stopped behind the Caddy, was looking at the running car with the open door, but seeing her approach, he eased himself back into his own car.

"Everything alright miss?" he asked, lifting a white boat hat from his nearly bald head. "I was about to call the triple-A."

Tanis slid the gun behind her back. "Sorry about that. I felt sick. I'm alright now."

If you're a Gorgon cocksucker, I will put an extra pair of nostrils in your head, grandpa.

He smiled and settled back into his compact Japanese car, hand up in a neighborly wave. "Feel better. God bless."

Okay, so not a Gorgon cocksucker.

She got behind the wheel and slammed the door, taking off for home as fast as her old wheels would carry her. She dialed Naree's cell, counting the five rings out loud before she was dropped to voicemail. While it was likely Naree was asleep, her ringer off, Tanis's stomach sank with the possibilities.

If they scried for Cassandra's heart, they'd have found her first...

119

Or if Ma found out I don't shoot blanks, she might have sent someone...

Stop borrowing problems. Just stop.

"Sweetheart. It's me. I'm on my way. Pack some clothes, the money, the guns. That's about it. We need to get the hell out of Percy's Pass. I'll explain in the car, okay? I love you. See you soon." She hung up and redialed, twice. Each call ended the same way. After the third attempt, her phone rang, and her breath caught, thinking it was Naree, but no such luck.

She answered it anyway.

"Bernie. Bad timing. I'm being followed."

"*Shit. Me, too,*" Bernie said, shouting to be heard over whipping wind. "*Been driving for an hour to lose 'em. Went out to get some bandages, and a yellow Volvo followed me across three towns. I'm circling back now. I think I'm alright, but I'm afraid of leading anyone to the Den. If they don't kill me, Ma would.*"

There wasn't a lot of time to consider the options, and with Naree down for the count—*please be sleeping, baby, please*—there wasn't opportunity to consult her, so Tanis had to choose her path.

It wasn't a difficult decision.

"Meet me at the Walmart in the Pass. Go inside. Stay safe in the crowd. I'll be there in... fuck. Twenty minutes."

"*You got it. What do we need?*"

"Nonperishable foods. Medical supplies. You got a gun?"

"*I live in Florida, what do you think?*"

Despite feeling like she'd been kicked in the face with steel-toed boots, she found a smile. "Twenty, Bernie. Stay safe."

"*Twenty, doll. You got it.*"

SEEING NAREE'S SWEET profile against the pillow, her mouth open, snores rumbling forth like she was a drunken hobo and not a brilliant programmer, was the biggest relief of Tanis's life. She stared at her girlfriend, reassuring herself that she and the baby were safe. Happy, even. It quelled some of the panic that had been suffocating her since she left Goodwill. She ran her hand down her face and closed her eyes. Deep breaths to ease her pulse, in through the nose, out through the mouth, reacquainting herself with her zen before she reached out to shake Naree's foot.

"Up. We have to go," she announced, turning for the closet and grabbing their duffel bags from the floor. Hers was plain black, Naree's was pink with white checkers and an N-shaped keychain attached to the zipper.

"Huh?" Naree grumbled and hunkered deeper into their bed, her arms wrapped around Tanis's pillow in protest.

"You said we should take the risk and move, and you're right. We're getting out. I was followed."

That got Naree's attention, and she darted up, her palms digging into her eyes to rub the sleep away. "When? Where? By who?"

"Gorgon priests, I think. First at the second-hand store, second at the intersection downtown. Bernie's being followed, too. I told her to wait for us at Walmart. I can't leave her behind. Maybe I should, but..."

"No, you can't," Naree said, which was what Tanis suspected she'd say, because Naree was elementally a good person and leaving Bernie to languish while they hit the highway was a death sentence for her. It still could be if Lamia lost her shit about them leaving and sent one of her brute squads, but their chances were better together than apart.

Bernie's strong. She knows how to fight.

Naree rolled from bed to pull on her pajama pants. Tanis tossed her the pink duffel bag, and Naree crammed as much of their overflowing laundry basket into it as she could, not paying too much attention to ratios of her clothes to Tanis's or pants to underwear and bras. Tanis worked on the other essentials: the pistols, the ammunition, the cash, the jewelry they could pawn, the cigarettes. If she couldn't smoke with all the mounting stress she'd probably have an aneurism, if lamias could even have those. She'd never heard of it before, just like she'd never heard of lamias getting cancer or having heart attacks, but hey, as of one day ago she also believed lamias couldn't impregnate their girlfriends.

Anything was possible.

Naree darted into the bathroom for their toiletries, storing them in a Ziploc and throwing them into her bag. Her laptop came next, along with their phone charger cords. Lastly, she collected the heart from the freezer, walking back to the bedroom to offer it to Tanis.

Tanis looked at it like she was giving her a vial of Ebola.

"You think?"

"Prophet tells you to keep her heart, you keep it. Your words," Naree said. "I'm assuming you believed at least part of what she told you, otherwise you're a really screwed-up person for ripping it out of her in the first place."

Good point.

Still, she hesitated. "I'm afraid they could track us through it."

"Maybe, but they found you when you didn't have it on you, so maybe not."

Naree tucked it into Tanis's supply bag, along with the guns. Looking at it there, realizing it'd stink sooner than not, Tanis texted Bernie and told her to get a small cooler and ice at Walmart, too. It wouldn't last long, but maybe long enough to get them to a motel and a mini-fridge.

Naree zipped up the duffel bag and tried to haul it. Tanis waved her off, carrying it and her own bag out to the living room. There, Naree rifled through her papers, retrieving her birth certificate and credit card and stuffing them into her purse.

Tanis glanced at the clock. Ten minutes. She'd get to Bernie on time.

"Do you have your insurance card still?" she asked.

Because you're probably going to give birth really soon and you're going to need it.

"Yeah, in my wallet. Which I should grab." Naree stopped to slide her feet into a pair of flip-flops and collected her glasses case from the coffee table. Tanis headed out of the apartment to wait at the top of the stairs while Naree performed a final sweep. Seemingly satisfied, she looped her purse over her shoulder and jangled her house keys. "Bye, TV. I'll miss you. Maybe I'll see you again one day. Shit. I better be able to stream *Game of Thrones* on my laptop. I'm in Season Four now."

"You're taking this fairly well," Tanis remarked, watching Naree lock both locks. It wouldn't do any good against snake women, but it was the principle of the thing, she supposed.

Naree shrugged. "I'm trying to look at the positives."

"Which are?"

"If we survive, we'll be free of your bitch mother."

They hurried downstairs. Tanis threw their stuff into the back of the Caddy and closed the trunk. Naree climbed into the passenger's side. Before joining her, Tanis walked around to the front bumper. An '86 Cadillac would be easy to spot on the road no matter what, but every advantage counted, and if the priest had used the dealership plate to identify them, it was better to lose it. Her fingers curled beneath the rusted metal. She pulled, and it bent at the middle before the screws popped from the holes.

"And the other positives?" she asked, sitting beside Naree and putting the Glock down between them. The engine roared to life and she tore out of the apartment's dusty parking lot to go back, yet again, to America's superstore, possibly for the last time ever.

Strange to think about, but then, so much is strange these days.

Naree settled into her seat, her head resting against the dented leather headrest. She let out a laugh as arid as a mummy's ass crack. "Well? At least we've got enough guns to blow our own heads off before your mother can eat us alive. That's a bright side, isn't it?"

Tanis glanced over to see if Naree was joking. The small smile on her mouth and the worry lines in her brow told her nothing.

CHAPTER FOURTEEN

"BERNIE'S FUNNY. YOU'LL like her," Tanis said. It was the first time she'd introduced Naree to anyone from Adder's Den, always insisting Naree was too fine a spirit to have to suffer Lamia's lot. It wasn't fair in a lot of ways—many of her sisters were decent—but Lamia was a stain. Everything she touched, she poisoned, and Tanis wanted to protect Naree from her reach as long as she could.

"How snaky is she? I'm assuming not very if she's waiting for us in Walmart." Naree frowned. "I didn't mean that to sound... I'm a dick. Wow."

"I know what you meant. There are scales on the back of her neck, but if she wears her hair down you can't see them. She looks like someone's fitness-obsessed grandma, otherwise."

"Oh. She's old?"

"Older, yes. Probably seventy? But don't let that fool you. She's tough as nails." Tanis pulled into the fire lane in front of the store and texted Bernie. A minute later, she appeared, limping her way out through the front doors with a zillion bags in hand. Her eye was blackened still, now eggplant and sickly yellow at the edges, but the swelling on her nose had gone down and her swollen lip looked alright. Floral leggings, a fluorescent yellow tank top that fell to her hips, bright orange sneakers—she didn't blend. That would have to change, with the whole being-followed problem.

"Tell me you bought clothes that can't be seen from space?" Tanis asked, climbing from the car to pop the trunk. She scanned the parking lot, looking for leering eyes among the glimmering cars, but spotted none.

"Yeah, I did. Here, slap these in the back seat and I'll change. Got your cooler and ice, and enough food to feed us for a week." She ripped open one of the bags of ice and poured half the contents into the cooler. Tanis tucked the bag under her arm so she could fish out the Tupperware from her duffel bag. She wedged it in, and Bernie topped it off with the rest of the ice, throwing the empty plastic bag to the ground. "Need to hit my car for the guns. One second—" She jogged off, still stiff, and Tanis climbed back behind the wheel, throwing Bernie's clothes behind her. Naree fanned her face, hot from sitting in the sun for those few minutes without a breeze.

"We'll get you an iced tea on the way," she said.

"Thanks." Naree reached out to squeeze her knee. "Where are we going, anyway?"

"North," was all Tanis said, because it was all she knew. Up north was colder, and snakes hated cold. Alaska, maybe, after they got close enough the flights wouldn't cost all their savings. It might not be a forever deterrent, but it was another thing in their favor and they'd need all the help they could get. The prospect of being hunted for the rest of their lives—if not by the lamias, then by the Gorgons and their groupies—was terrifying. Tanis wouldn't be able to let her guard down, ever. Not with Naree and a baby. Which...

I have to tell Bernie about the baby.

Balls.

Bernie pulled two big duffel bags from the back of her ancient hatchback, then limped over and tossed them into the back seat, the contents clicking and clunking as they settled.

"What is that, an arsenal?" Tanis asked.

Bernie climbed in behind Naree and grinned, revealing the giant gap in her bottom teeth. "Pretty much. I'm not a pistol girl. Shotguns, that's where it's at." She leaned forward to slide a hand over Naree's shoulder, offering a shake. "Berenike. Bernie, to my friends, and if you're a friend of Tanis's, you're a friend of mine."

"Naree. Nice to meet you. Tanis has said a lot of nice things about you."

"She's probably lying to you, doll, but that's okay. She does it 'cause she loves you best."

Bernie slunk back into her seat to sprawl out, her head tipping back toward the ceiling. She inhaled deeply. "Ah, nothing beats the smell of Walmart in the morning. Except maybe sweaty armpits and a turd factory."

Naree's eyes widened. She looked over to Tanis, mouth open in delight, and giggled. Tanis managed a smile, too. "Bernie's colorful. I think you two will get along."

"Hell, yes, I'm colorful. Speaking of which..." Bernie pulled new, less-hideous clothes from her shopping bag. Tanis took that as her cue to get driving and pulled onto the road, heading for the highway. It'd take them awhile to get there, but that wasn't such a bad thing. Small country roads meant tails were easier to spot—and dispatch.

"We have some news," Tanis said, the wind whipping through the car and tousling their hair. "It's going to shock the hell out of you."

"I'm all ears," Bernie said from a tangle of T-shirts.

"Naree's pregnant."

Bernie poked her head up through the neck hole of one T-shirt while still wearing the second underneath. "Oh. Uhh... congratulations?"

"It's mine," Tanis said, filling in the blank.

"...oh. Ohhh. Oh, shit. How?"

"The usual. In and out over and over again," Naree quipped.

Bernie boggled at the back of her head before bursting into guffaws. She ducked back inside T-shirt Two to complete removal of T-shirt One, and upon divesting, tossed the DayGlo eyesore out the car window. "I wondered why you went to running so easy. Sure, the Gorgons, but we could have moved out with the group. Safety in numbers and all that shit. Makes sense now. Ma would be all over you like white on rice; you'd be the Sperminator of choice."

"She would." Tanis turned off the road at a drive-through to get Naree her promised drink. "Probably worth noting she's gestating quickly. The baby is. It's a girl. You want anything?"

"Nah, thanks." Bernie popped back up from the back seat to put a hand on Naree's shoulder. "How you holding in there, girlie? Knowing all this?"

"Best I can. I've got questions about it, like how long it'll take and what to expect and all that, but I don't think anyone would know how to answer them." Naree frowned. "The doctor kept talking about five months from now and I think I've got more, like, five minutes, you know?"

Bernie looked thoughtful. "A witch could probably help out. They're good with childbirth. All the bloody stuff."

"Witches?" Naree accepted her iced tea from Tanis before turning in her seat to address Bernie. "Wicca stuff?"

"Nah, that's bullshit." Bernie held up a finger. "Well, it's not. It's a belief system just as valid as any other, and the goddess and Green Man are old, old druidic deities, but the magic side—those Raven MoonFucker books? All crap. I mean a *real* witch. Like, one who can hear the gods, sometimes bargan with them. I'm sure there are Wiccan witches who can, but most I've met are naked ladies who buy too much patchouli and like shiny rocks a lot."

"Oh." Naree smirked around her straw. "I was into that once, when I was thirteen. Enya was my homegirl until my super Catholic mother found out and threw my stuff away and made me go to confession. I had no idea any of it was for realsies."

"Like, lamias and Gorgons, cool, but witchcraft is crazy talk?"

Naree shrugged.

"Point is, if you want to talk to a witch, I know one. Sort of. Might help on a few fronts. With this Gorgon crap, too."

"Do we have time?" Naree's hand slipped over her stomach, over the gently rounded dome of baby pressing against her shirt.

Tanis watched her and then glanced in the rearview mirror to look at Bernie. "Where?"

"Two towns up. Keep climbing Seventy-Five."

THE HOUSE LOOKED like something out of *The Amityville Horror*. Boarded-up windows on both stories, a wraparound porch with holes peppering the boards. White paint peeled from everything—the rails on the stairs, the stairs themselves, the fence, the shutters, the house-front. Half of the roof shingles were gone. Some of the windows on the second story were lacking glass altogether, thanks to asshole kids throwing stones. There was a car parked in the driveway, but whatever it had been was hidden from view thanks to the nipple-tall grass poking up from the cracks in the pavement.

"You know, this is a little cliché," Naree said, eyeballing the house. "If I was a kid, and walked by this house, I'd totally say a witch lives here."

"Right? I told Astrid that, the last time we had coffee. That's her name: Astrid. She's a völva, a Norse witch." Bernie bummed a cigarette from Tanis and leaned against the Caddy, eyeballing the house façade while she puffed. "Expect a lot of runes and blood and bird bones. Oh, and cats. She has like nine of them."

"How'd you meet a völva in Florida?" Tanis demanded. "How is this even a thing?"

Bernie snickered. "Yoga."

Tanis was incredulous, but she probably shouldn't have been. For all that Bernie and she had been friendly, they hadn't really ever been *friends*. It was more a passing "Atta girl" and a few swapped stories before they went their separate ways.

Bernie winked at her. "I gotta keep these old bones in shape!

I guess she thought the same thing. Old dame trying to stay nimble. Anyway, we did the class together. She sensed I was different from the other old bags in there. Asked what I was, we got talking. Not exactly BFFs, but friendly enough. She'll probably do you a solid. For a price."

Tanis wasn't happy about the thought of a 'price,' but she wasn't getting anywhere standing on the overgrown walkway getting dive bombed by black flies either. She headed up the steps, avoiding rusty nails and broken boards to knock on the front door. She half-expected Cousin It to answer, and turned out not to be too far off her guess. The door cracked open a couple of inches, only as far as the chain lock would allow it to go. A green eye. A tangle of curls that spilled over one half of her face, most of it more white than blond. Dark circles and deep lines spoke to her age—sixties, maybe; possibly seventies. A small nose, a small mouth, a pointed chin. Her dress was royal blue and hung to the floor, the spaghetti straps showing off toned, freckled arms. She smelled like herbs and old blood. And meatloaf. Meatballs, maybe.

The witch let her gaze drift over Tanis, from the sneakers up to her head and back down again. "What, snake thing?"

Thing? Well fuck you, too.

"Astrid? I'm Tanis. Bernie's here. You know her from yoga?"

Because yoga is a happening place where snake women and Norse witches like to hang out, I guess. Maybe Starbucks was closed that day.

Astrid craned her neck, and seeing Bernie waving at her from the Caddy, grunted. "Fine. Come in. Wipe your feet. Mind the cats."

The chain on the lock jingled and the door was cast wide. For all that the outside of the house looked like it'd been shot at and missed (and shit at and hit), the inside was beautiful. The living room was tufted leather furniture with brass buttons, with a couch against the far wall, two chairs angled toward the fireplace. Wooden bookshelves occupied the corners. A glass-fronted cabinet held strange statues and scrolls that spoke to old magic. Tapestries covered the walls, hung on wrought-iron rods, the designs capturing famous scenes of Norse mythology, specifically Ragnarök. On one piece, woven in blues, grays, black, and white, Fenrir devoured Odin's prone corpse. In another, a golden Thor with his hammer held aloft was wrapped in the emerald coils of Jörmungandr, the Midgard Serpent. The red fire giant Surt cast Freyr's broken body into orange and yellow flames; and in the last tapestry, above the mantel, a purple-clad Loki thrust a spear through Heimdallr's middle while the mounted god, on his trusty steed Gjallarhorn, pierced Loki's heart with a sword.

The rug on the hardwood floors was teals and purples and golds, with ornate diamond medallions from one end to the other. It was also home to two cats, an orange tabby and a fat black-and-white one with no tail.

Tanis turned back to the front steps, offering a hand up to Naree. Naree picked her way around the weakest boards and hopped up to the porch, cringing when she felt the wood beneath her feet bow. She leaped into the house and paused on the threshold to admire the living room, peering through into the kitchen, with its clusters of dried herbs and baskets full of exotic roots.

"It's beautiful in here," she said.

"Thank you. Sit, please."

Naree moved to the couch and Tanis followed, Bernie pulling up the rear and closing the door behind her.

"Lock it, please," Astrid said. "My wards are good, but an ounce of precaution is worth a pound of cure."

"'Course. Good to see you, doll."

"You as well. Are you still going to class?"

"Nah. Whole place went to shit a couple months after you left. Bunch of moms who'd sit around bitching about their kids in daycare took over. I didn't last long after that."

Naree nestled into Tanis's side, and Tanis slung an arm across her shoulder, rubbing at her bicep. The witch motioned Bernie into one armchair while she claimed the other. Her hair swung away from her face, catching on her ear, revealing not a second eye, but a crisscross of black stitches sewing the socket closed. Tanis tried not to stare, but must have failed, as Astrid snorted and tapped at her cheek.

"I traded it for a set of ancient runes. To gain one sight, I gave up the other. I wasn't expecting company, so I didn't bother with my patch."

"Sorry. Didn't mean to be rude."

"You weren't. But you wore your question on your face." Her eye narrowed and she craned her face toward Naree. "She grows fast, the child. Eager to be born."

Naree nodded and hesitated, looking from Tanis to Bernie. Bernie nodded encouragingly, and Naree sat up straighter in her seat, her hands running over the thighs of her pajama pants. "That's why we're here. I want to know about her. If you can tell when she'll come? Or anything, really. Doctors aren't really useful for my particular situation."

"No, they wouldn't be. I can help, but my labor is not free. What do you have of value?"

Tanis leaned to the side to reach for her wallet, but the völva tutted and waved her off, her nails short and efficient and clean, her fingers adorned with stacks of silver rings, some with gems, others with sigils Tanis couldn't identify. "I don't need money. What do you have *of value?*"

"What do you want?" Tanis asked.

"*It,*" the witch replied, grinning. Her teeth were stained yellow from too much coffee, but they were straight, and in that moment, seemingly endless, filling her mouth and then some. She was equal parts Cheshire Cat and shark. "What is it? I sense it, but it's not clear. Powerful, though. It's very powerful." She leaned forward, her elbows dropping to her knees, her fingers lacing together and making her palms kiss. Her expression grew sly. "What do you bring to my doorstep, snakes, to tantalize me so?"

CHAPTER FIFTEEN

ASTRID REMOVED THE heart from the Tupperware. She bare-palmed it, twisting it this way and that beneath the kitchen light to get a better look. She seemed in awe of the thing, her expression so reverent, Tanis thought maybe the mysteries of the cosmos rested somewhere within that single lump of flesh. The old adage about one man's trash being another man's treasure came to mind; to the völva, it was a mystical something-something to be studied and appreciated. To Tanis, it was a stinky inconvenience she wanted out of her trunk.

"Old. So old," Astrid crooned, one of her fingers coursing over the rubbery nub at the top. Rusty snow rained upon the table, some parts ice, more parts blood. A meaty tendril dangled from the bottom to twine around her wrist like a slimy red worm.

Tanis could have mentioned Cassandra, or the Gorgons, or any number of things at that point, but she didn't. Astrid asked no questions, Tanis volunteered no answers. It was simpler that way, for all parties. Body parts in Walmart coolers were surreptitious affairs that painted no one in a good light, and really, it was safer for Astrid.

Well, safe-ish. If the Gorgons are eating Cassandra's dead body and searching for the heart, they'll come here.

Do I care?

...no, not really.

Astrid sniffed at the heart, and then licked at it. She shuddered with rapture, her eye closing, her breath quickening to short, fast pants. Her nipples pebbled beneath her dress, her free hand coursed down over her stomach and meandered straight for witch parts unknown, and Tanis wondered if they should leave her alone with her new favorite organ. Naree jerked her face away from the sordid scene, and Tanis couldn't blame her; it wasn't pleasant to behold, especially when Astrid rubbed the heart all over herself, smearing the thin fabric with gore from breast to crotch. Tanis eyed Bernie, Bernie shrugged, but no one dared say anything. It was a fundamental truth that witches were fairly disgusting. You didn't bargain in flesh and blood and come out smelling like a rose.

You might, however, come out smelling like day-old sirloin.

"It has so much power. Yes. I... it's a good barter. Good." The witch's eye opened and she reached above her head for some dried herbs, snatching three very specific clusters and laying them on the counter. She never loosed her grip on the heart, not as she went to the cabinet to retrieve a big box of kosher salt. Not as she washed out the Tupperware and wiped it dry. Not as she arranged her supplies on the counter in neat order. It was all a bit too Gollum and Precious for Tanis's comfort, but at least the damned thing had found a good home.

The heart was rolled in salt—covered like a big slab of steak—before being placed back into the container. Layers of herbs came next, followed by more salt, like she planned to sauté the damned thing. Maybe she was; eating the heart was the secret to magical prowess, if Cassandra was to be believed. Tanis watched the preservation process with morbid fascination, reaching for Naree's hand and clinging as Astrid replaced the lid on the box and wrapped two big rubber bands around it. She then carried it back to the living room to the locked cabinet of miscellaneous fuckery, where she displayed it between a ram's horn and a dagger in a jeweled sheath.

Astrid's fingers caressed the glass, a faraway look on her face. Another shiver, another inappropriate self-fondle, and she returned to the kitchen to clear the table of refuse. She stayed silent, disappearing from the kitchen to go into a room with a closed door. Rummaging sounds, clamor, a rattle, a squeal. She returned with a black cloth stitched with golden symbols along the edges and a great green tree at the middle. She laid it out before Naree, placing a flat, tin pan over the tree symbol.

"Spit," she said.

"What?"

"Spit. Blood's better, but spit is often more tolerable. People are squeamish." This declaration was followed by Astrid presenting a small checkered bag with a drawstring top. She opened it and upended twenty-four runes into the pan, the sigils hand-painted in white on black tiles. She motioned at them. "Well? Don't be shy, girl. No one's delicate in this house."

Naree cast Tanis a look before doing as she was told, spitting as politely as possible.

"No loogies?" Bernie asked.

Naree wrinkled her nose. "Ewww, no!"

Bernie winked at her and Naree went rosy in the cheeks, her ample ass shifting in the kitchen chair and birthing a squeal. Astrid ignored the banter, intent on her preparations, most particularly the butcher's block on the kitchen counter behind her. She never batted an eye as she pulled out the big butcher's knife and closed her hand around the blade, the steel sliding across her palm and bisecting its meatiest part. Blood pooled quick, and she drizzled it into the pan, curling her fingers into a fist. She waved it back and forth like she was dressing a salad, covering the runes, Naree's spit wad, the bottom of the pan, with slow, deliberate movements and a steady drip.

"Shake the pan," she instructed, jerking her hand away and holding it up, above her head, to force the clot. "Close your

eyes, breathe, and shake it. Don't stop until you feel ready."
Naree picked up the edges of the pan, her thumb slithering
through a dollop of Astrid's blood as she tossed the runes
around, rearing back when blood splashed up and nearly
struck her chin. She cringed, but kept going for another twenty
seconds before putting it back down on the embroidered tree
on the table. Astrid, meanwhile, rinsed off her hand in the sink
and wrapped it with some medical tape she kept on the nearby
window sill.

Astrid sat at the table across from Naree, leaning forward
to eye the placement of the runes, some upended, some on
their sides, some double stacked and leaning. Tanis knew it
all meant something, just not what, but Astrid looked totally
comfortable with her gooey, nasty pile of painted rocks. Her
finger came out to stroke the tiles, hovering over foreign,
blood-splashed shapes. She hummed quietly to herself, a
tune Tanis didn't recognize, and rolled her head around on
her shoulders. "It's a girl child. Healthy." She paused. "Days.
Three to her birth? Maybe, but that is all. It comes soon. As
does..." Astrid peered at the runes and then back up to Tanis.
"Who is this that comes for you? Who are the seekers?"

Tanis could have played coy, but even she knew a witch was
not a thing to be trifled with, and she wasn't big on wasting
anyone's time. "It could be my mother's people. It could be the
Gorgons."

Astrid glanced back down at the pan, her expression
darkening. "Gorgons. Monsters. They are angry with you?"

"Pissed."

"Why?"

"Partly because I'm a lamia and they hate my kind. Partly
because I spied on them and stole the heart." Tanis motioned
at the living room. "Belonged to a prophet they had chained in
the basement. She begged me to kill her and said Naree would
die if I didn't take her heart. She said I'd need it for trade. I'm
guessing she meant to you, but I can't be sure."

"Mmmngh. No. No, no, no." Astrid pushed herself away
from the runes. She stalked out to the living room, opening the

cabinet and retrieving the heart from inside. Her hand pressed to the closed lid, her head forward until her chin touched her chest. "I want it to be mine. It *should* be mine," Astrid insisted.

Tanis frowned. "Okay? I already gave it to you?"

"It's not for me!" Astrid barked, stomping back in to slap it down on the table. "It's not for me. They say it's not for me, so you will take it with you when you go, and you'll go now. Before they come."

"They who?" Bernie asked.

"The Gorgons. Your lamias are too busy slithering about inside their dens in a panic to be a concern for now, but the Gorgons come. I'll not be involved in your war. I'll not be your collateral damage." Astrid pointed at the pan of runes and then at Naree. "Her fate is good. You, snake things, not good. I see grief and pain and death and blood. Out, out. Out of my house before you bring folly to my door."

"Well, shit." Bernie pushed herself away from the wall she'd been leaning on. "I'm sorry about that, doll. I didn't realize... nothing we can do about the Gorgons?"

The witch snorted. "Can you kill an immortal? No, you can't. They are that which cannot die."

Tanis raked her fingers through her hair. "Fine, can we outrun them, or hide from them, or stop them in any way? I don't care if they die. I just want to live with my girlfriend and my kid, and see my friend safe. Death would be handy, but it's not a requirement."

The witch's eyes narrowed as she fingered the bloody patches on her dress, the fabric dried stiff where the heart flesh had been ground in. "Sleep, perhaps. Like Cronus. He swore upon the River Styx and broke his bond, and was banished to Tartarus for a long sleep. It is not death, but it might as well be."

"How the hell are we supposed to get a Gorgon to swear on shit?" Bernie asked. "Or for that matter, on the River Styx?"

"That is not my problem. *You* are not my problem. Don't seek me out again, Berenike. You brought danger here." To emphasize the point, she collected the Tupperware with the salted heart from the table and jabbed it against Tanis's chest, whacking her with it until she accepted it back. "Damn you for having this, snake. It's worthless in your hands."

Tanis scowled. "You're telling me."

"Yeah. I... yeah. Sorry about this. Thanks for the help. You take care, okay?" Bernie put her hand on Naree's back and guided her toward the door. Naree looked Tanis's way, her brow furrowed.

"Go ahead," Tanis said. "I'll be right out." She eyed the tin pan on the table. She wanted the secrets of its contents. She'd have done anything for clarity regarding Astrid's ill tidings, but divination—hearing the gods' voices—was not her gift. To Astrid, the runes were harbingers. To Tanis, they were blood-spattered dominoes.

"You're walking a thin line," Astrid said from behind her. "There's death all around you. Eihwaz. *He's* waiting for you. You'll have to be quick, little snake. Quicker than the shadows to survive this."

"What does that even mean?" Tanis said, whirling on her, but Astrid shook her head and walked to the living room, standing beside her open door and motioning outside.

"Go. Please. They're coming, Tanis. You need to go *now*."

CHAPTER SIXTEEN

IT HAPPENED AT a gas station off of Seventy-Five at six o'clock, when the sun broke the horizon and the mosquitoes swarmed in black clouds. They'd driven for hours, until the empty light came on in the Caddy and they couldn't avoid a stop. There'd been little chatter; Astrid's decrees were a pall upon an already shittastic day. It was better not to talk about it and to let the radio fill the awkward silence.

Naree was in the front seat, chomping on her second cheeseburger, a vanilla shake clasped in hand. She was hungrier than usual—ravenous, she said—which made a certain amount of sense. There was a reason Lamia devoured a whole man after her breedings. Yes, it neutralized the threat of a crazed snake-man crawling around the Den, but more than that, it was a hundred and seventy-five pounds of protein. Fast gestation took a tremendous amount of energy and food was energy.

A heck of a lot of cows were about to die to feed Tanis's insistent offspring.

Naree swallowed and groaned, her head flopping back against the headrest. "Is Bernie getting more Ritz crackers?"

Tanis was fueling the car, leaning against the big fat trunk with the nozzle notched into the gas tank. She desperately wanted a cigarette, and would indulge when she wasn't quite so flammable. She craned her head to the side. Bernie was inside the convenience store, standing in line behind three old men holding scratch tickets. She could be there the rest of her life; for some reason, old guys took six years to play their lottery.

"I think so. We'll know sometime next year. Long line."

"Okay, cool. Thanks." Naree crumpled up the bag and handed it to Tanis through the window.

Tanis eyed it, then her girlfriend. "...thanks?"

"You're standing right next to a trash barrel."

"Lazy."

"Look, I'm like twenty pounds fatter than I was yesterday and I just found out I'm going to have a baby sometime in the next twelve minutes. You can throw my trash away for me." Naree slurped on her shake, grinning around her straw as she peered out the open window at Tanis, brushing bugs away from her face. "*Checkmate, bitch.*"

"Yeah, yeah."

Tanis smiled, but she had to force it. How was Naree so calm? Was she putting on a brave face because she thought she had to for Tanis's sake? Was she actually excited about it, despite the threats? It was hard to say because they hadn't had time to *talk* since the shit hit the wall. It'd been doctor to nap to flying out the door because Gorgons were coming and then straight to a witch's house. Tanis pulled the nozzle from the Caddy and capped the gas tank, walking around to the other side of the car but still near the trunk to keep her smoke away from her best girl. She lit up, filling her lungs with smoke and relishing the familiar burn.

"How are you doing with this?" Tanis asked. "I'm worried about you."

And me, honestly. What kind of parent am I going to be? Will I even be around to help you with our daughter? Is the kid going to be weird thanks to her lamia blood and you'll have to figure it out on your own? Who'll watch out for you?

Her? What happens if Lamia comes for you both and I'm gone? Hell, what'll happen if Lamia comes for you both and I'm alive? There's only one of me. Bernie's here, but...

"I might still be in shock, if I'm being perfectly honest," Naree said. "Like, my brain knows it's happening, but I'm not sure it's registered in the feelings factory. I'm numb. I know we're running from a bunch of angry snake women, but it's not yet... maybe it's because I can't feel the baby yet. Or maybe it's because I kinda like kids, so the idea of having one isn't such an awful thing, even if the circumstances are messed up. I'm not unhappy about it, if that helps at all. I'm just not sure I'm happy about it yet, either."

"That's fair." Tanis puffed on her cigarette once more before stubbing it out on the heel of her sneaker. "Are you scared?"

Naree nodded. "Sometimes. Astrid was something else. She... yeah. That was creepy. They can be wrong, right? About stuff? Like what she said about you and death?" She slurped the last of the shake from her cup, eyed it, and then stretched out to offer it through the window. Tanis ignored it just to be contrary, so Naree chucked it at her head. Tanis caught it before it struck her nose and put it in the trash barrel along with her dead cigarette butt.

"They can be. Divination isn't exact, and she said I was walking a thin line, so there's hope there. We'll be smart, or as smart as we can be. I'll help you as much as I can either way," Tanis said.

"I know. We'll figure it out, babe. We will." Naree sat up straighter in her seat. "Okay, seriously, where's Bernie with my crackers? Because if I don't get them soon, I'm going to cut a bitch."

Tanis looked back. Bernie still had one old timer in front of her and she didn't look too happy about it. When she noticed she had Tanis's attention, she pantomimed gagging with her free hand, the red Ritz box tucked into the crook of her elbow.

"She's got them," Tanis said. "One guy left."

She circled around the car and was about to climb in when a gray Nissan with a cardboard-and-plastic-bag-covered rear window pulled up in front of the store. It didn't park in one space, but stretched across two. Two men climbed from the front seats, a tall black man with long arms and large hands and a short white man with orange hair and a face full of freckles. Both dressed casually in T-shirts and jeans, the black man wearing a cowboy hat, the white man sporting an earful of silver piercings from lobe to upper cartilage. Tanis watched them circle the back of the car and open the trunk. Someone barked at them from the back seat, behind the cardboard window covering. Whoever she was, she wore far too much floral perfume. Imitation rose scent was not kind on a lamia nose.

There was something about the set-up that bothered Tanis. It looked too much like they were gearing up for something—a robbery, a confrontation, a drug deal. Whatever the circumstance, it wasn't *normal*, and she reached into the car for her pistol, her back to Naree as she surveyed the newcomers. Bernie was finally at the head of the line, was paying for their things, when the short ginger man broke away from the car to go into the store. He perused an aisle, selected something, and stood behind Bernie.

Maybe I'm wrong. Maybe I misjudged.

Except the man in the cowboy hat walked her way, his long arms swinging. If he'd been in his car and pulling up close for gas, she wouldn't have been so on edge, but he walked straight at her, no gas can, no nothing.

"Get down, Naree." Tanis kept her attention fixed on the stranger, but didn't pull the gun on him yet, in case this was one of those have-you-heard-about-our-Lord-and-Savior-Jesus-Christ speeches, but...

CRASH!

Tanis looked up as the window of the convenience store exploded. Glass rained down, glimmering beneath the sun, and the red-headed man flew out, nearly striking the parked Nissan in his trajectory. He landed in a heap midway between the store and the gas pumps, grunting with the impact. Tanis wanted to check on Bernie, to see what had happened, but the black man took the opportunity to run at her, something silver glinting against his palm. She lifted the gun, aimed it at him, but he crouched and kept coming. She fired the shot. It took him in the side of the leg and sent him sprawling. She kept the pistol aimed at him and he lashed out at her again, his cowboy hat rolling off of his head to land on the pavement. He slashed wildly as he crawled toward her, desperate to make contact with her leg. It made no damned sense—the thing in his hand was tiny, looking like a dinner fork or a miniature back scratcher...

Something's wrong with it. It smells off. The danger isn't the weapon, it's what's on it.

The same odor had been in the basement of the Gorgon house, though she'd only caught a hint in passing; Cassandra's rot had overpowered pretty much everything else. But as Tanis had made her escape, on her way through the basement to meet Bernie at the bulkhead door, she'd caught a whiff of a strange, chemical funk. It came from upstairs, specifically the room with Ariadne's body: a wicked combination of bleach and lemon and cat urine. Bitter, unpleasant. She'd associated it with the Gorgon—not her priests, but the monster herself—and she'd dismissed it at the time as a pheromone scent marker similar to her mother's.

It's the green shit on the end of Euryale's fingers. It's how she slow-petrified Ariadne. It's a venom.

Realizing it, seeing how close the man came to her—and, worse, Naree—she shot him through the cheek. There was no dramatic death scene, no twitching or rolling or thrashing. The bullet went clean through, into his brain, and he slumped forward, a small trickle of blood slithering out from beneath his body and traveling, slowly, down, to settle into a crack.

"MOTHERFUCKER!"

Bernie. Tanis cast a wide berth around the body, putting an insurance bullet into the back of the man's brain before eyeballing the gray car, the crumpled redheaded man on the pavement, and the shattered storefront. A woman in a white robe now sat in the driver's seat of the Nissan. Perfume girl. She had a shaved head, the home-tattooed circle symbol behind her ear. Tanis lifted the gun right as the woman threw the car into drive, circling it wide and, in the process of veering off for the main drag, running over her own compatriot. He screamed, but Tanis ignored him, shooting at the back of the car in an attempt to take out the back wheels. She was a good shot, excellent really, but a moving car was not as easy to strike as the movies made it appear. The Nissan got away in a screech of burnt rubber and dust clouds.

"Son of a bitch cocksucking thundercunt. What'd you do? Eh? What'd you do?"

Oh, shit.

Tanis turned around to see Bernie stalking from the blasted open storefront and through the sea of shattered glass to dive on top of the redhead. He breathed wet and hard, his midsection having taken the brunt of the car's weight when it passed over him. Bernie didn't care. She grabbed him by the face with her left hand and bashed his head back against the pavement. It hit hard. He bellowed in agony, so she did it again, up, down, again and again, crunching wetly, until his screams dwindled and a messy puddle formed beneath him.

It was only when she sat up, straddling his limp body, that Tanis noticed her gray right hand.

No.

No, no, no, no, no.

"Stay in the car, stay low. Keep this. If anyone comes near you and it's not me or Bernie, I don't give a fuck who they are, blow their heads off," Tanis instructed Naree, who crouched best as her round body would allow in the footwell of the car. She raised miserable eyes to Tanis, bottom lip quivering. Tanis's heart constricted in her chest seeing her so scared, but she knew she had to check on Bernie, and so she opened the driver's side door to lean across the seat, offering Naree the gun grip first. "It'll be okay. I'm okay. Bernie needs help, alright?"

Naree nodded, holding the gun to her cleavage, and Tanis closed her in before jogging Bernie's way. Bernie was red-faced and furious, her good hand rubbing over her limp arm. It was dead weight from her shoulder socket, wobbling around whenever Bernie moved. Her knees were to either side of the redhead's lean hips, and the blood from his pummeling was creeping toward her leggings, threatening to ruin the floral print.

"Bernie. Probably want to move or you'll get blood on you. *More* blood on you."

"Fuck you," Bernie snapped. She immediately winced and shook her head, her gray hair flying wild around her shoulders. Her face screwed up into a thousand wrinkles as she tilted her head back, dark eyes pointed at the sky, the edges rimmed red and glossy with unshed tears. "Didn't mean that, doll. My arm hurts. That asshole poked me with something and I lost all control from the shoulder down. Within seconds. It burns like I got fire ants eating at my skin from the inside."

Tanis winced. "Shit. I'm sorry. Other one tried to do it to me. I think it's the shit they used on Ariadne to do the slow poison thing." Tanis eased Bernie's way, afraid to get too close in case Bernie lashed out, though beating her attacker to death seemed to have taken some of the edge off. Ish. She was still tomato-colored, blotched with hives, but she was breathing slower and she wasn't cursing up a storm anymore. "It's probably temporary?"

"Don't bullshit me, doll. Gorgons don't do anything temporary." Bernie looked down at her useless arm, pinching it, poking it. She tried lifting it up and letting it go, and it swung down hard like it was lead. Sometimes, the fingers appeared to spasm, which accompanied a murky, navy blue tinge settling into the very tips around the nails. "Why would they bother with this poison shit? Eh? Why not just shoot us?"

"Don't know. To neutralize us, maybe. Take us back to the Gorgons. We've got the heart. Maybe they thought we'd tell them where the Den was if they poked at us enough. I can't be sure, but... there's..."

"Get me out of here," Bernie said, cutting her off. "Just get me out of here. If I'm going to die, it won't be in a Quik Mart parking lot because a redneck cop decides he feels sorry for the bad guys that poisoned me. I got some dignity, you know."

Tanis managed a flat smile. "You're not going to die. You'll be fine," she said, looping her arm around Bernie's waist and helping her to the car.

"*There's death all around you. Eihwaz. He's waiting for you.*"

Don't make promises you can't keep, Tanis.

CHAPTER SEVENTEEN

THEY DIDN'T HAVE two double-bed rooms at the motel, so they got two rooms side by side instead. It was a mom-and-pop-owned and -operated place called the Honeybee, with a yellow brick exterior, floral wallpaper in every room, and a solid market share of dried flowers and Yankee Candles. The furniture was covered with plastic, which Naree on a brighter day would have called "couch condoms," but after what happened at the gas station, she wasn't in much of a jokey mood. Neither was Tanis, for that matter; Bernie's injury was serious, like 'need a mystical healer' serious, and even then, magic didn't fix everything. Gorgon toxin wasn't something people had handy antidotes for.

Maybe she'll just lose the arm. Maybe it'll stop there.

"Just" an arm. "Just."

Hell.

"Are you hungry?" Tanis whispered in Naree's ear after check-in.

"Yeah. Yes. Please," she replied, voice small, her face swollen from crying in the car. Tanis handed her the room key,

146

eyeballing Bernie. A chicken-foot worry mark indented the middle of her forehead, and every few seconds she shuddered, a full body thing that made her back hunch and her eyelids flutter. It was obvious the arm was hurting her, the gray stain up to her wrist now and running into her forearm. Her veins bulged beneath the skin, black instead of blue. Her fingertips had blackened too.

"You two head to the room. I'll get some food. Bernie, you hungry?"

"I'll eat," she said flatly.

The woman behind the counter, a middle-aged Latina with graying hair at her temples, a sensible white linen suit and a nice string of pearls, pointed down the far hallway. "Our restaurant is there, and takeout or room service is available. Our fried chicken is the best in the county. Miss Belle's an artisan with a fry pan."

"Nice. Thanks, Miss"—Tanis glanced at her tag—"Miss St. Charles." She turned back to Naree. "I'll see you at the room. Lock the door, maybe take a bath while you wait for me, okay? To relax? Text me if you need anything." Naree nodded and headed down the hall, her pony purse clutched to her chest. Bernie went with her, not looking at Tanis, not saying much of anything. She carried a single bag, too, but hers was full of guns. Big guns, heavy guns. The kind that blew off body parts. It'd been that kind of day.

It took a half-hour for their dinner to be ready. Tanis used the time to empty the car of hearts and bags and Walmart snacks. Naree had taken her advice and climbed into the tub. When Tanis dumped off the luggage, Naree was sprawled out, submerged, her head back, her eyes closed, with earbuds in her ears. Tanis left her alone to the dulcet screeching of the Misfits to wait outside of the restaurant on a golden bench someone had hand-painted with cartoon bees. It was cute, in a kitschy way.

Well, except for the bee with the huge dick dangling from its undercarriage. That wasn't so cute. It was, however, funny.

The dinner was well worth the wait, by the smell of it. Tanis headed back to the rooms with three styrofoam containers and a plastic bag full of soda machine Cokes, knocking first on Bernie's door.

"Yeah, one sec." Bernie sounded as haggard as she looked. She opened the door and stepped aside to let Tanis in. The room was as floral-ridden as Tanis and Naree's, the print on the wallpaper the same pink and orange blossoms with big, tropical leaves and flowering vines. The bedspread was fuschia to match, the art on the walls all want-to-be-but-not-quite-Monets. Bernie's guns were wildly at odds with the decor; she had eight of them laid out on her bed, organized by size, the top one looked like a goddamned bazooka.

"I'd ask how you're feeling, but I don't want you to punch me," Tanis said.

Bernie snorted. "I won't. Feel too shitty for that. I'm tired and I can't tell if it's the awful couple of days, me being older than dirt, or whatever's in my system. Maybe all three. Who knows." She settled down at the table. A carton of cigarettes was giving her difficulty—the little pull on the plastic wasn't easy to tear off if you couldn't secure the box with a second hand. Tanis opened it for her, pulled out a cigarette and lit it for her, *No Smoking* sign be damned.

"We should look at getting you to a healer or—"

"No," Bernie said. She smiled around the cigarette as Tanis slid her dinner across the table before her and stuck a fork in the top like a flag. "You need to see what you can do about the Gorgons. You got a kid on the way. I'm an old lady who's doing what old ladies do best: falling apart."

"Bernie," Tanis said. "Come on. We at least have to try."

Bernie puffed on her cigarette. "Could, maybe, but it's in my bloodstream. I can feel it, Tanis. I can feel it in me. Moving. The burning is creeping. Shit, maybe if we could do something *now*, it'd matter, but by the time we found someone? Where will it be? If it hits my chest, it'll hit my heart. My head, my brain. I already feel..." She paused, lips pursing. "Heavier. All over. Like there's sediment settling into my hand. Like it's weighed down by concrete."

Tanis immediately thought back to what she'd seen of

148

Ariadne through the floorboards at the manor house, the weighted coils of her bottom half stuck to the floor. If that was happening to Bernie, she could be right. It could be half over already. Maybe it'd slow creep and turn the arm to stone and it'd fall off, like Ariadne's breast.

I don't know what the hell I'm supposed to do.

"Maybe whoever we talk to can point us in the right direction—"

"Stop, doll." Bernie shook her head. "Focus on you and Naree now, and that sweet baby. I'll come along for the ride, as long as I can. If we stumble across somebody to help me along the way, grand, but the priority is that kid, not my old ass. What about a death dealer to help? With the River Styx thing Astrid mentioned?"

A death dealer was what normal people, the unawakened masses oblivious to the existence of gods and monsters, called 'psychics.' Just like anything else metaphysical, a lot of psychics were charlatans, but sometimes, you found the real deal, and the first sign that they were real deals was they forsook terms like 'psychic' and 'medium' and called themselves death dealers. They were favored by the death gods for one reason or the other—maybe they'd made good offerings, or maybe they'd looked extra nice in a party dress. Whatever the reason, the gods had granted them the ability to see past the veil splitting life and death. The spirits favored them.

It must be one of the shittier talents to have. Who'd want to be bugged by the restless dead all the time?

"We could hit the psychic shops along the interstate, see if we can find one? Would take some luck," Tanis said. "Since, like, ninety percent of them are crap."

"Or you could go to death dealer country." Bernie stubbed out the cigarette so she could attack a piece of fried chicken, making yummy noises as she tore a fat chunk of meat off the drumstick. "It's only a nine-hour drive from here and you pretty much trip over 'em every street corner."

Tanis hadn't considered that, mostly because she'd been intent to get north, into the cold. But going west into bayou country wasn't a terrible idea. It altered the plan a little, sure, but they could still get to less agreeable climates via Chicago instead of New England. "We could. Nothing ventured, nothing gained."

Bernie smirked, a big chunk of fried chicken skin gobbing up her bottom lip. She lashed her tongue over it, not letting a single crumble of Miss Belle's artistry go to waste. "True enough. Besides, there are worse places I can think of to croak than New Orleans. Take me down to Delta town."

"I WAS STARVING to death," Naree announced, the entire lower half of her face covered in chicken grease. "Like, it was coming. I saw the big white light. I may have to give up on atheism now; I know Jeebus is real and he wanted to take me home because I had no chicken."

Naree joking around was infinitely better than Naree huddled into a ball in the footwell of a Cadillac with tears running down her face. Or Naree looking out the car window and crying as the adrenaline drained from her system. Or Naree who, seeing the deterioration of Bernie's arm, walked up to her and hugged her, despite barely knowing her, her voice breaking when she said, "I'm sorry." It would have been nice if it'd been hormones making her sniffly, but no. The day had been that fucking foul.

"We'll go to church when we get to New Orleans," Tanis said in return, scooping up the last of the potatoes in her box. The dinner really had been good, even if it'd been lukewarm by the time she left Bernie's room. They'd talked a bit more about which death dealers to look for once they got to the Crescent City, and they both agreed when it came to hearing the spirits, you'd do a whole heck of a lot worse than a vodouist. Tanis knew next to nothing about them, but she was willing to see if they'd help her.

She had some money. She had a heart in a box. What could possibly go wrong?

"I'll change my mind by then, just so you know." Naree

reached over for Tanis's biscuit, claiming it for her own. As she leaned back, Tanis noticed that the T-shirt could barely contain her middle, the fabric stretched so taut, the lettering on the screenprint had cracked, making the words illegible.

She's swelling again. Growing.

Oh, baby. Slow down. Be nice to your mother.

"I think, maybe, I'm sated. For now. Ask me again in an hour," Naree said. "Or don't. Because I'm thinking sleep would be good. Really good. Best thing ever, really. Today was balls."

Tanis got up to prep the room, hanging a *Do Not Disturb* on the door and locking it down. She and Bernie had come up with a plan to block off their room entrances with heavy furniture. Unless the Gorgons themselves appeared, which would put them front and center of the human populace and possibly land them in an Area 51-esque zoo, they were safe. Ish. The priests didn't have super strength. That didn't mean they weren't smart or dangerous, but it did mean they wouldn't be able to get past the dressers pushed up against the door and window without for-sure waking someone.

The way Bernie had her guns laid out, anyone stupid enough to break into her room would be peeing out of a new hole pretty quick. Tanis was just fine with her handguns, though she did put the Colt beside the bed in lieu of some of the more delicate pistols.

Tanis ducked into the bathroom so she could rinse off, not bothering with clothes when she got out. The room was cool enough, the air conditioner functioning, but there was still that hint of Florida swamp that said she wouldn't need pajamas, especially not curled up with Naree's radiating body.

She padded back into the bedroom, expecting Naree to be asleep, but she sat up in bed looking at her cell phone, intently reading from the screen. Tanis took that as her cue to plug in her own device, pointedly ignoring the new-voicemail icon at the top. Everyone she'd want to talk to was gathered in two rooms at the Honeybee Motel. Everyone else could wait a few hours for Tanis to distance herself from the last disasters before introducing new ones.

"The interwebs say I'm extra horny during the second trimester. Or second day, if you're spewing lamia babies. They also say I could get nosebleeds, gum bleeding, heartburn, headaches, hemorrhoids—oh, fun!—and bigger boobs. Also my stomach will feel harder and at some point it'll flutter. Wow, Mother Nature is a douchebag. Wait, is she real? Like do I have to worry about insulting her? If so, sorry Mother Nature. I was funning. We cool."

Tanis smirked and climbed into bed, rolling Naree's way to press a kiss to her cheek. Naree turned her face at the last second to catch her lips, blindly sliding the phone onto the end table, her hand reaching up to sweep through Tanis' hair. Her fingers felt amazing on Tanis's scalp, skimming over, rubbing circles before gliding down to Tanis's neck to hold. Lips to lips, Tanis's tongue flickering out to steal a taste. Naree sank back down into her pillow, flattening out on the bed. Tanis broke away from her only long enough to shut off the light, but then she was on her, crawling over her, her lean muscle fitting against Naree's swells and valleys. She tugged the shirt off of her body and threw it to the floor.

"I need to purge it," Naree rasped, her mouth moving to Tanis's shoulder, her tongue slithering over her skin. "To make today go away. I need you."

She didn't have to ask twice. Tanis's mouth found hers again, opening her up and claiming her, her hands sliding over Naree's sides and down to her soft legs with their softer down. She hiked her up on one side, lifting her leg and opening her, filling the air with the sweet smell of wet human female. Tanis worked her way down. From the mouth, all minty with toothpaste, to the warm neck, with its jumping pulse. Tanis placed a kiss to that hard thud, to the pounding life, giving it a gentle suck. Naree bruised easily, as Tanis had found out in the past, and while she liked to mark her, it was better when it was colder out, when Naree could cover it up if she saw fit.

Down, down, down. Heavy breasts, breasts that filled her palm and fingers and still squished out over the sides. Tanis placed her face between them, licking over the inside curves,

Naree breathing harder beneath her, her hands raking over Tanis's shoulders. A nipple in the mouth, lathed, sucked, worshipped, then the other. Naree's sex scents grew stronger, filling Tanis's nose and thickening her, growing her, her hips humping down at the bedsheets below.

She kissed down over Naree's stomach, over that firm mound where their daughter grew. She rubbed her face against it, her nose and her mouth and her tongue, realizing for the first time that she, too, was feeling maybe just a little eager for this thing. This little girl. It was theirs. It was as many parts Naree as it was Tanis, and that was sexy. Yes, it was terrible timing. Yes, it was terrible circumstances. But in some ways—more than Tanis had realized—it didn't matter so much. The trials and tribulations were secondary to the beauty of their creation.

I want more of her. Need *more.*

Tanis's hands went to Naree's thighs, stroking over them and spreading them wider before she was kissing the very heat of her. Tanis buried her face in her girlfriend, drowning herself in the familiar wet. Naree moaned, body rising to meet her mouth, and Tanis closed her eyes, falling into the rhythm of pleasuring her. Falling into abandon.

Falling into Naree and the love they shared, no matter how fucked-up their circumstance.

CHAPTER EIGHTEEN

THE CELL'S RINGER was off, so Tanis missed the first four calls from Number Unknown. It was only when she woke up early to drain the pants weasels that she saw the string of attempts, and even then she put it off, taking care of personal business first. She pulled on her jeans and Naree's discarded T-shirt before snatching the phone and her cigarettes. There'd been no disturbances during the night, no Gorgon priests tapping at their window panes, and so she moved the dresser away from the front door. For safety's sake, she kept a gun in her waistband, which would, she knew, eventually misfire and blow off her ass, but beggars and choosers, and Florida didn't have open-carry.

Not that she would have dared. She didn't exactly have a permit.

She lit up and called her voicemail, surprised to hear the slow, steady cadence of the female mountain herself on the line, Fi. Fi had that low, booming voice, and on a phone call, it seemed somehow bigger than usual. It was a six-foot-tall, six-foot-wide wall of muscle, just like its wielder.

"Tanis, Mother wants you. We are discussing a new Den."
Call one.

"Where are you?" Call two.

"This is important. Please call." Call three.

"She has seen your departure. She is scrying now." Call four.

"She knows, Tanis. About you and the child. She wants to send me for you. I can only stall so long."

Call five sent a shiver of apprehension down her spine. *Of course* Lamia would send one of the few people in the Den Tanis actually talked to. Of course she would, because she was an awful, insidious bitch who cared nothing for loyalty or sisterhood. All she cared about were results, and Tanis might—*might*—hesitate to fight if it was someone she liked tracking her down. Lamia was nuts if she thought anyone would trump Naree, but it made a modicum of sense.

Tanis didn't call her back, but she did text; Fi deserved at least that.

I can't. I hope you understand.

The answer was efficient. Fi was an efficient person.

I know.

Tanis finished her cigarette and promptly headed for Bernie's room, pounding on the closed door. "You up?"

"Yeah. Coming. Bit stiff today. Ha. Stiff, get it?" Bernie chuckled quietly from inside her room. There was the slide of the dresser and the jingle of latches. The moment she opened the door, Tanis winced. Bernie was gray. Not statue gray yet, but the tint was there, in her skin, in her face, and worse, the blackness at the tips of her fingers had crept up her arm overnight, to her elbow. People would mistake it for gangrene, but it didn't smell like a moldering limb. It smelled... dusty? Like sand? Dry. *Dry* was the word, even though dry didn't have a proper scent, but it was there. It was what Tanis thought of.

"As you can see, we've had a fantastic night." Bernie lifted the dead arm and let it swing from the shoulder, back and forth like a fleshy pendulum. Bits of dust crumbled from her fingertips. "I do believe we are on the last train to Shitsville, doll." Bernie smiled and motioned her inside.

"Fuck. Bernie, I'm sorry. I'm so damned sorry."

"Meh. We all gotta go sometime. I'm getting comfortable with the idea." She shuffled back to the bed, slower than usual, her spine extra rigid as she slid her shotguns back into her duffel bag, one at a time.

"Fi called. Ma's coming for me."

Bernie didn't look shocked, but she did look tired. "It's ridiculous, when you think about it. She's got Gorgons sniffing around and she's worried about securing her baby daddy."

Tanis cringed. "Don't use that term. Please."

Not daddy or father or... no. Mother. I think? But Naree's mother.

It probably won't matter. I probably won't be around to see my daughter grow up.

"Sorry, sorry. Didn't mean to be insensitive, doll. I'm just off." Bernie glanced over at the alarm clock by the bedside. It was half past eight, later than Tanis expected to be on the road, but after yesterday's steady progression of awful, they'd all needed their sleep. "Give me twenty and I'll be set to go. I got donuts yesterday. That should hold us over until lunch?"

"Sounds good. I'll go wake the princess. She was drooling into her pillow last I checked."

Bernie grinned. "I like her. She's good people. I'm glad you've got each other."

"Yeah, she is. I need her to be okay."

Which might mean giving her up.

Naree.

WHAT NAREE DID to the donuts was unseemly. The powdered sugar everywhere made it look like she'd used her face to bulldoze a mountain of cocaine, but she didn't care. She merrily popped another, her free hand resting on her belly, which was, Tanis noticed, bigger. Big enough they had to get her some new shirts soon for fear of her popping out of all the ones she owned.

Or, why bother? Just let her stretch them out. The kid's due within a day or two anyway.

With a cloudless sky, the windows down to keep it cool, and enough junk food to cause a diabetic coma, it should have been a dream of a road trip, but every car that passed had Tanis peering suspiciously at the drivers. Every car that followed them for any length of time had her reaching for the gun on the seat. Every one of Bernie's pained sighs made her flinch. Naree's fretful Googling about baby things, about the rapid changes she experienced in her body, made Tanis's temples throb. She couldn't relax, no matter how much she told herself that they still had a shot—that they were going to New Orleans to see a death dealer and maybe, just maybe, they could get one of the two sets of snake people off their asses.

Tanis drove on. Sometimes there was chatter, sometimes there was music. There was Popeye's chicken at their afternoon refuel, and fast food burgers for dinner. When the sun disappeared and they were left with a starless sky and the wafting stench of Mississippi, Bernie sat up in the back seat, grunting and yelping. There was a cracking sound, followed by a hard *thunk* of something hitting the car floor.

"What happened?" Tanis demanded, eyes fixed on the unlit expanse of black pavement and bright yellow road paint. Naree flipped around in her seat to look in back and gasped.

"Her hand," she whispered. "Oh, Bernie. I'm so sorry."

"Eh. I wasn't using it anyway," Bernie croaked. She tried so hard to sound blasé, like this was just one of those things that happened because it was a day ending in Y, but the pain was there, an unmistakable undercurrent soiling her sweet, raspy voice.

"Christ." Tanis didn't know what else to say, because what was there to say? Her friend was falling apart in the seat behind her—literally, chunks of her body crumbling—and there was nothing Tanis could do.

Except drive faster.

It should have taken another two hours to get to the city, but Tanis cut that by forty-five minutes, pulling into a motel not in the expensive tourist part of town, but north of, where the houses were small and the roofs needed replacing. Forty dollars a night seemed like a good deal to her, and she got them a single room with two double beds. The carpet was old but the sheets were new, and there were three locks on the door and barred windows. It didn't say much about the safety of the neighborhood they were in, but that didn't bother her. Humans weren't the real danger. Not this time.

Bernie had set herself up in an overstuffed recliner pointed at an old boxed TV set in the corner. It was on a metal cart that didn't look strong enough to hold the TV's weight, but by the layer of dust on the second shelf, it'd been doing just that for a long time. She'd wrapped her arm in a scrapped T-shirt, from shoulder to the stub at her wrist, mummifying it either so her bits didn't fall to the floor like in the car or so no one asked questions about her condition. The black veins were up to her shoulder and stretching along her collarbone, spidery and pulsing fit to explode. Naree was settled on one of the beds with a big bottle of water between her legs, her phone connected to the charger she'd just plugged into the wall. Her eyes glazed over as she stared at a newscaster predicting a ninety-four-degree day with six trillion percent humidity.

"I have to go out," Tanis said. "Going to try to find a vodou shop."

It was a hit or miss thing with the shops, but the good news about being half-lamia was that people who didn't quite fit recognized each other quickly. If she walked into a place that catered to the erudite, they'd see she was special. Maybe it was an aura thing, or maybe the spirits were chatty, but she knew if she found the right place, she'd know.

Hopefully.

"Okay, text me if something comes up. Please be careful?" Naree climbed off the bed to waddle over to Tanis, her belly hanging over her drawstring pajama pants. Her T-shirt had rolled up off it, exposing a gently furred belly button that looked like it was pushing forward inside her navel. Tanis wrapped her arms around her and took a big sniff of her hair, getting a potent waft of hormone that she knew now as 'human mother.'

"I will, love. I promise." Her gaze drifted over to Bernie. She had her head back, her eyes half-mast. She lifted the shotgun at Tanis in a show of solidarity.

"Anyone comes near your family, I got a new face hole for them."

"You're a gooder, Bernie."

I'm going to miss you.

AFTER WHAT BERNIE said, matters of mother and father were on Tanis's mind as she wound her way through the streets of New Orleans. The French Quarter was bustling; not in the way the pictures of Mardi Gras portrayed it, with bare breasts and beads and drunken revelry, but the sidewalks were packed, the spill-over bodies walking mid-street without much care. The smells were plentiful—there was that below-sea-level funk of the river and old city sewer stench rising from certain parts of the narrow streets, but there was also the sweetness of confections and good fried food and fruity drinks. The novelty shops all smelled like candy. The titty bars smelled like cigarette smoke and perfume.

Naree's the mother. She is Mother. She gets dibs on that title for having to carry the baby. I don't want to be Father, even though some would say, biologically, I fathered the baby. I reject that. It doesn't feel honest. It makes me feel... wrong. I am a daughter of Lamia. I parented the baby, yes, but fathered...

I don't like it.

I'm Mother, too. Right? Right? I can say that?

Fuck, does any of it even matter? Will I even be there for it to matter?

She wedged her hands into her pockets and kept her head

down, her cigarette a long pillar of ash threatening to tumble with every step. She'd never before had to consider her gender in these terms before. There was a safety to the lamias' seclusion, to their keeping only their own company. How they were was how they were, the paradigm was created and maintained by the daughters. But her biology allowing her to impregnate her girlfriend had inadvertently brought a certain dysphoria into her life, and wasn't *that* a keen new problem?

Thanks, dicks.

She took a turn onto Rue Royale and walked on, searching for the ineffable in the long strip of stores. New Orleans didn't sleep. It was the type of city that breathed its best breaths at night, and so, even at quarter to nine, business blazed on. She looked in open doorways of stores, she peeked into tourist traps, searching for the otherworldly among the carnival-colored banality of a tourist town.

Instead she found a chicken—a big black rooster that pecked at the sidewalk, seemingly oblivious to the chaos of the world around it. Tanis stepped over it, not thinking much of it, even if it was a chicken in a place where chickens ought not be, but three feet on she heard a musical voice call out to her, stopping her dead in her tracks.

"Are you looking for me, koulèv?"

CHAPTER NINETEEN

IT WASN'T A vodou shop at all. It was a bar, nearly empty, tucked in between a closed art gallery and a T-shirt shop with the customary tourist trap beads in the window. Behind the bar was a short, fat black man with a perfect fade and a mole on his temple. The piercing in his septum was shiny gold, and a dragon tattoo wrapped itself around the back of his neck. His T-shirt was royal blue, as was the rag in his hand that he used to dry shot glasses.

The woman who'd called Tanis was one of the most beautiful women she had ever seen. She was short, barely five feet, with mahogany skin and cornrows tied behind her neck with a colorful scarf. High cheekbones in a heart-shaped face, a broad nose with a diamond stud on the left side, big brown eyes that looked black in the dim light of the bar, lips panted a bright scarlet. Her body was thick all over, curvy up top, curvy down below, with a wasp-thin waist between. She wore a white halter top that ended just below her breasts to reveal her flat stomach, and from hips to her bare feet she was wrapped in a crinkly skirt with red, yellow, and orange diamonds of alternating sizes.

"Sit, koulèv. Talk to me. The spirits say you have great need. Let's see if I give a fuck about it." The woman smiled as she slid onto a bar stool. The barkeep pushed a drink her way, a glass of rum topped with an angry-looking green pepper. She sipped it as Tanis circled the barstool and sat astride it, shifting to get comfortable.

"Tanis Barlas. I'm a lamia."

"Yes, snake girl. I know. Koulèv. This means 'snake.' You've come far to see me, eh?"

"From Florida, if that's far."

"Oh, far enough." The woman crossed her legs, her elbow drizzling across the bar and putting her in a half-slump. Her finger whirled above her head, motioning at the walls. Tanis looked up. The bar was decorated with black chickens, like the one she'd stumbled over outside. "I am Brigitte, but you may call me Maman. Everyone does. Now talk. I am a busy woman."

Considering the bar was empty besides the barkeep, Tanis wasn't sure how true that was, but she was also smart enough to not question it aloud. "I need a death dealer."

"Fooor?" Maman's face split in half, revealing two rows of perfect teeth. "Losing interest, koulèv. Delight me or get the fuck out."

"Gorgons are after me. The lamias, too. The Gorgons because I stole the heart of a prophet when she begged me to. The lamias because I abandoned them and"—she sucked in a breath, her shoulders aching with tension—"I think I'm the only lamia who carries potent seed. My mother will want me to breed her, but I have a mate. Who's pregnant with my daughter. I love her."

Delight. Utter delight. Maman tilted her head back and laughed, the sound filling the tiny bar and spilling out into the street, like tinkling music. It made Tanis think of wind chimes, which was strange, but there was something about the tones that spoke to gentle breezes on summer nights and chiming bells. "Ah! That is interesting. Did you hear that, Renaud? She is the great cock of the lamia."

The bartender's lip twitched, but he said nothing, concentrating on the line of glasses before him.

Maman drained her rum and bit into the hot pepper, never flinching despite the pungent juices drizzling down her lips. She tossed the stem into the empty glass and smiled. "So you are hunted. How can a death dealer help this? They are not dead things, your snakes. We are masters of the dead."

"There's no way to kill a Gorgon. They're immortal. But there was a witch—a völva—who said if I could get them to swear on the River Styx, they'd be banished to Tartarus. I want to know if that's true."

"Aaah, I see. Clever snake, to find a way around immortality." Maman reached out to bop Tanis on the nose, as one might do to a particularly precocious child. Tanis crinkled her nose, so Maman did it again; her fingernails were curved talons painted the same crimson as her lips. "You are right that this oath will send anyone below for long, long years. But sad news, koulèv. I am not a guardian of the dead rivers. The answers you seek, the very waters you seek, belong to the lords of the dead, and I am not a lord."

"Oh." Tanis ran her hand across her brow, fingers stopping at her temple to massage the throbbing vein away. How the hell was she supposed to keep running around looking for answers, looking for the right people, when everything was on such a limited time table?

Maman seemed to pluck the thought straight from her head. She leaned forward, closing the distance between them, until her nose nearly touched Tanis's own. "I can get you an audience with my husband, but no one labors for free. Especially not a lwa."

Lwa? Oh, fuck. Oh, fuck, fuck, fuck.

Tanis's first instinct was to lean far away from the predatory gleam in the woman's eyes; to Hell with that, her instinct was to *flee*. A lwa wasn't just some death dealer nobody, it was a *fucking god*. But what was she supposed to do? What other options were there? She was running out of time and resources. Bernie was dying, Naree would pop within days. She was stuck and she knew it. She forced herself to remain on her barstool despite the hot pepper stink scorching her nostrils. Despite the leering predator in front of her.

"The heart?" Tanis croaked. "Is that what you want?"

"Fuck the heart. No, I seek something baser." Maman's hand dropped to Tanis's knee and then glided up, over her thigh, and higher, until she was cupping Tanis's crotch, her palm rolling against her cocks through her jeans. "This. One night of pleasure. You would do anything for the girl, and this is your anything. Fuck me. Tonight. Upstairs. I demand my due."

TANIS STOOD IN Poul Mwen's one-stall bathroom, her hands clasping the sides of the sink, staring at her reflection. Hair mussed. Eyes pinched at the corners with strain, plum-colored circles and puffiness beneath them after days of too much stress and not enough sleep. She bared her teeth to the mirror, eyeballing the faint yellow tinge of too many cigarettes and too much coffee.

Can I do this to Naree?

Can I do this for Naree?

"She won't know," Maman had insisted, withdrawing her hand from Tanis's crotch. "It is between you and me, you have my word. I swear on the graves of the good dead. But you wish for my help? This is my price. Pay it or get out."

"What can your husband do for me?" Tanis had insisted, desperate for a reason to say no and hie herself to the hills.

Maman had laughed at her, climbing off of her bar stool and heading toward the back room of the bar, slipping behind a curtain of clicking wooden beads. "Everything. I will be upstairs. You have five minutes. If you are not there, I am not there, koulèv. Do not waste my time." There was the squeal of floorboards as Maman climbed stairs unseen, and then the sound of footsteps as she walked over Tanis's head. Renaud poured Tanis a single shot of vodka, saying nothing as he slid it across the bar. Tanis downed it, appreciative of the stabbing sensation in the pit of her stomach.

Too bad I need the bottle to feel anything.

Mouth on fire, stomach churning, she'd ducked into the bathroom of the bar—the name translated to 'My Chicken'—and suffered an abbreviated attack of conscience. Gods never asked for what was easy, like a heart in a trunk or a hundred bucks or a cheeseburger. They wanted blood. Literally or figuratively—they thrived on the ugly choices that left indelible scars on the soul.

If the lwa can help me, I have to.

Gods help me, I have to.

She splashed her face with water, raking her fingers through her hair to flatten it to her scalp. A mouth rinse later, she reappeared in the bar long enough to see Renaud flipping the *Open* sign in the front window. She followed Maman's trail through the beaded curtain and into a back stock room. She ascended the narrow stairs like she was mounting the gallows, her heart in her throat, each footstep met with the screaming of the boards that perfectly encapsulated her inner monologue.

Maman waited.

She was glorious in her nudity. Large breasts with prominent nipples, broad hips, an untamed bush of pubic hair between her thick thighs. She lounged like a queen in wait of her court, propped on her elbows, her braids fanned out behind her. It was a large bed, king-sized, with a red velvet coverlet and throw pillows stacked high, each decorated with fine embroidery or beading. The windows had similar velvet drapes. The art on the walls was all portrait work, black faces in period clothes, some of them smiling at the artist, some stoic and aloof and looking elsewhere.

The room was cool, air-conditioned, with no hint of the sweaty spring night just beyond the brick walls. It smelled of stale perfume, good booze, and female, but not human female. This was something other—bigger. Still essentially woman, but there was a spiciness that spoke to more.

Godliness. You're smelling godliness.

God cunt.

Fuck, what's next?

"You look so sad, little koulèv. Come to Maman. She will make it better."

Maman slinked across the bed, motioning Tanis close. Tanis dropped her pistol on the bureau and glanced behind her. With no door separating the bedroom from the stairs, she worried Renaud would discover them in a compromising position, but again Maman sensed her thoughts, chuckling as she reeled Tanis in by the belt loops on her jeans. Her hands settled on Tanis's hips, fingers kneading the lean muscle before snaking around back to cup her ass.

"Firm. So firm. Do not worry, Miss Tanis. Renaud is gone, gone, gone. Done. We will not be disturbed. You are *miiiine*." The last was said with sinister promise, the lwa unbuttoning Tanis's jeans before her warm hands swept up to grab the hem of Tanis's T-shirt and tug. Tanis's arms went up and Maman rose to her knees to jerk it over her head. Seeing Tanis's bare chest, the abdominal muscles so firm and defined, the modest breasts with the large areolas and small nipples, she gasped and leaned forward, those red lips closing around Tanis's flesh and sucking. Tanis grunted, eyes fluttering, her hands limp by her sides. Maman didn't seem to mind, content to suckle her, her free hand moving down to stroke over the front of Tanis's pants, palm rolling over her crotch.

"Firm little titties you have. I like, I like." Maman explored her with her tongue, from the contours of her breasts to the ribs and hard muscle below. When she licked over Tanis's navel, Tanis's stomach muscles spasmed. Maman liked that, and she cooed, kissing it again as her hands worked at Tanis's fly.

Sneakers. I have to… fuck. I don't want to like this.

But she did like it. How could she not? An expert mouth tasted her skin, feasted on her. Tanis kicked off the Chucks as Maman's hands looped in the waistband of her jeans to pull them down. Tanis stepped from the pool of denim, her body rising to the touches, the sighs, the sensations. Maman again cupped her, kneading her as her mouth traveled back up, this time to Tanis's neck to lick and suck and kiss. Her jaw. Her ear. Her mouth latched onto her lobe as her fingers plunged inside of Tanis's shorts, groping. She grabbed the top-most cock and then the bottom, laughing against Tanis's ear.

"Naughty secrets. Maman's spirits said you were special. *Giiifted.*"

"Yeah, I'm dick gifted. Gets me far in life," Tanis said, her voice gruff. Maman chuckled and gave her a stroke, and then another, and Tanis crawled up onto the bed beside her. Maman peeled her boxer briefs down, tossing them into the corner along with her own halter top and diamond skirt. She skimmed her hands over Tanis's body and rose up to straddle her knees. Tanis watched her braids with their shiny bead caps glimmering in the dim light of the room, and then she watched the sway of Maman's breasts as she leaned forward to place another kiss to the flat of Tanis's stomach.

It was strange; the moment Maman's mouth traveled down to the upper cock, to close around it, Tanis's mind went to Naree. Naree was soft with her, gentle, always delicate when she tasted her, never quite losing that sweet curiosity she had for Tanis's body. Maman had no such hesitation. She was loud, growly, her hand ducking underneath to pump the second shaft. Tanis draped an arm across her eyes, wincing at the sounds of her flesh being gobbled. Devoured. It was terrifying in its own right, wet and nasty and brutally efficient. She peeked down, staring at the lwa mastering her. Hard. Harder. Hardest. Tanis grunted, her hands dropping to the coverlet beside her and bunching it up in her fists. Her toes curled, Maman's cheek bulging lewdly, her black eyes pinning Tanis to the pillows and daring her to escape.

Part of her wanted to. Part of her wanted to run from the French Quarter and never look back. To go home to Naree and snivel a thousand apologies into her sweet girl's hair. But another part, the part that existed in the far back recesses of her mind where things like conscience and reason gave way to instinct and physical need, wanted to stay right where she was, pinned. Worked.

Used.

Maman tore her face away, Tanis's cock shining with her spit.

She reached between her legs, rubbing hard at the sodden flesh and filling the room with her sex. Potent. Sweet and sour. Tanis gasped as Maman crawled over her, settled over her, aiming herself down and sheathing herself with one hard shove of her hips. Maman threw her head back and moaned, impaled on the lower of the two, her hand curling around the upper piece.

Tanis's hands settled on her hips. She'd been passive before, allowing this thing to happen to her, but they were past the point of no return. When Maman rose up, Tanis jerked her down again, slamming her home. Maman rode her hard, working her with both her recess and her hand, her body rippling with every heave. Her breasts, her thighs, her hips. Every part of her was in motion, and Tanis pushed up, panting, her heart slamming in her ears as the lwa used her. There was no mistaking who was in charge, who owned the scene, and Tanis gave herself over to it because the only other choice was to keep running forever.

Slap. Slap. Slap.

Maman groaned, angling her hips forward and gasping as she raked her sweet spot over and over again. She licked her lips, smearing her lipstick past its perfectly drawn boundaries and up to her cheek. She rocked hard, fast, satisfying her body, Tanis clinging to her and feeling herself rising. She was tense all over, every muscle coiled and ready to spring. Her breathing came fast, her own sweat rising as Maman forced them both towards the end.

Over, over. Make it be over.

"Yes, yes. This. This. *Now*, koulèv. Give to me. Honor me. Give me tribute."

Tanis yelped as the orgasm crashed through her, dragging her into a perfect moment with an imperfect partner. Both of her shafts pulsed, one filling the woman above her, the other spurting hot trails across her own belly. Maman's hips jolted as she joined her, her head tilting back, mouth agape as she screamed, joyfully, her lover's peak erupting in a victory cackle that would, Tanis knew, follow her into her dreams and possibly her nightmares.

CHAPTER TWENTY

SHE'D TEXTED NAREE after the first round, telling her she'd met someone who could help her with the Gorgon situation. She offered few details, wrestling with the wriggling worm of guilt as she was, which only worsened when Naree professed her love and told her to come home soon, that she and baby missed her.

I think I felt her tonight. The flutters.

I love you both.

Because it was true, she did. More than ever. Being used by a lwa made your dear ones dearer.

We love you too. Bernie says hi. She's hanging in there.

Good.

And that was it. Maman climbed atop her twice more after the first coupling, each time as insistent and as aggressive as the first. It was intimidating, ferocious, and devoid of the sweetness she had with Naree. When Tanis finally passed out at half past three, she was physically spent and too tired to dream. She woke alone in the sullied velvet bed, the black rooster feather on the pillow beside her head the only indication Maman had thought of her at all beyond their fucks. She didn't get the chicken thing, but she also didn't have to. Some stories weren't for her to understand, and the lwa were beyond her scope.

She stumbled to the shower, scrubbing off the crusted sex remains and smeared lipstick, not feeling clean even when she'd rubbed her skin red. Her clothes were wrinkled and smelled like incense. The shirt smelled like Maman's perfume. That shit wasn't going to fly, so Tanis grabbed her gun and headed down the stairs and left the bar, the rooster feather in her pocket. She found a twenty-four hour store along the strip and bought herself a Crescent City T-shirt. She also bought a triple-extra-large NOLA shirt for Naree in case her stomach looked like she'd swallowed a beachball.

She changed right on the street corner, not giving a single iota of shit whether or not anyone saw her. It was pre-dawn, the sky that hazy purple gray going gold at the fringes. Street cleaners were out and about already, sweeping and hosing down the sidewalk in preparation for another busy day. Tanis slapped at her pocket for cigarettes, but finding that she'd left them in the car or at Maman's, she grunted, surly, and crawled up the sidewalk, stepping over the revelry of the previous night's tourists. Sparkly confetti, a spilled drink or four, empty cups, beads broken off their string, a condom wrapper.

All of it spoke to fun she hadn't had in New Orleans.

She'd parked off Canal, six blocks away. As she turned the corner to navigate back to the Caddy, she smelled pipe smoke. It was a sweet blend, something pleasant and grandfatherly, and she inhaled deeply, appreciating it against the mustiness of old city. The low humming and footsteps started a moment later. Tanis's hand moved back to hover over her pistol, just in case, which bought a low, masculine chuckle from behind her.

"That won't do you much good, koulèv."

She whirled around only to find herself looking at the chest of a tall black man with short-shorn gray hair wearing a pair of aviator sunglasses, an ornately carved ivory pipe clenched between his teeth. Her nose was assailed by the smells of fresh-turned earth, cologne, and tobacco. It was odd that he got so close to her so fast without her sensing his approach, but there he was, a foot away, when she could have sworn there'd been at least twenty feet separating them before. He was tattooed seemingly everywhere, starting at the bottom of his chin and stretching down, past the crew neck of his black T-shirt. Skulls, snakes, crosses—the images bled one into the next, black and white and red inks whorling together. He wore an open tuxedo coat with tails over his T-shirt, a pair of blue jeans, and black dress shoes.

Tanis didn't know much about the lwa, but anyone and everyone knew about Him.

"I thought you had a top hat," she said in greeting.

He chuckled and plucked the black feather from her pocket to stroke it along her jaw. She winced at the touch. The pipe fell from his lips and he caught it without ever looking down, upending it to rain burnt tobacco on the pavement below. "We adapt to our circumstances. Let's say I look different at parties. Call me Papa, koulèv. You are the gifted one, yes?" To demonstrate his meaning, he groped himself, giving his crotch a squeeze before bursting into laughter. "Maman is pleased with you."

"I'm—yeah, I suppose." Tanis sucked in a breath, embarrassed, heat climbing her face.

Shy, Tanis? You're shy?

"You're still around? I heard the really big gods were gone?" she asked, desperate to change the subject.

"Only the daddies. Dumballah is gone from us. Ayida grieves." He fell in beside her and motioned at her to keep walking. Tanis did, her shoulders hunched, her head down. Papa side-eyed her, twirling the rooster feather between his fingers with a jaunty skip in his step. "Maman says little koulèv wants to know about bonds made on the rivers of death. What you heard is true. If you break a bond by the dead river, you are dragged into its depths until it sees fit to release you, which can take a very, very long time. Immortals are no different than mortals. They just have the benefit of escaping one day. Any mortal that touches the waters dies instantly."

"Makes sense." Tanis licked her teeth, instantly regretting the decision. *Must find a toothbrush.* "Not sure *how* it helps, but it must somehow."

"Consider this: you don't need to take someone to the river. You can take the river to them. Then it's just a matter of getting them to vow."

Tanis jerked her head up at that, peering at the Baron's profile. It was hawkish in a way, his nose long and sharp, his forehead prominent with fiercely arched silver brows. "How?"

"You go to the river, you collect the water. If they know it's the water, they will be suspicious, of course, but no one said they have to know what they swear upon." Baron's smile stretched from one ear to the other. "Can you be tricky?"

"...sure. I guess. But how do I get the water?"

"There's the rub." Papa broke into dance beside her, doing a bit of a shuffle jig before he twirled ahead, pirouetting his way into her path and stopping her short. He loomed over her. She was a tall woman, so it was odd for her to have to raise her chin to look someone in the eye—well, sunglasses—but he had at least five inches on her.

"I can get you there. For a price," he said.

"What price?"

If I have to fuck you, too, I'm out. I'll just send Naree to parts unknown and give up now.

"What do you have to offer?" he countered.

"...I have a heart. A prophet's heart. In the trunk of my car. Cassandra's."

He looked thoughtful, which surprised her. After Maman's dismissal, Tanis had come to the conclusion that the damned thing was useless beyond getting her hunted by Gorgon priests, but Papa stroked the sides of his mouth, his head tilted. "That is powerful magic. So let us say six hours in the dead lands to get your water for... half a heart. You go in, you get out. Simple."

Whoa. Half a heart gets me six hours? Maybe it's worth more than I realized.

"Okay, so what's the small print? Because there's always small print."

Papa grinned at her, walking backwards and beckoning her to walk with him. Not once did he misstep on an ending sidewalk or a fire hydrant. It was like he had eyes in the back of his head—for all Tanis knew, he did; gods were tricky things. "Small print. Good question. Well, aaah... The dead lands are dangerous, but you know this. You'll have to be quick and clever. And if you cannot make it back to the portal through which you came within the six hours? You stay. Forever."

"What about the Orpheus shit with the no looking back and Eurydice getting stuck there?"

"Singular deal for him and her. You can look back all you want."

"Cerberus?"

"A silly puppy. He won't bother you."

One more block and she was at the car. She pulled her keys from her pocket and jingled them in her hand, trying to think of other loopholes. It was always up to the bargaining parties to ask the right questions during negotiations. If she was too blind to see, that wasn't Papa's fault. "...if a mortal touches the water, they die, you said. How do I collect it?"

"Ah. Well." He shrugged, a big roll of his wide shoulders. "You need a proper container to hold it. Something that can touch death that will not decay."

Tanis nodded, spotting the Caddy, untouched, in the line of cars where she'd left it. She swept the area to be sure they weren't being watched, but by all appearances, the world, for the most part, was still asleep, including the snake women and their priests. "Fine. A half a heart for six hours and your ivory pipe, and you have a deal."

The baron's brows shot high as he looked from her to the pipe in his hand. "My pipe? Why?"

"You're death. It touches you. It'll hold the water."

Papa smirked as he tapped the last of the tobacco from the

pipe's bowl. "Touché, little koulèv. Touché. You are clever. Do we shake on it, then?"

"Nope." Tanis opened the trunk of the car to pull out the heart. "I'm not touching you either. Figure out another way."

"This is not my usual way, koulèv, but if you insist," Papa said, flourishing a contract he'd conjured out of ether and whimsy. "Were you mine, I'd be insulted."

"My own gods have made me distrustful," she said. "No reflection on you. I've heard nothing but good things about the lwa." That seemed to placate him, and Tanis read both sides of the page, including the small print. There wasn't anything in it they hadn't discussed, no sly side-clauses, no double talk, and so she signed, witnessing him as he put his signature beneath hers. From there it was taking out a switchblade she had socked away with her weapons and sawing the salted heart in half. She kept the Tupperware container for herself and offered Papa his due in one of the Walmart bags, which amused her on a sick level.

"Good doing business with you, Tanis Barlas. Tonight, midnight, Poul Mwen's. Maman will help you cross over with my blessing. Six hours, but no more. Six hours, but no less. I wish you luck in your endeavors."

Before she could answer, he, the heart, and the contract were gone, leaving her alone in a sea of pollen-covered cars. "Plant spooge," Naree called it, and Tanis smiled faintly as she climbed behind the wheel. The sun was up, creeping past the trees, and soon would shine down a zillion watts of almost-summer. She drove back to the motel with the windows down, the radio loud to keep her awake. It was six-thirty when she parked, and after collecting the heart from the trunk, she rapped her knuckles on the door. Shuffling inside, the smell of cigarettes. Bernie.

"It's me," Tanis whispered.

"Thank Christ." The locks rattled and Bernie pulled open the door. She was grayer than the day before, especially around the face, and had lost more of her arm at some point. Still she wore the wrapped, tattered T-shirt, now tied off at the elbow. The forearm was nowhere to be seen.

Tanis leaned in to hug her, gentle with Bernie's decrepit body, and Bernie slapped her on the back affectionately, if awkwardly.

"None of that shit. Get in here."

Naree snored from the bed. Tanis slid the heart, the ivory pipe, and the trinket shop bag with Naree's T-shirt onto the table, peering at her across the room. She was peaceful, glossy black hair covering half her face, mouth open. Every once in a while, she rumbled like Gentle Ben, but that was okay, because it was Naree, and she was perfect regardless of her Weed Whacker sounds.

I'm so sorry for what I did, sweetheart.

So sorry.

Tanis's eyes stung. She'd taken no other lovers in her life, not among her sisters, not among the humans. There'd been Naree and Naree alone, and she'd gone and sullied the purity of that bond. She hadn't wanted to, hadn't sought out the affair, but it'd happened anyway and she'd have to live with it for the rest of her life. She could tell Naree, she supposed, to assuage her guilt, but what would that accomplish, besides making Naree upset and potentially hurting the baby?

No, I'll keep it to myself.

Not because I'm noble, but because I'm a coward. I want her to remember me fondly.

She sniveled as she climbed into bed behind her girlfriend, her arm sliding over her waist. The stomach was bigger, rounder, and so warm. She dropped her face into Naree's hair and breathed her in, relishing her sweet scent, the mix of ripe hormones and hotel shampoo. Maman had been something different, something spicy and musky and laden with sex. She had her own appeal, but this was home. Naree was what she needed.

She fell asleep surrounding her. When she woke hours later, at nearly eleven if the digital clock was to be believed, Naree and Bernie were sitting together in the second bed, side by side, doing despicable things to a pile of beignets while they watched game shows on the ancient TV. Tanis sat up, yawning, and Naree grinned over at her, handing her a half-eaten beignet powdered with sugar.

"There's a bakery across the street. I couldn't resist."

Tanis accepted the offering, jamming hot, greasy deliciousness into her face. Naree gleefully plucked another from the pile, her hand resting on her bare belly. She'd foregone trying to cover her roundness, instead tying her T-shirt off beneath her swollen breasts.

"I got you something," Tanis said. She got up, rubbed the sleep from her eyes, and fished around inside the bag for the T-shirt. It was purple, Naree's favorite color, with fancy script lettering and a glittery crescent moon. Naree wasted no time changing. The stomach still protruded, but not so much that the T-shirt's seams screeched in agony.

"Oh, thank God. The girl at the bakery saw me with my shirt tied up and probably figured I was one of those hippy moms who draws globes on my preggo gut. Which, all power to the hippies, but I think I littered twice on my way across the street alone."

Bernie reached for another beignet but winced and stiffened. Naree tucked one into a napkin for her and handed it over, patting Bernie's upper thigh.

They're getting along. Good. Bernie's good people.

"So where was the mighty hunter all night?" Bernie said, chomping on her breakfast.

"Making a deal with a death dealer. Maman Brigitte." Tanis paused. "She's a lwa. Met Papa—Baron Samedi—today to hash out the details."

"What details?" Naree paused her feasting to eyeball her. "Aren't lwa vodou spirits?"

"Gods, really, but yes." Tanis sat on the edge of the bed, leaning forward with her elbows on her knees, her hands clasped together. What spilled from her mouth was a loose plan that sounded like gibberish even to her ears: have Bernie drop her off at the bar, go into the afterworld, get some water from the Styx in a six-hour window of time, bring it back, put it in something, eventually make the Gorgons swear on it, hope for the best. The blank stares she got were not encouraging, but then, nothing about the situation was encouraging.

They look how I feel.

"...how are you going to get the Gorgons to swear on anything?" Bernie demanded.

"I don't know yet."

"So you're risking a trip into the underworld with nothing to go on for what happens next?"

"Pretty much."

Bernie said "Why?" at the same time Naree said "No."

"You can't," Naree said. "It's dangerous."

Tanis sighed. "So are Gorgons and lamias. I have an idea. It's not much of one, but it's something, and it might take care of both problems, but I have to get the water first." She eyed them both. "The less I say, the better. Don't know who's scrying. So here's the deal: I go tonight, at midnight. If I am not back tomorrow by, say, eight o'clock, go north. Chicago, the Pacific Northwest. Take the money and go. Alaska is probably your best bet. It's cold and anyone following would have to fly or get through Canada to get you. The Gorgons probably don't care about Naree, but Lamia—I don't trust her. *Do not* wait for me. It's a death sentence if you do. For you two, for the baby. And staying anywhere for too long is risky right now, so we're probably going to want to switch motels at the very least. We should pack it up, and soon."

Naree studied the beignet in her hand instead of looking at Tanis. Tears trickled down from behind her glasses and over her rose-kissed cheeks, a few sprinkling her new T-shirt. "This is the only way?"

"I'm afraid so. I can't kill something unkillable, but I might be able to trap it long enough it can't hurt anyone for a lifetime or sixty."

Bernie grunted and dropped her head to the headboard, powdered sugar dusting the bottom of her face and her LA Lakers T-shirt. "Alright. It sucks, but alright. I'll do what I can to get her out of here. We'll go at eight tomorrow without you. I don't have much left in the old gas tank, but what I've got is yours."

"Thank you. Truly. Thanks."

"Tanis. No. Please, no." Naree burst into sobs, body shaking, the donuts teetering precariously on her mountain of stomach. Tanis wedged herself onto the bed beside her, handing the beignets to Bernie so she could pull Naree in against her chest. She murmured against her girlfriend's neck, her hand stroking over her back as Naree pleaded for her to stay. Tanis said nothing, holding her close, and for the first time, with that big belly pressed to her side, she felt her daughter move.

CHAPTER TWENTY-ONE

POUL MWEN HAD been quiet the night before. Not so the second night; it was packed. A writhing throng of bodies pulsed inside and just outside of the door, people congregating with plastic cups full of frothy gasoline. Renaud was behind the bar, along with a short, skinny white girl with a blond French braid, both slinging drinks and smiles. Lively jazz music played over the speakers. Once a barstool was vacated, it was quickly filled.

Seeing Tanis pushing her way through the crowd, Renaud raised his hand to catch her attention, pointing her toward the back room. Tanis signalled Bernie away from the curb. It was hard to watch the Caddy's taillights disappear up the street, the gesture speaking to goodbyes she wasn't ready to say, but there was nothing she could do about it now. The deal had been struck.

At least it had been a good day. They'd spent it walking around New Orleans, alert and anticipating trouble, but there'd been none, not as Naree waddled along the Moon Walk holding Tanis's hand, not as they'd enjoyed crawfish at a restaurant overlooking the Mississippi. After ice cream dessert and Naree bursting into another crying fit that saw Tanis tearing up, too—she couldn't witness Naree's hurt without feeling like shit—they'd gone to a boarding house in the Tremé to rest. Naree passed out in their room, face buried in the pillows. Tanis sat with her for hours, holding her hand. She never let go, not until eleven o'clock when it was time to leave for the bar and Bernie gently guided her out the door.

"The sleep is good for the baby," she said. "Let her rest."

"But she's alone in there."

"I'll be back in twenty minutes. She'll be okay. You focus on getting your ass back to us, you hear? No dying. I won't allow it."

"Do my best. If she goes into labor—"

"I'll get her to a hospital."

"Good." Tanis paused. "She has insurance. Make sure she brings her card."

Bernie flicked her on the ear. "Stop fretting."

Easier said than done.

Naree was all Tanis thought about as she shouldered her way through a gaggle of yapping college kids to get to the back room. Past the beaded drape, into the storage room. She eyeballed the stairs leading to the bedroom, but then noticed that the back door of the building was propped open with a concrete block. She could hear voices outside. There was the smell of wax and herbs and things Tanis couldn't immediately identify, and she followed her nose out to a modest courtyard. There was Maman, seated on a plastic chaise longe with rusty hinges, people surrounding her and hanging on her every word. Maman looked totally at ease holding court. She sipped her drink and smiled, intently listening to her flock, a pepper adorning the edge of her drink glass like a lime would on anyone else's. She'd wrapped her hair in a bright red scarf and wore a royal blue sundress with white flowers all over it, the skirt flirting around her knees, her feet bare.

Spotting Tanis, she sat up.

"Koulèv! So glad you could join us. I ache from your fuck. You are surely blessed."

There were easily a dozen people in the courtyard and every single one of them turned to ogle Tanis. She wanted to melt away right then and there. Her hand went to her mouth, her face radiating. She expected censure or mocking from her gawkers, but there was none. An unspoken current passed through the crowd and they parted to reveal an altar against the back wall, draped with black, purple and white cloths, complete with candles, funereal crosses and skulls. There were offerings, too, of rum and peppers and cigars and pieces of silver. On the right side was a vase full of black feathers, perhaps for Maman; on the left, beautifully decorated bottles. There were flags tacked to the brick exterior of the building next door, showing skulls and crosses and what looked like saints, picked out in sequins and bright threads. It was beautiful, even if Tanis knew nothing about what any of it meant.

Maman glanced at her wrist, at a fine gold watch, and offered her hand to one of the people standing nearest her, a darkly tanned, heavyset woman with a port wine birthmark on her neck. She pulled Maman to her feet with minimal struggle.

"You want the most of your six hours, I'm sure." Maman winked and drained her rum glass, giving it to the closest worshipper and sauntering Tanis's way with an exaggerated sway of her hips. She placed her warm hand against Tanis's cheek, pursing her ruby lips together in obvious appreciation.

"You are most fine, Tanis. Most fine indeed."

That's the first time she's used my name.

"Manbo, what do you need?" a male voice called.

"A cloth for the koulèv's eyes. What is ours is not hers. To the floor, koulèv. We will get underway." She grabbed Tanis' hand and led her to the center of the courtyard, everyone stepping back to give Maman room to work. The bricks below Tanis formed a circle, and Maman positioned her in the middle of it, on her back, looking up at a star-riddled sky and a moon closer to full than not. The heavyset woman who'd pulled Maman up from the chair offered Maman a pillow, and Maman knelt by Tanis's head, the pillow tucked beneath her body to keep her comfortable.

An older man with glasses produced a strip of purple fabric for the Manbo. She leaned down to fasten it over Tanis' eyes, whispering into her ear.

"Heed me, little koulèv. Be ready. Be wary. I have fondness for you, yes, but I cannot protect you beyond the gate. Track your path, don't get lost. Your eyes will deceive you. Remember, the deadlands are full. You are never alone, no matter how it appears." Maman pressed a soft kiss to Tanis's forehead. "Keep the blindfold on until the water comes and no sooner, yes? And when you are done, find your way back to your starting point. That is where I will wait."

"What do you mean by 'until the water comes'?" Tanis asked, smelling tobacco on the air; it was similar to what Papa smoked earlier.

Maman chuckled. "You will know. Do not worry. Do you have your pipe?"

"In my pocket. The gun's in my waistband."

"The gun is worthless. The pipe, not so much. At ease, koulèv. At ease."

There was shuffling all around, bodies moving in close. Tanis could smell the strangers' skin, their sweat, the last meals they'd had for dinner or their minty gum. A drum sounded, then quieted, as Maman's voice rose in a beautiful prayer that Tanis had never heard before and couldn't understand; it wasn't English or Greek. It was sing-song and lovely, and every few lines, the people gathered would answer Maman with similarly musical lilts. Sometimes there was more drum, but then it would go quiet again, letting Maman continue her veneration. This went on for a while, Maman guiding the ceremony as their Manbo. Tanis listened, and as she listened, her body rhythm dropped to the tune of the ritual. Her breathing slowed, her heart rate slowed. She was caught in a current of prayer and song, her nose full of candle wax and incense. She felt swimmy, not quite right, like she was drunk but, at the same time, totally aware of every part of her body in relation to everyone and everything around her.

How is this possible?

It wasn't comfortable, she didn't like it, and she almost asked Maman to stop; but then the water came. It struck her face, her shoulders, her upper body. It was freezing, a complete body shock, and Tanis darted up, cold needling her skin and making her teeth chatter. She slapped at her chest, realizing that she wasn't actually wet. The sensation abated as the seconds ticked by.

The voices are gone.

She rolled the blindfold up and off of her face. Darkness everywhere, as far as she could see—or, more appropriately, not see. Her eyes adjusted, and she was able to make out the black tones on blacker tones. It was a field of tall grass, similar to what she'd trekked through in the Glades, except touching the blades proved it was all dry and dead. Spartan, mangled trees dotted the flat landscape. A crow cawed and cut across the starless, moonless sky. Charcoal clouds scrambled in the distance, a flash of lightning zapping the ground every few seconds, but there was no thunder behind it.

Silence.

Tanis stood, whirling to see if it was all endless dead fields forever, but no, behind her were mountains. They were enormous, touching the sky, their peaks angry, jagged teeth jutting up from the earth. She tilted her head back and inhaled. It wasn't hard to catch the scent of the river—water, but soiled. It was shit and death and blood and putridness. She gagged, covering her mouth, and stepped forward only to remember at the last second what Maman said about tracking her path back to the starting point. With few landmarks nearby, with nothing on her to act as breadcrumbs, she did the only thing she could think to do given the circumstances.

She bit into her own finger and bled on the ground, squeezing the tip. Every few feet, as she walked in the river's direction, she made sure she splashed a few more drops. She wouldn't be able to see them, but she'd be able to smell them, even with other blood stench nearby. It wasn't as good a marker as piss, but she wasn't about to whip out her dicks in the deadlands of all places.

Something could bite them off.

Through the grass and toward the mountains. More crows screeched, some settling on the emaciated carcasses of the here-and-there trees to witness her passing. Tanis had to keep gnawing on her finger to coax more blood out, but the temporary pain was worth the knowledge that, when she was finished with her grim business, she could find her way back.

Six hours, Papa had said, and she pulled out her cell phone to check the time. It should have occurred to her to bring a manual watch; there was no signal in the deadlands, and for the first time ever, her clock showed straight hash marks for time. Annoyed and unnerved, she shoved it back into her pocket, the one on the left, because the one on the right had Papa's pipe. Her hand brushed the gun at her hip. Useless, Maman said.

But I like it there anyway. It's like a Tanis-sized pacifier.

There was no path forward, no clear way to go, and so Tanis trod toward the mountains, grass as high as her hips and breaking beneath her shoes but never making a sound. Walls of black flies greeted her a short while later, but she pressed on through them, their feathery wings striking her face, their spindly, silken legs tickling her neck. She batted them away, keeping her mouth closed so they couldn't sail in and choke her. One flew into her eye and she cursed, her voice the only thing to break the stillness surrounding her as she plucked it out and flung it.

The river felt like it was forever away, but she knew she made progress by the size of the encroaching mountains and the rising stink. Still she bled, ever wary of the deadlands with its grass, its dead trees, its crows. "You're never alone," Maman had said, and she knew that was true despite the quiet. It seemed like a forgotten place, a void of nothing, but there was a heaviness on the air, a thickness and energy that spoke to things bigger than what she could perceive with the naked eye. She felt it on her skin. She breathed it into her lungs and knew the Other was nearby.

The first finger stopped donating blood so she bit a second, and it drizzled true all the way to the mountain. It was hard to say how long had passed: two minutes, two hours. The timelessness was not her friend, and so she started to trot, the grass giving way to a rough black gravel and a thick soot that sank beneath her feet. The water was close, that she could tell, the smell so overwhelming she took to breathing through her mouth so she didn't gag. The incline got steep and hard to navigate, and she had to stop to assess her approach. It took her a bit to spot the pass; it was narrow and tucked behind a line of dead shrubbery, a spindly fence cutting out the right side from the rest of the mountain. She jogged for it, dismayed to discover that the fence was not made of wood, but bones tethered together with spindly red twine.

That's pleasant.

She followed it up, following the slope to the left and down, until she crested a rise in the path and finally laid eyes upon the river. It was black and raging, the current far faster than any river she'd ever seen before. Clots of gray foam formed along the banks, snagging on jutting rocks and fallen tree limbs covered with unpleasant green slime. Bones littered the shores, some skeletons scattered like an animal had been at them, some in repose and unmolested, and by the lack of clothing or artifacts, they'd been there a very long time.

Tanis didn't have to stretch her imagination too much to see herself among the debris, lost and forgotten, arms forever reaching for something just beyond her grasp.

She worked her way down the mountainside, her feet sliding through soft, eroding silt. Her hand gripped the bone fence beside her for purchase, finding it surprisingly sturdy. It was perhaps strange, but the logistics of her trip didn't occur to her until her descent. A lwa had granted her passage to the River Styx. Did Papa have access to Tartarus because he was a lord of the dead? Did he sneak her in under Hades' nose? Or were all deadlands one land, only the names and gods ushering you across changing? She had questions she probably should have asked back in that parking lot on Canal, but there'd been so much whirling around in her skull, so many possible ways their bargain could have gone wrong, it hadn't occurred to her. And frankly, it wasn't important.

She was where she needed to be to get what she needed to get. That was all that mattered.

She hit the flat ground below, almost stepping on a skull. She picked her way around the bones best she could, but there were so many in every direction, sometimes she had no choice but to crunch over them. When she picked her way to the riverside, it occurred to her that the Styx made no sound at all, despite the churning violence of the current. No hissing or spitting or whooshing. It was stone silent, and remained that way as Tanis crouched down in more soft, black silt. It wasn't wet at all, feeling more like sand beneath her, which was probably good because wet meant dead and she liked being not-dead.

She wanted to get home to Naree.

She reached into her jeans pocket for the pipe and drew it forth. She watched the flow of water, how it broke upon the juts along the edges of the banks and splashed up in places. It'd do no one any good if she was stupid and got her hand splashed while she collected her sample, and so she waited for the right time, for a stretch of calmer water. It wasn't exactly predictable, but there were some spots that lulled more than others, and she crouched in wait, pipe lid up, her arm poised and ready for the dash.

"Here goes," she muttered to herself. She counted down from three. On "two," she lashed her arm out, dunking the pipe into the black water, and for a terrible moment, when she broke the surface, she saw the souls trapped below. Twisted faces, mouths agape, eyes white and forever staring, cheeks hollow. They were there, hundreds of them. Thousands, millions. Toiling and trapped in the savage pull of the water. Tanis only spied them for a heartbeat, but even that was too much, and she scampered back from the shore, her pipe full, a splash of water arcing up and damned near sprinkling her foot.

"Shit, shit!" She looked inside the bowl of the pipe. It wasn't full anymore, but it was close enough she didn't have to dip back into the Hell waters. She held the pipe away from her body as she regained her feet, abandoning the shore, content to never look back at the Styx. Back to the mountain, holding onto the bone fence and pulling herself up the side, exerting herself on the steep slope and soft ground.

It was only when she reached the peak where she'd seen the river that she heard the squealing. It was a shrill, high-pitched shriek, echoing from the hills and carrying across the deadlands, diminishing to a terrible hiss. Tanis' eyes jerked to the mountainside, at the black monolith shape before her, searching the landscape for its feral secret.

"You are never alone, no matter how it appears," Maman had said.

Tanis pulled the gun from her waistband seconds before the mongoose lunged.

CHAPTER TWENTY-TWO

MONGOOSES WEREN'T SUPPOSED to be six feet long and hundreds of pounds. They weren't supposed to have glowing golden eyes and inch-long fangs. They certainly weren't supposed to bleed into the shadows so it was impossible to anticipate where they'd strike from next.

There was an exception to every rule.

It isn't a mongoose at all. It's shaped like one, but it's something else. Something worse. Something that took the form of a snake killer to hunt me.

Tanis's first gunshot blasted through its head, and in any normal creature, that would have been the end of it. It barely slowed the damned thing. The bullet parted the dense blackness, creating a ravine through its big, weaselly skull, but it reformed seconds later, the mongoose bellowing with rage as it lunged for Tanis's legs. She sidestepped, but one of the front paws had enough reach to rake her across the back of the calf. The claws shredded her jeans, the thick fabric protecting her skin, but another strike like that and she'd be shredded to the bone.

The pipe slipped in her grasp and she adjusted her grip, taking off running for the path ahead. The mongoose was quick and it was agile, keeping pace with her despite the steep incline of the mountain. It screamed again, its deafening cry echoing in the stillness. It had no scent, because it wasn't real. It wasn't an actual creature, but the shadow of the deadlands itself coming for her, and shadows had no smell.

Shadows shouldn't have claws either.

Tanis's feet pounded the soft dirt of the mountain pass. She skimmed her hand over the top of the bone fence as she ran to the bottom, using it as a guide as she worked her way down. As she hit flat land, the mongoose leaped from the stony crags to cut her off. It blocked her way, hunching its back, hackles up, eyes huge and rimmed red, jaws slathering. The claws slashed out, smacking at the air and promising menace, and she had to duck and roll to avoid them, her grip on the pipe wavering.

If one drop escapes, I'm done. It's all over.

Fuck.

The mongoose circled her, lunging and biting and gnashing its teeth. Instead of running at the grass where her blood trail was, she took off alongside the mountain to try to zag her way around the shadow creature. It was fast, not as fast as she was, but it was a good jumper; any distance she made, it recovered with a few lunges. It shrieked at her back as she sprinted, her breath coming fast. The thick deadlands air filled her lungs, her nostrils flaring as she tried to pick up her own scent markers. Nothing yet, she wasn't close enough, and she veered back toward where she thought she'd come earlier. The landscape wasn't kind to her; the grass extended for miles, the trees few and far between. One of them, some yards up, looked vaguely familiar-ish, and she headed for it, the crows standing sentry on the branches squawking irritably that she'd led the mongoose their way.

Another wheezing snarl behind her. Tanis pointed the gun back and fired off three shots. They obliterated the shadowy beast, but it coalesced against in moments, picking up its pursuit like nothing had happened.

Maman said the gun was useless. She didn't say tits-on-a-bull useless.

The mongoose lunged at her left side and so she veered right, the grass pushing against her, a tide that had been ignorable before but not so with a nightmare on her heels. She was slowed by the tiniest of fractions, but enough to count. The mongoose lashed out, snarling, caught the back of her T-shirt in its grasp and jerked back. The pipe flew from her hand, but she didn't dare try to catch it in case the cap unlatched and water drizzled over her hand. She fell forward and the thing was on her, claws digging into her back, pain tearing through her body. She grunted, pushing herself up onto her forearms as the jaws clenched on her shoulder, teeth sinking into the meat. It shook its head back and forth like a dog worrying a bone, trying to tear pieces of her away. A hot wash of blood poured down her neck, her arms. She nearly buckled from the pain, but she couldn't. She had to stay up.

I have to get out from under this thing or I'm going to die.

She reached over her shoulder, getting a fistful of oily, furry scruff, the texture unlike anything she'd encountered before. Solid shadows were dense and slick—all she could think of was the gooey, pasty leavings in a fry pan after making hamburgers. Her fingers sunk in, past the skin and into the actual body until she encountered something firm inside, a spine of sorts, and she looped her fingers around it. She heaved it forward, using the strength that let her bend metal and pick up dumpsters. She threw the thing as hard as she could. The teeth slid from her flesh, the sensation a singular agony she never wanted to repeat again, the mongoose screeching when it landed some feet away.

Tanis eyed it, gasping, wounds burning. She crawled toward the pipe to see if it'd all been for nothing, but somehow, magically, the damned thing was still capped. She stole a peek, relieved to see the water safe inside, and refastened it with careful fingers. Back on her feet, back to her escape. The scent of her blood was ripe in her nose, coming off her shoulder in waves.

How the hell was she supposed to pick up a few drops in the grass?

Still she ran, past another tree that looked familiar-ish. The mongoose shrieked behind her, undoubtedly readying itself for another charge. She made as much distance on it as she could, pushing her body to its limits. Her chest hurt from exertion, her back ached from the gouges. Her T-shirt was glued to her body with blood. Her eyes swept the fields looking for the familiar, her path home lost to her, thanks to the attack. She could hear the mongoose coming for her, and she put her head down to focus on staying ahead of it for as long as she could. Feet became yards, yards became miles, Tanis lost in a sea of dead grass with no idea if she was going toward her starting point or away from it.

I'm going to die in here.

Oh, Naree. I'm so sorry.

Her jaw set, her eyes narrowed. The mongoose behind her hissed and chittered, with an eerie, hyena-ish quality that suggested it knew she was stuck there, and it would relish what it did to her when her body finally gave out. Tanis kept moving, pushing past the pain, pushing past the point where she wheezed for breath. The grass went on forever and one tree looked like all trees. How many had she passed? How many were ahead?

It's pointless. This is all so pointless.

A rooster crowed.

In the weirdness of her day, in the vast scheme of talking to lwa, fucking lwa, making deals with Death, crossing into the deadlands, looking into the River Styx, and being mauled by giant shadow weasels, a chicken was pretty banal by comparison. A chicken in Tartarus, however, was noteworthy, especially as all Tanis could think of was Maman Brigitte and her black feathers.

Another crow.

She's calling me.

She could have been wrong—it could have been a four-foot-tall rooster waiting to peck her face off—but she was willing to take a chance. She followed the call, shadow in tow, burning the last of her reserves. Another caw and she saw it, thirty feet off and standing on a rock surrounded by grass. It was black and glossy and as shadowy as anything else in the deadlands. As she neared it, daring to hope and dreading the worst, the rooster fluffed itself up. Tanis watched it grow, tall first, then wider. Legs stretching, comb smoothing over to become braided hair, tail feathers curving inward to form an ass. Maman was there, not articulated as she was at Poul Mwen's—there were no pretty dresses or lips as red as a cherry popsicle—but it was her form with golden eyes, and she pointed at the mongoose, chopping her hand down as Tanis collapsed at her feet.

"Kanpe la!"

The creature shrieked and sniveled, rearing back and away from the lwa, becoming less ferocious and more wheedling. Maman looked unimpressed. She shooed it off and crouched before Tanis, cupping her chin in her oily hands, her thumbs brushing over Tanis's cheeks. There was a break in the shadows of her face, revealing white, straight teeth, and then she was leaning in, kissing Tanis full on the mouth, that same shadowy greasiness translating to Tanis's lips.

"Close your eyes, koulèv. Close your eyes."

Tanis did, swallowing back a sob, as she was splashed on the upper chest with cold, frigid water.

TANIS'S EYES FLUTTERED, but she couldn't keep them open, not yet. She was too spent, too pained. Too... everything. She heard the singsong prayers, and felt a cool cloth dabbing at her brow. Another swept over her shoulder. A warm breeze brushed her body, bringing with it the smell of rum and incense. She was bare from the waist up, that she knew, even as warm hands pushed her up onto her hip. Another cloth pressed against her back, putting pressure on her still-tender skin where the mongoose had raked her. She hissed, but didn't pull away, vaguely understanding that these were helping hands, not hurting ones.

They're tending my wounds.

A new herb scent, something fresh and good, filled her nose. It was everything that the deadlands hadn't been, and it was all over her, overriding the tang of blood. Dispelling the stench of the River Styx.

"Easy, koulèv. Let the pipe go. If you squeeze much harder you'll break it and all Maman's work will be for naught. Give to me. Give. Good. Good, girl." Tanis's fingers relaxed on the pipe, her palm dented from the carved sides of the bowl. Someone took it away. She opened her mouth to protest, but no words came. Her body was there, present, but unwilling to cooperate with her mind, which was telling her to sit up, get up, get moving, go home.

Soon. I can't yet. Soon.

"You are pushing too hard. I have closed all the nasty wounds and if you tear them open again, I will be irritated. Cock-blessed or not, I will not have my time wasted," Maman chastised. Tanis immediately stilled, mostly because she was too damned tired to do anything other than sprawl limply anyway. They worked on her awhile, Tanis fading in and out of consciousness until finally, after what could have been days, Maman leaned down to whisper in her ear.

"Wake."

And she was awake. Her eyes popped open, her vision swimming into focus. Her body ached, but in a way that suggested old hurts, not new ones. The sky was clear and blue above with nary a cloud in sight. Birds chirped in the nearby trees, oblivious to anything but the spring sunshine.

"What time is it?" she rasped, pushing herself up into sitting position. Her back screeched in protest, but when she ran her fingers over a sore spot on her shoulder, where the mongoose had torn her open, there was fresh, slick skin. She looked down at herself. No shirt, just her sports bra stained brown with old blood, but she was clean otherwise. The bite mark, where the shadow thing had gnawed on her, had scarred over to a tender patch of pink against her skin.

"Early still. I gave you an hour to sleep. You barely made

it out on time." Maman loomed over her, smiling. They were alone in the courtyard with only the chaise lounge, the altar with burned-down candles, and the art on the walls. Tanis pushed herself up, looking at a hand-sewn flag showing a saint, complete with a halo.

Tanis motioned at it. "That looks Catholic."

Maman followed her gaze. "When my people were brought to Haiti as slaves, the French king demanded that they only worship the Roman Catholic God. They would not lose their lwa, and so they depicted us as saints, to appease their oppressors." Maman collapsed into her chair, using her red scarf from the night before to dab the sweat from her forehead. "We are resourceful people."

"Clever."

"Mmmm. Indeed."

"Thanks, by the way." Tanis ran her fingers through her hair, cringing at the oiliness there. "For everything. I need to—Naree. My girlfriend." She slapped at her pockets, looking for her phone or the pipe but discovered neither, nor her gun. Maman chuckled behind her.

"Here, koulèv. Here." Maman motioned to her left, at a wrought-iron garden table with a mosaic top. She pushed forth gun, phone, and a small, olive-green bottle shaped like a snake with a cord around the narrowed top. It was simple enough, with its red eyes and glazed exterior, but if it could hold water from the River Styx, it was obviously blessed or magical in some way. "Papa will want his pipe back. I took the liberty of moving the waters into a proper vessel. Dumballah the snake. He would not mind being used thus, considering what you are."

"Right. Thanks again." It wasn't that she didn't appreciate what Maman had done, but she was cautious by nature and she had too much at stake to not check her hard-won prize. She uncapped the bottle, muttering, "I don't mean to be rude, but..." and sniffed the contents. The concentrated foulness of the River Styx assaulted her senses, and she closed up the statue, rubbing her nose like a dog who'd been blasted in the face by a skunk.

"Serves you right for not believing Maman," the lwa said, grinning. She crossed her legs and leaned back in her lounge chair, pretty face tilted toward the sun, arms stretched over her head. "Renaud is out front. He will take you home if you like."

"I—thank you." Tanis tucked the gun into her waistband and snagged her phone to look at the time. Half past eight. Her heart sank; she'd told Bernie and Naree eight, and she'd slept right through deadline thanks to the mongoose bullshit. Her thumb hit Naree's speed dial, hoping to catch her, but no answer. A second call, no answer.

Out of service range?

She tried Bernie's cell, with the same result. Maman opened a single eye to peer at her, looking much like a contented cat as she waved Tanis off, yawning in her patch of sunlight. "Go. See Renaud. Perhaps I will see you again, koulèv. My cunt will remember you fondly." She paused. "Do you still have your black feather, koulèv? The one I left for you on the pillow."

"No. Papa took it."

"Oh, that brat. Take another from the altar. For luck. Then get home to your girl. She needs you."

What does that mean?

But Maman was not forthcoming.

"Thanks. I—thanks."

Tanis snagged one of the feathers from the vase on the altar and then hauled ass to the back door of Poul Mwen. Through the stockroom, to the bar itself. Renaud was behind the counter, lining up bottles on the shelves, a pen tucked behind his ear, a notepad clenched in hand. Seeing her, he stopped and smiled, motioning at the whiskey glasses.

"Thirsty?"

"No. Maman said you could give me a ride home? Not home. The Tremé. We're at a boarding house there. Or they might be. Shit."

They could circle back around to get you. Leave them a message. They're not far out.

Renaud tossed notebook and pen onto the counter, grabbed his keys and unlocked the bar's front door, leading her out to a yellow pickup truck with too many bumper stickers. He was quiet as Tanis called Naree's and Bernie's cells, leaving similarly panicked messages telling them that she was fine, that she was on her way back to the Tremé, and if they'd be so kind, to turn around to pick her up. It only occurred to her as she ended the second message that maybe something had happened to them. Maybe they'd had to run. Maybe they'd gotten killed. She'd been gone all night, and if the priests had turned up...

"Maman likes you," Renaud said. "She said you gifted her."

"Gifted?"

Oh. My dicks. Go me. I'm dicktastic.

"That. Yeah, it's... yeah."

Renaud chattered on about Maman, the bar, New Orleans. Tanis looked out the truck's window, grunting answers when appropriate, telling him the address of where they were staying when he asked, but she couldn't concentrate. Her brain was on fire. When Renaud pulled into the parking lot twenty minutes later, the Caddy was in the corner spot they'd been assigned when they'd accepted their rooms. Tanis mumbled a "thank you" at Renaud and ran for the door.

She was halfway up the stairs when she heard Naree's scream.

CHAPTER TWENTY-THREE

IT'S ODD TO barge into a delivery room wearing a sports bra crusted with blood and holding a gun, but it wasn't even the strangest thing that had happened to Tanis that week. The fact that the woman giving birth was her girlfriend, and the baby crowning was her daughter, probably moved it into the all-time top fifty, though.

"Push. Push!"

"I'M FUCKING PUSHING!" Naree let loose with a bellow that would have done an angry bull proud. She hunched up on the bed, body supported by her elbows, her knees splayed while she bore down. Bernie sat to her left, holding her hand. She looked rough—her skin was gray and riddled with black veins and patches of dusty-looking charcoal-colored lesions. A pile of dust pooled beneath her feet, her body flaking away bit by bit.

Tanis frowned at her, and then at the stranger at the foot of the bed. She was a round, dark woman with a port wine birthmark on her neck—

She's from Maman's. She was at the ritual.

Did Maman send her? She must have.

She sat on a stool, her gloved hands between Naree's legs, cupped in wait of the coming baby. Around her neck was a stethoscope. At her feet was a bag full of medical supplies.

"You're doing great," the woman said. "Almost there. Push on the next contraction."

Naree's head lolled back, her brow glossed with sweat, hair plastered to her neck and upper chest as she panted. Tanis was gawking—at the sight of their daughter eagerly shoving her way into the world. At Bernie and her decay. At the helping stranger. She put the gun on the bureau and rushed to Naree's side to take her free hand.

"Naree. Sweetheart."

"Oh. Oh, hey. You made it. Keen. Fuck you for doing this to—*AIEEEE!*"

Tanis cast Bernie a grateful look. Bernie winked at her, but said nothing, enduring their mutual finger-crushing with grace. Tanis looked down Naree's body, over her swollen breasts and stomach to her knees, and to the woman positioned between them. Naree strained, her body shaking, her mouth opening to let loose with another scrotum-shriveling screech that ended with a lusty cry from a baby and Naree collapsing onto the bed, staring at the ceiling and laughing in a way that spoke to equal parts relief and trauma. She grunted a second later, tensing again for a few seconds before going completely limp, her lashes fluttering against her flushed cheeks.

The room smelled of blood and piss and sweat.

Life. It smells like life. Funny that death is so similar. We fall back to the place from which we rise.

"There she is, there she is. She's beautiful, beautiful," the woman said. Tanis leaned down to kiss Naree's face all over, squeezing her hand, her gaze swinging between her exhausted girlfriend and the small, thrashing, slimy creature held by the stranger

"I'm so sorry I wasn't here," Tanis whispered into Naree's ear.

"I don't care. You're back. That's all that matters. You came back."

Naree's tired smile made Tanis's breath catch.

She's beautiful. They're both so beautiful.

"Just in time, koulèv. This one got two pretty mamas, doesn't she?" The woman cut the baby's cord and clamped it off. The baby let loose with a primal scream that rivaled Naree's own before being carried from the room and into the bathroom for clean up. Faucet running, another big cry, and all went still. Naree peered at Tanis, brow furrowed, but the corners of her lips were curled into a smile.

"Thank you," she said.

"For?"

"Sending Esther. She's been wonderful."

Tanis's first instinct was to deny her involvement, but she didn't want to paint anyone a liar in case that was the cover story that got Esther through the bedroom door in the first place. She kept quiet, waiting patiently for Esther and the baby to reappear. It took a few minutes, but Esther emerged shortly thereafter with a tiny, black-haired miracle swaddled in a soft towel, the baby's eyes a murky gray-brown and barely open, her fist waving, her skin ruddy.

"She is perfect. Perfect," Esther crooned.

Bernie and Tanis helped Naree prop herself up on a small mountain of pillows. Esther laid the baby across Naree's chest, Naree's arm circling the infant, cradling her close as her lips skimmed over the soft head.

"You have to support their necks," she said. "I read that last night. They can't hold their heads up yet."

Tanis smiled.

Bernie did, too. "That's a fine looking puppy you got there, doll. Doesn't look a thing like Tanis, which is good; she's uglier than a dog's ass-end."

"Fuck you, Bernie." Tanis immediately cringed, because shouldn't she stop cursing in front of her newborn kid?

So much has to change. If I'm around for it, I'll do my best. Be my best.

No butts. No swears. No leaving the bathroom door open while I piss.

Bernie sank back into her overstuffed chair, eyes closing like she'd fought hard to stay awake for so long. "Seriously, though. Gorgeous, girls. Gorgeous."

"Thanks." Tanis was grateful Bernie couldn't see her frown; the Gorgon poison had taken a visible toll overnight. Her bad arm was completely gone, the open shoulder socket a circle of crumbled stone that reminded Tanis of Ariadne's ruined chest. Dust littered the floor, gray particles of stone covering the end tables, the entertainment center, the desk in the corner. Her ankles were oddly swollen, her bare toes turning black, the pinky on the left gone already. Her right earlobe was missing, too, the fragile shell above chipping along the uppermost curve and giving it a strange point.

Tanis swallowed past the lump that formed in her throat and swung her focus over to the tiny person she'd helped make. She ran her fingertip over the newborn's chin, over the fat waddles in her neck, over her chest. She was pale, like Naree, and had a little upturn in her nose, also like Naree. Tanis struggled to see herself in her until the little hand closed around her finger and squeezed. Strong. Not too strong, not anything freakish, but firm.

There I am.

"She's beautiful," Tanis rasped, her voice thicker than she expected. "Like her mother."

"Mothers. I want to call her Bee. Beatrice. For Bernie." Naree glanced Bernie's way, smiling, oblivious to Esther wadding up the soiled sheets at the foot of the bed.

"Well, aren't you sweet. That's a fine name, doll. Just fine." Bernie never opened her eyes, resting against the headrest of the chair, shoulders slumping as she dozed off. Tanis studied her profile, studied the slow rise and fall of her chest and the angry, pulsing veins in her neck. In that moment, sandwiched between her newborn daughter and a dying woman, she realized what a gift a life was.

ESTHER CHECKED THE baby over; not only was she a skilled vodou healer, she was a nurse in an intensive care unit by day.

While she still recommended getting the baby looked at in a hospital or a pediatrician's office for blood screens, she was confident saying she was healthy and hardy and had all the proper functioning baby parts.

"Her vitals are perfect," she said. "I'm sure she'll thrive. Congratulations." She handed her back to Tanis, careful to adjust her in her arms before packing up her medical bag. She eyed Bernie in her chair, frowning as she slid the stethoscope from her neck. "Old woman. You should come see Maman. She might be able to do something about that curse. Or if she doesn't, she'll know someone who can, yeah?"

Bernie smiled faintly, rolling her head but not lifting it from the back of the chair. She cracked one eye to peer at her. "You're real sweet to say so, but I'm not sure I want to keep going. There's too much of me gone. It's more'n an arm. I won't go into detail, but unless she can grow a new me, I'm... I'll pass. Thank you, though. You're a doll for offering."

"You're sure?" Esther pressed, her hand hovering over the doorknob. "She deals fair."

"I'm sure, doll. Sure as sure can be."

Tanis offered Esther money, but she refused, saying she was grateful for her service to Maman. Considering the only service Tanis had provided was a few sweaty, regrettable tumbles, she was quick to see her out, doing her best to ward off the guilt so it didn't ruin the one truly good thing that had happened to any of them over the last few days.

She shut the door and drew a deep breath.

You had to. It's in the past. This is the future.

"So I was thinking about the two moms thing," Naree said, the baby on her breast. They were lucky—she'd latched easily and Naree's milk had come quick. "What if she calls me Umma, which is 'mama' in Korean? You can be Mom. Figured that'd keep us straight?"

"Yes, keep us straight. Straight's a word I think of when I think of us." Tanis smirked her way, and Naree burst into giggles, utterly delighted.

"Touché, my big dyke-y love. Give me a kiss."

Tanis readily complied, her fingers sweeping over both Naree and Bee's brows. "I love that, though. Umma and Mama. It's great." Tanis watched Bee working at Naree's nipple, her rosy lips pursed, her eyes closed.

"When did you go into labor?" she asked. "I'm sorry I missed it."

"Six-thirty?" Naree narrowed her eyes thoughtfully and nodded. "About, anyway. I got upset when we didn't hear anything from you and my water broke. It was quick after that. Esther showed up, told us you were fine, told us you'd sent her to help. She actually knows the lady who owns this place—she said the Tremé is a close neighborhood. Anyway, she talked to her, told her what was going on with me, and then helped me deliver. And here we are."

"And here we are." Tanis nuzzled Bee's fuzzy head.

Everything was, by all appearances, going well. Well enough that Tanis dared to dart off to the grocery store, buying pads for Naree, diapers, powder, formula, bottles, and a pacifier. She was wary of leaving her family alone yet again, but what could she do? They needed stuff, and Bernie was in no condition to go in her stead, stiff and uncomfortable and sleepy. She'd insisted she was alert enough to shoot a gun if needed, hefting one of her shotguns as proof, and after a quick shower, Tanis had ventured out, exhausted but happy, especially when, in her travels, she passed a baby store. She stopped to pick up a car seat, a blue one with cartoon elephant print all over the interior.

As she parked the Caddy at the boarding house, she had the creeping worry that they should move again. Not far— just enough any scrying would be too late to catch up with them. But Esther had said to keep Naree planted for a day or two. Naree looked okay, but after they'd put her in the bathtub post-delivery, the water was full of blood and floating tissue. She wasn't outright hemorrhaging, but it *did* look like something from *Friday the 13th*.

They couldn't risk it. And yet.

Those fuckers are coming. I know they are.

I'll need to be alert.

...after I get some sleep.

Tanis helped settle Naree into bed, the baby propped on her chest. Bernie was drinking beer and watching a baseball game on the television. Tanis climbed into bed beside her girls, allowing herself to doze, only waking a few times when the baby chirped because she was hungry or cried because she'd peed herself. Naree had to show Tanis how to change a diaper, which was considerably more unpleasant when you had a super-nose, but she muddled through, managing to not tape her kid's eyes shut or powder her armpits. The whole family settled down for nap together after that, only waking when Bernie reached out to shake Tanis's shoulder.

"Tanis," she hissed, head cocked to the side. She inhaled deeply and shook Tanis's shoulder again. "Tanis!"

"What?"

Bernie said nothing more, but she didn't have to. Tanis saw her sniffing the air, and she did the same, searching for whatever it was that had her friend reaching for her shotgun by her seat. She moved to the window, pulling the drape back. Tanis did the same, quiet as she reloaded her Glock. She inhaled again and was met with a familiar sour, lemony scent. Not pheromones, but sweat. A particular type of sweat that was more pungent than most and unmistakable, especially so far from home.

Lamias.

CHAPTER TWENTY-FOUR

RHEA AND PRISKA didn't bother breaking into the boarding house. They walked through the front door, up the stairs, and knocked. Tanis looked calm as she shook Naree from her sleep, pressing a finger to Naree's lips when she started awake. She motioned at the bathroom. Naree's eyes widened, but she said nothing as she climbed out of bed, the sheet draped over her shoulders to protect both her and the baby's bareness. Tanis cupped her elbow and led her inside, pointing at the bath. She even went so far as to provide her with two pillows so she'd have something to rest against, settling the girls into the tub and pressing the Glock into Naree's hand. Bee slept against Naree's chest, undisturbed, her little fist curled over.

They'll smell them both, but maybe they'll assume it's another guest next door.

Unlikely. But maybe.

Tanis closed them in and surveyed her surroundings. Directly across from the bedroom door was the bed, flanked by end tables, double windows beyond it. To the left, the bathroom entryway, a bureau and, in the corner, the overstuffed chair, with Bernie dust all over it. To the right, a second bureau and a pullout couch where Bernie had supposedly slept. In the far corner was a flat-screen television and a short book shelf full of inspirational Christian novels.

No cover. Nothing to hide behind.

Balls.

She went to her stash. Luke's Colt, a Desert Eagle magnum she'd gotten from Nicholas Pope before Lamia had fucked him to death last month. Bernie had backed herself into the corner of the room with the TV, shotgun at the ready. Tanis couldn't keep her hands steady as she put one gun in her back waistband and held the other behind her. She crossed to the door, sucked in a breath, and opened it, the weapon nestled into the small of her back.

"What?"

"You know what," Priska replied.

Priska sounded and looked annoyed. She was a humanoid daughter born in the same clutch as Tanis and, in some ways, similar to Tanis: no scales, no claws or protruding fangs, no visible snakiness to her at all. That was where the similarities ended, though. She was on the short side at five-two, unusual for a lamia, with a riot of brown curls and big brown eyes. Tanis figured she more resembled their mystery father than their mother—Priska was fairer and slighter in stature than she was. She was wont to dress better, too. Whereas Tanis wore a Rolling Stones tank top with the giant tongue lolling out and jeans, Priska wore black slacks, a white top, and sensible black flats.

To what was, at its core, a kidnapping. Which said a lot about Priska.

Rhea was taller than Priska by a foot, and heavy. She wasn't fat per se, but she was padded, with thick hips, thick arms, thick neck, and a belly roll. It was deceptive; beneath that squishiness was a lot of muscle. Tanis once saw Rhea deadlift a pickup truck for fun on a dare. She was one of the few blondes in the lamia den, and she wore it short, cropped around her ears, and slicked back. Her face was all broad features and moles with big green eyes—another standout feature among Lamia's brood. She had huge feet and hands the size of oven mitts. Unlike Priska, she dressed casual: a black T-shirt, a short-sleeved red checkered shirt hanging open, jeans, sneakers. She was more Tanis's ilk, all salt-of-the-earth and comfortable, but that wouldn't matter. She was on a retrieval mission.

Under better circumstances, they may have had something worthwhile to say to one another.

"Can we do this easy, please?" Priska said. "For all of us?"

"No, doll. We can't. There're circumstances."

Priska and Rhea looked over at Bernie in the corner; neither could hide their shock. She was a gargoyle version of herself: haggard, tired, far more gray than fleshy. Spidery veins crossing every inch of visible skin. Her hair looked like silver straw, and her fingernails were putrid green on black fingertips.

Priska jerked her face away, but Rhea was not so polite. "What happened to you?"

"Gorgons," Bernie spit. "They're the priority, not Tanis. Sending you here was stupid. It's not getting Ma moved, not getting the Den safe. Daphne was petrified outright, one stare. Ariadne they tortured to death by turning her to stone piece by piece. Me? Their priests carry the venom. One nick is all it takes. I can feel myself going to stone. I've lost an arm, a toe, part of my ear. My lady junk is falling out. It's painful, y'all. Like lava in your veins. Every movement burns, so maybe we can look at the bigger picture and stop this nonsense?"

"Jesus Christ." Rhea glanced at Priska, eyes wide. "You hearing this?"

"Shut up. Just shut up. It doesn't matter." Priska jabbed Tanis in the chest with a manicured finger. "You have to come home or it's our asses. You know no one gets to run. Doesn't matter if the world is on fire, you come home."

"No," Tanis said. "Leave."

"We can't," Priska insisted.

"Yeah, you can. You can run. What's Ma gonna do if we all just up and take off?" Bernie waved the shotgun around. "She'll run out of helpers. You can go be somewhere else. Be free."

"No, we can't." Priska shook her head and sucked in a breath, her chin rising, her jaw grinding. "I can't."

Ma's got something on her. It's all over her face.

"Who's she holding?" Tanis asked quietly.

"She took Zoe." Zoe was a younger snake, ten maybe, who Priska had taken under her wing at hatching. She was different from most of the lamias; she had one human leg and one that was was, for all intents and purposes, a snake tail without scales. No foot, no toes—a long, prehensile, fleshy extension she'd wrap around your wrist or wiggle into your pockets to steal your pens. Lamia wanted to drown her like the runt of the litter, but Priska had insisted she could care for her. Lamia agreed so long as it didn't interfere with Priska's service to the Den, and so Priska stole Zoe away, to her house somewhere on the outskirts of Adder's Den. It wasn't Percy's Pass, but close by. She'd hired one of the other lamias to act as nanny while she worked her day job, fitting in among the humans like one of their own with her fancy clothes and articulate speech.

Priska wasn't a bad sort, really. She was generous to Zoe and a hard worker. It was unfortunate that she'd been given such a shitty mission.

Tanis shook her head. "I can't. I've got my reasons."

"Yeah, what are they?" Rhea demanded. "You always did your duty. You were never a deserter. Now this? What's going on?"

Lamia didn't tell them. She's keeping it to herself.

They probably assume she's going to devour me, but I'm willing to bet she won't. Wouldn't.

I'm not going back. They'll have to kill me first.

"I have a gift she wants and she can't have it," Tanis replied, careful with her words. She swung the Colt around and pressed the fat barrel to the middle of Priska's forehead. "Leave."

"Don't make us do this," Priska said through gritted teeth.

"Oh, fuck this." Bernie raised the shotgun and pulled the trigger. Rhea and Priska dropped, as fast as Tanis, diving to either side of the doorway The boom echoed through the house and there were screams down the hall. Naree yelped.

Bee cried from the bathroom. Tanis spun around to fire at Rhea, but Rhea lunged at her legs, tackling her and wrestling her to the ground. Tanis was strong, but Rhea was stronger, and she grabbed Tanis's wrist and pinned it above her head. Tanis's knee came up, catching Rhea hard between the legs.

She oomphed, but wasn't crippled.

No dick. Well, shit.

They wrestled like cats. Tanis couldn't see anything other than Rhea, but she heard Bernie fire another shot, followed by the sound of furniture crashing and breaking. The baby wailed from the bathroom. It was all so hectic and chaotic, especially as a blur of woman raced by—Priska, undoubtedly. A chair flew through Tanis's peripheral vision as she struggled against Rhea's hold. Rhea reached up, prying her fingers away from the gun and shoving it away. She punched Tanis in the face, and Tanis's nose exploded, her eyes rolling up into her head at the pain as Rhea's other, huge hand grabbed her hair and lifted her head up, smashing it down against the floor.

And again.

And again.

It vaguely occurred to her, as Rhea beat the shit out of her, that Rhea could have grabbed the Colt at any time and put a bullet in her. But she didn't. She'd been told to bring Tanis in alive.

Which gave Tanis a very strange advantage.

"Stop, stop," Tanis mumbled.

Rhea paused above her, fist drawn back and ready to strike again. "You going to come nice?"

Another shotgun blast and a howl. Tanis' world whirled around her. She couldn't tell who screamed or why, but there was a thud, followed by a groan. She tasted blood in the back of her throat, and Rhea's visage swam above her. It was odd to be so helpless; even with the Gorgon priests, she'd had a speed advantage, a strength advantage. Against another lamia, though, it was blessing against blessing.

Lamia sent a superior fighter to take down her favored hunter.

Formerly favored hunter.
I'm in the shit now.

"Come nicely, please," Rhea pleaded. A plaintive whine and a gasp sounded from the corner. Rhea looked over. Tanis would have liked to follow her gaze, but she was still chained to the bottom of a tornado, and she was pretty sure turning her head would make her puke. "Priska? PRISKA!" Rhea's brows knit together into one long, golden strip of fur.

"She's hurting, doll. Could use some help." Bernie. She sounded tired, weak. Like she had gravel in her throat, which was a possibility, considering her ailment.

Rhea reached for the Colt and pushed herself to her feet. Tanis had the vague notion that she might not shoot Tanis, but Bernie was probably fair game, especially if she'd gutted Priska. Tanis rolled Rhea's way and looped her arms around her knees, getting a solid hold and jerking back. The nausea hit full throttle and her lunch tickled the back of her throat, but it was worth it. Rhea went down hard, felled like a high tree. She struck the floor like a rock and Tanis was on her, a hand bunching in her hair and shoving her face down. She whacked the Colt away, the gun sliding under one of the bureaus and striking the wall. Tanis reached into her waistband and pulled the magnum, pressing it to the base of Rhea's skull, the barrel parting that fine, curly brown hair.

"I don't want to do this," Tanis spat. "But so help me, I will kill myself before you take me back to the Den, and then what? What'll you have to show? You're in the shit either way. There are three options as far as I can tell. One, I blow you away. Two, I blow myself away. Three, I let you walk out of here with Priska. Pick one." She jabbed the gun into the base of Rhea's skull. "*Pick one!*"

Instead of begging or fighting or doing any number of things Tanis expected, Rhea went to pudding beneath her, her big hand pointed at the corner. "Priska," she said. "She needs help."

Tanis blinked the world into better focus and swung her gaze over. There on the floor, curled into a ball, was the slight lamia. There was blood, and a lot of it, but it was hard to tell where it was coming from, the way she'd huddled in on herself.

Bernie filled in the blank, the shotgun still in her hand, bits of smashed TV littering the floor by her feet. She leaned against the wall and sucked in a ragged breath. "Got her in the chest. Right side. Lung's probably collapsed." Bernie wheezed again, rasping in a way that suggested she might be laughing. "Interesting thing. Hitting a statue hurts you more than it hurts the statue."

She cast Tanis a wan smile and winked.

Looking between her sisters, all four of them fucked up in some way—Tanis's face a mess, Bernie nearly petrified, Priska rocking a hole in her chest, and Rhea pinned at gunpoint—Tanis's revulsion for her mother roared to the surface. None of them were bad people. Rhea and Priska weren't bad. Rhea was worried about Priska; Priska was worried about Zoe; Bernie and Tanis worried about each other. In Lamia's mission to satisfy her needs, she'd pitted good women against other good women, and none of them really wanted to be fighting. It was all so *pointless*.

It was all in service to a woman none of them loved, but all of them feared.

Bernie is right. If we all just left, what then? She can't go out in public, not as she is. She'd be alone. She'd be desperate.

But that was the thing about abuse, wasn't it? It was so insidious, because the obvious answer is to get away, but you give yourself a thousand reasons why that's the worst idea in the world. That all of those reasons boiled down to fear was secondary to the survival instinct.

Fuck you, Lamia.

Enough is enough.

"Go," Tanis said, climbing off of Rhea. "Get out of here before the police come. Get her to a hospital. Go. And whatever you do, don't go back to the Den. The Gorgons are coming. *Will* be coming. I... go."

Rhea said nothing as she climbed from the floor, crossing the room in three strides to pick up Priska, disregarding the blood, disregarding Bernie and Tanis both. Priska's head rolled back against her shoulder, her eyes big, her panicked gaze swinging from Rhea to Tanis.

"Zoe!" she whispered, the sound wet and raspy. "Zoe."

Right, the kid.

Tanis looked her dead in the eye, reaching out to clasp her hand, Priska's fingers slick with warm, wet blood. "I'll get her out. I promise. You have my word." She squeezed Priska's fingers. "Just go and whatever you two do, *don't go home.*"

CHAPTER TWENTY-FIVE

TANIS LEFT FIVE hundred on the bureau before they screwed out of the boarding house. It wasn't enough to cover all the damages, but it at least took care of the decimated TV. She didn't like leaving it in such disarray, but every cop in the world would be looking for them soon and her family's safety came first.

She piled the four of them into the Caddy and took off, not toward the highways and main routes, but to the hot, dusty back roads of Louisiana. Naree's Google Mapping kept them off the radar. At one point, about twenty minutes from the boarding house, they pulled into an empty driveway with a four-door white Honda parked on the side lawn, a *For Sale* signed wedged beneath its windshield wiper. She cased the house and, finding no one home, told Naree to drive the Caddy into the woods a ways up the road, to go as far as she could and to wait for her there. Naree did as she was told while Tanis broke into the house through a screened back window. A quick sweep and she found the Honda's keys dangling from one of those pegboard things near the side door.

She could have hotwired it if she had to, but this was infinitely more convenient.

Tanis drove up the street in her new wheels, joining Naree on an overgrown hunter's trail that looked like something from *Apocalypse Now*. Seeing the Caddy nestled among all the greenery, her grille gleaming, her rusty fender pert despite all the miles, Tanis felt heavy all over.

All things had to end. Gods. Monsters. People. Even Cadillacs with mighty hearts for engines.

She patted the trunk fondly before unpacking their weird miscellanea from the trunk, a cigarette hanging from her mouth all the while. Bernie sat shotgun in the Honda while Naree and Bee nestled into the back. It wasn't a bad car; only fifty-thousand miles, though the upholstery was dingy and the radio didn't work. Those were minor faults, though, and they drove out of the woods and onward, as fast as Tanis dared, stopping fifteen minutes later at yet another empty-looking house so she could pry a licence plate off of a pickup truck and slap it on the Honda.

It wasn't much protection; it wasn't enough. But it was better than nothing. They couldn't avoid the highway forever, and she didn't try to. As she hopped onto I-10 to leave New Orleans, she realized she knew what she had to do, despite the tightness in her chest and the awful, sinking feeling in the pit of her stomach. This was no life for her or Bernie or their sisters, and it most certainly wasn't a life for Naree or little Bee.

It took her an hour to get to the Gulfport-Biloxi International Airport in Mississippi. Naree was in the back seat, asleep. Her color was good despite the chaos of the morning, despite being moved during her recovery. Bee was against her chest, face tucked against her breast, little eyes closed, rosebud mouth open with milk crusting her bottom lip.

I don't want to do this.

I can't do this.

I have to do this.

Tanis parked the car and, with girlfriend and daughter still asleep, took the guns out of the duffel bags. The black bag she stuffed full of money, snacks and Bee's baby supplies. The pink one already had Naree's clothes. She heard a car door open and prepared herself for a squabble, but it was Bernie, dragging her left leg, her gait stiff. Every time she stepped, Tanis could hear the *clunk* of stone meeting pavement.

"You ready to go, old woman?" Tanis whispered.

"Yes, but not in the way you're thinking." Bernie opened up one of her own bags. She pawed through her shotguns and a few pairs of underwear to pull out a gray metal box the size of a shoebox. She handed it to Tanis. "Put that in there for Naree. There's about forty or fifty grand. Let me... got a pen?"

Tanis didn't answer her, opening the box and peering inside at perfect rows of hundred- and fifty-dollar bills. Banker stacks, where the money was real flat and pristine. "Cocaine stacks" Naree would say, because she always pointed out, whenever they watched movies together, that the only people to have money sorted that way were drug dealers and bank robbers.

Tanis's shoulders tensed.

I won't cry.

I will not fucking cry. She's going to cry, you don't cry.

"What's this?" she warbled instead.

"Can't take it with me." Bernie had found a pen in her bag and tried to scrawl something onto the corner of a pizza menu, but her fingers were too stiff, and she handed both pen and menu to Tanis. "Four-six-six-two. That's the pin. Write it down for her." The pin to what became evident when Bernie produced a debit card from a wallet. That she'd secured a bank account, a real license, and a few credit cards over her years spoke to an interesting life Tanis knew next to nothing about.

Visas, Mastercards, debit all went into the metal box, along with the money.

"Aren't you going with her?" Tanis clasped the treasure box in her hands, peering at her friend. Bernie wouldn't look her in her eye when she shook her head and headed back to the front seat, climbing into the Honda without another word. The slam of her door woke Bee, which woke Naree. Tanis braced herself for the inevitable. She hated it; she wanted nothing more than to climb in next to her girls and hold them until her arms couldn't hold anymore.

But that wasn't keeping them safe.

"Babe?" Naree sounded tired.

"Come on out, Naree."

Tanis closed the trunk, the two duffel bags by her feet, Bernie's box in her hand. Naree opened her door and stepped outside, the sun bright against her glossy hair. She twitched the nursing cloth over Bee's head so she wouldn't get burned, adjusted her glasses on her nose. The moment she realized where she was, took in the terminal, the tower, and the line of silver planes, she started arguing.

"No. I won't. Come on, Tanis. We've been over this."

"Yes." Tanis motioned her close.

Naree scowled. "I can't. We just had her. No! We're in this together, remember?"

"Listen to m—"

Naree stomped her foot. "No, I'm not leaving you!"

"*You have to or you're both going to die!*" Never in all of their time together had Tanis raised her voice to her. Never had she felt the need to, but with her family on the line, with Gorgon priests and two of her sisters already come a-calling, she needed Naree to hear her. "Listen to me, sweetheart, okay? Listen. I don't like it. I hate it. I hate losing you, and her, when I just got her, but this is never going to stop."

"We could go north," Naree protested. "You said snakes hate the cold."

"We could, but we'd still have to move around. Always. And I can't let either of you live like that, always running. I can't let our daughter live like that. She can go to school. She can have a life. She can maybe go to college one day, if she's smart like you. And hey, maybe she'll like video games like both of us, huh? She should get to play them without always worrying if someone's going to come steal her or her mothers away at night. She's... normal, Naree. Normal-looking. Normal everything. She's got ten fingers and toes and no scales and no nothing that speaks to her snake. She's got a chance at a real life. With me around, unless I can fix this, there's no normal. None. And I think, deep down, you know it."

The baby started fussing and whimpering against Naree's shoulder, and Naree bounced her gently, her hand stroking along her back. "I can't, Tanis. I can't. Okay? Not yet. Maybe just another day or two and we can—"

"We don't have another day or two." Tanis opened the top of the box and showed Naree the money, the credit cards, the debit. "The pin's on the pizza menu. Use the money first, then the credit cards. It's from Bernie. She wants you to have them."

"Doesn't she need them?"

Tanis gave her a hard look. Naree immediately caught on, flushing pink and looking away. "Oh."

"So, listen. Get a flight to Atlanta and then you can go anywhere, yeah? Go to Connecticut maybe, with your parents for a little while. I know you hate them, but they'll take you in until you figure out where you want to go next. You can get Bee a birth certificate. Get her a real identity. With the Gorgons in the picture, I don't think my mother's going to spend the resources to hunt you two down. I'm the much bigger prize, so you should be fine, but... get a gun. In case. Keep your eyes peeled. Just—" Tanis's voice broke, and she swung her eyes up at the sky, at the puffy clouds above that looked so goddamned cheerful when she felt so goddamned terrible. "Take care of yourself. And her. If I can, I'll come back. But I can't do that until I know you're safe."

"You have a plan," Naree whispered. "Don't you?"

Tanis swallowed past the lump in her throat that threatened to choke her. "Yeah. Yeah, I do. It might be a bad one, but it's all I've got."

"Are you going to die?"

Tanis closed the distance between them, wrapping her tattooed arms around Naree and Bee, holding them to her chest. She inhaled Naree's scent, sucking it in and trying to keep it with her always. She kissed her daughter's fat cheek. She waited while Naree said a tearful goodbye to Bernie, and she carried Naree's bags up to the United ticket counter so Naree could purchase her flight to Atlanta. She kissed her stupid, right up until Naree had to go to the security line practically bawling the entire time. Bee was crying, too, because that's what babies did. She watched them walk from sight, and she stood in the airport until they were too far away for her to smell them anymore.

And she never, in all of that time, answered Naree's question, because she couldn't bring herself to say it.

SHE DIDN'T CRY, she sobbed. Ten full minutes, non-stop, until her head hurt and her hands were covered in snot and she couldn't see. She blew her broken nose on some McDonalds napkins Bernie found in the glovebox, blasting it with blood, and then, when she was through or at least clotted, she guzzled two bottles of water, ate a Twinkie, and got back on the road, driving silently from Mississippi to Alabama. When night fell, they crossed into Florida. Bernie rested beside her, silent, chest barely rising and falling. Tanis eyed her here and there, to see if she was still breathing. She was, but it was a struggle. There was an echoing rattle and a whistle with every breath.

She stopped by a drive-through for dinner. Bernie declined; Tanis gobbled a couple of cheeseburgers, doing her best not to think about her girls. She'd gotten a text when they'd landed in Atlanta, saying Bee had been good on the flight and slept through most of it, and when she did cry, the other passengers were nice about it. Tanis expected another message when they got to New York, but that wasn't for hours yet.

Safe. Safe and away.

It hurt, but it was right. There was some consolation knowing that.

She'd just gotten back onto the highway, ready to squeeze another few hours of driving time in before a motel stop, when Bernie grunted beside her. "The ocean."

"Eh?"

"Let's go to the ocean. I like it. Always did. Don't even mind the sky-rats so much..." It sounded like there was something else she wanted to say, but the sentiment faded to a weary sigh.

Tanis eyed her in the passenger seat. Bernie was so still, so gray. Another person might have mistaken her for dead or truly a statue, but there were signs. The veins all over that pulsed, not often, but often enough. Her tics, like when her finger tapped against her thigh. The subtle swell of her nostrils when she breathed.

She's fading.

A beach stop would delay her return to the Den, but Bernie had been a good friend. She'd done so much, sacrificed so much, that granting her something so simple was a no-brainer. Tanis veered off the highway and drove toward the coast. The Pensacola night was warm and humid, but there was a Gulf wind coming in that made it more bearable. Past picturesque manicured lawns and vague Spanish architecture, and homes worth more money than Tanis would ever see, in this life or next. Past hotels and restaurants and bars playing Latin music and other bars playing contemporary country. She drove to a public beach closed hours ago, a sign threatening fines for anyone caught after sunset.

She parked in the space furthest from the road, turning off the engine and peering out at the gentle, rolling waves. Salt air, the slightly rotten tang of low tide. Bernie's hand fumbled with the door beside her. It swung open and she heaved herself from the car, using the grip handle to gain her feet. Tanis followed, pausing to grab her cigarettes and the American Eagle, sliding it into her pants just in case. Once the parking lot pavement became sand, Bernie needed help, the uneven surface setting her pained gait off-kilter. Tanis offered her an arm, surprised at how heavy Bernie's body had become. Her left leg was completely stiff, no longer capable of bending at the knee, but she limped along anyway, undeterred.

The ocean whispered invitation at them, not angry and roaring but whispering sweetly as it lapped at the shore.

Hush.

Hush.

Hushhhh...

Bernie collapsed ten feet from the water, and Tanis sat down beside her. When she lit a cigarette, Bernie grunted, and

Tanis plucked the smoke from her lips to place it between Bernie's. All was silent save for the ocean and Bernie's labored breathing. The cigarette wasn't helping any, but there wasn't any point in bringing it up, not anymore, and when her pillar of ash threatened to break off at the end, Tanis grabbed it, flicked it for her, and put it back.

When she'd smoked it to the filter, Bernie spit it out, her eyes fixed on the smoldering orange stub flaring red with every gust of wind.

"I can sing, you know," she said.

Tanis turned her head. "Eh?"

"I used to go down to Barbara's, when all y'all were babies. I'd sing you to sleep. I even joined one of those Baptist revival churches so I could sing in the choir. I was real good, too. Didn't care much for the Jesus stories, and they were way too hung up on who was fucking who else, but the music was nice. The hymnals are beautiful."

Tanis gathered her knees to her chest and watched the water. Bernie hummed a little, and then, for the first time that Tanis could remember, she sang. Her voice was probably less perfect than it would have been pre-Gorgons, but it was still lovely. Raspy, throaty, all sweet and grit twisted together to make a honeyed melody.

> *Abide with me; fast falls the eventide;*
> *The darkness deepens; Lord, with me abide;*
> *When other helpers fail and comforts flee,*
> *Help of the helpless, oh, abide with me.*

> *Swift to its close ebbs out life's little day;*
> *Earth's joys grow dim, its glories pass away;*
> *Change and decay in all around I see—*
> *O Thou who changest not, abide with me.*

"Pretty," Tanis said, because it was. The song, the voice singing it. Bernie smiled, and, as she did, a quarter-sized flake of gray skin tore away from her face, fluttering away with the wind. Tanis watched it go as Bernie rolled onto her hip to push herself up, struggling in the sand. Tanis immediately went to her side, hefting her, her sneakers digging deep under the burden. They stood together, Bernie's arm clinging to her waist, her head heavy against Tanis's shoulder. There were a million stars before them, and a fat white moon that hung so low they could reach up and pluck it from the sky.

"You're a good kid. Don't die on that girl of yours, you hear? And that sweet baby? Try not to fuck her up too much," Bernie rasped, her eyes squinting. Her silver hair whipped around, sometimes smacking Tanis in the face, but she didn't care. This was Bernie's moment, not hers.

"I'll try."

"Don't try. *Do* it. Live. Cheat, lie, steal; do what you gotta do. You only get one shot at this. Don't blow yours." Tanis examined Bernie's profile—the slope of her forehead, the prominent nose, the wide lips. The years had taken their toll long before the venom had, but still she smiled, showing off the gap in her teeth where Lamia had taken her due a few days ago. Particles of dust flaked off her body with the wind, pieces of her rippling across and then lying to rest on the beach forever.

Bernie shrugged Tanis off and started walking.

"Bernie..."

"You ever read Kate Chopin?" Bernie shouted over her shoulder, dragging her petrified leg as she hobbled along.

"No. What are you doing?"

"They say if you don't fight it, it's the most peaceful way to go. Well, I ain't fighting anymore."

"Bernie!"

"You got this, doll. Now watch this stone do what stone does best."

And what stone did best was walk into the water, and keep walking, despite the incessant tide pummeling her shins. Stone took her time and let her weight anchor her as she pressed forward. To her knees. To her waist. The water fought her, shoved her away, but she plowed on, pushing, pushing,

pushing. Up to her chest and then to her chin. There was a momentary pause when it crested her mouth and a half-turn, one hand rising from the water to wave at Tanis one last time, before stone sank deep beneath the black, rippling surface, never to be seen again.

CHAPTER TWENTY-SIX

THERE WERE NO tears for Bernie because Tanis had none left to give; Naree and Bee had claimed them all at the airport. But her heart was heavy as she drove from the beach. It was dark, it was quiet—perfect feeding ground for sadness—and it mounted as the miles passed, a snowball rolling silently downhill and becoming a boulder. She was alone. She was vulnerable. In the face of Lamia and the Gorgons, she was a speck of dust on their shoes, powerless. And where once she'd had nothing to lose, now she had everything.

Which is why I'm going to them, to the monsters.

I might fail, but at least I tried.

She drove until her eyes wouldn't let her anymore, landing at a cheap motel just outside of Tallahassee. She slept poorly, the Colt on the bed beside her, her hand resting on its grip. She would have preferred Naree's warm curves and the softness of a well-loved T-shirt, but that was behind her for the time being.

Forever, if she couldn't get herself out of the mess she was about to make.

Breakfast at nine, Tanis reading a wall of Naree's texts while she stuffed herself with an omelet so big it had to be served on a platter. Naree and Bee had landed in New York at five in the morning. Their bus had arrived in Connecticut at six-thirty. Naree's father picked them up, nearly throwing up on himself seeing Bee for the first time, but the shock gave way to delight, and both of Naree's parents were already fawning over their first and possibly only grandchild.

Naree attached a picture of Bee against her grandmother's chest. Bee looked annoyed with her circumstance, and despite the sick feeling pervading her guts, Tanis actually managed a chuckle.

So much like her mother already.

Naree's questions started thereafter—what Tanis had planned, why, when she thought she'd be done. Tanis didn't know how to answer any of them so she changed the subject to Bernie, filling Naree in on what happened at the beach. Naree replied with a line of sad faces and a single Damn, which pretty much covered Tanis' feelings on it, too. She didn't feel good losing her friend, but in the face of a grueling, painful death, Bernie had chosen to let go, her way, on her timetable. Tanis might have done the same in her position.

Tanis fueled the Honda and hit the road south. She'd veer east to catch the seventy-five and follow it all the way down to the Everglades. She didn't want to go straight to Adder's Den, but somewhere nearish, maybe thirty minutes out, where she could park until the Gorgon priests came sniffing around. Hopefully they were still looking; she hadn't encountered them since the gas station a couple days ago, but that may have been because Tanis and company had kept moving. Scrying wasn't a perfect science, and they didn't have the lamias' sensitive noses to round it out if they lost the trail. Tanis had been able to avoid detection by being smart and just a little bit lucky.

She didn't want to avoid it anymore, though; she wanted to be found. But that wasn't for hours and half a state yet, and so she scrolled through her missed calls from the other day, finding Fi's number and dialing. Fi'd been kind enough to warn her about her pursuers. Tanis could, at the very least, return the favor, and maybe in the process have Fi get Zoe and the other kids away from the Den. The kid didn't deserve to suffer—hell, none of the kids did—and Tanis would have to figure out a way to pull off what she wanted without creaming the innocents, too.

Two rings in, Fi's line connected. But it wasn't Fi that answered.

"Is this you, traitor child? Deserter. DISLOYAL STAIN!"

There was a time that Lamia's anger would have turned Tanis's insides out. She would have done anything to appease her so life could go back to the atrocious reality of being abhorred and ignored until she was needed again. But so much had happened in the last few days, so many new feelings, so many new experiences, so many hurts, that Lamia didn't seem as scary anymore. She was the same horrific piece of shit she'd been before Tanis left, yes, but the notion of dying beneath her hands didn't scare Tanis as much, not with Naree and Bee away and safe.

"Knowing what you want from me, I'd be careful dropping insults, *Mom*."

There was a sharp inhale of breath on the other end of the line. Lamia was taken aback at Tanis' gall; or else formulating her next onslaught.

Possibly both.

Seconds ticked by.

"I ate her, you know," she said finally, her voice quiet and laced with an ugly purr. *"I found out she'd warned you so I gouged out her eyes and then I ate her. Feet first. She was a big girl and it took some work, especially with how she flailed, but I snapped her arms and legs like twigs. She screamed all the way down, bellowing like a cow. Hnnn. Hnnngh. Hnngeee."*

Fi. Oh, Fi. Fuck. I'm sorry.

Lamia kept up the horrible honking moos. Tanis wanted to pound the phone against the dashboard until it stopped, or reach through the line to pull her mother's tongue clean out of her fat skull, but neither was possible, and so she breathed deep, letting her mother put on her little show.

"I'm coming home," she said, finally, when Lamia's brays died out to a raspy chuckle. "I'm on my way."

"*Good. Make it fast. We're leaving soon. Kallie has made arrangements for my shipping.*" There was a pause. "*I've been dreaming about punishing you, you know. I've thought about it—thought about tearing off your arms and legs and feeding them to our first clutch. Thought about taking out your teeth and your tongue, leaving you a husk with just your cocks to keep you company. If I were you, I'd think long and hard about how you'd like to curry my favor. I am displeased, consort. Most displeased.*"

Consort? No. No, never, you loathsome twat.

Tanis ended the call without another word and focused on the road ahead. She pushed the Honda up to eighty, ninety. She'd had enough of Lamia's bullshit. For herself, for Naree and Bee. For Bernie and Fi. For Ariadne and Daphne who'd had to run because they loved one another. For Priska with a hole in her chest and Rhea who had to care for her.

Tanis Was Done.

And Being Done made what came next infinitely easier.

SHE STOPPED BY the apartment in Percy's Pass. The door had been jimmied open, and the inside was a disaster; the TV was toppled over, the kitchen cabinets all opened, the bureau drawers rifled through. Hell, even the sex toy bucket had been found and upended, raining Naree's rainbow of sparkle dildos across the bed. Whoever it was had been most thorough, going so far as to take their desktop computers and any receipts, probably looking for evidence of their plans. Tanis picked through the litter on the floor of her former life to find her now-dry alligator boots, her most broken-in jeans, and a Budweiser T-shirt. She didn't let her gaze linger too long on any one thing. There were too many feelings trapped between those four thin walls. Too many laughs and loves and ghosts of good times past.

She drove to the Value Mart and waited, the statue of

Dumballah tied around her neck and resting between her breasts. It was everything a mom-and-pop quick stop in Florida ought to be: six packs, cigarettes, junk food, Coke, jars of home-brewed moonshine next to a live-bait cooler. Tanis parked outside and off to the left, sitting on the trunk of her car watching the store's neon *Open* sign in the front window flicker. There were two gas pumps ahead of her beneath a rusted carport, the front one covered by a tied-off garbage bag with a handwritten *Closed* sign attached to it, the back one still in service and charging a buck more a gallon than anywhere else nearby. Two lightbulbs dangling on strings lit the whole place, dragging moths in to singe themselves and plummet to the cracked tarmac below.

Tanis was on her ninth cigarette, a full carton beside her and ready for smoking. She'd sit there all night waiting for the Gorgon priests if she had to. The only snag she could think of was if the lamias came for her first, but she'd told her mother she was on her way. Her sisters had no reason to retrieve a willing tribute.

A mosquito buzzed by her ear and she swiped it from the air, killing it before it got any of her blood. They'd been dive bombing her awhile, and she considered heading into the store for some repellent, but then a black BMW pulled up, not alongside the gas pump, but on the opposite side of the store. Tanis smoked her cigarettes and eyed them. The two people in the front seat didn't get out immediately. She watched them through the haze of smoke by her face and had the distinct impression they watched her right back.

"HEY!"

Her voice echoed across the empty parking lot, bigger thanks to the carport. Still the strangers didn't climb from their car.

"I NEED TO TALK TO STHENO AND EURYALE. WE GOT BUSINESS TO DEAL."

If they weren't Gorgon priests, no harm, no foul. They'd assume she spoke in tongues, might shout some random shit at her and drive off, and that'd be the end of it. But if they were...

She waited.

After another five minutes, a man climbed from the car and walked her way. He was polished—nice khaki slacks, nice pale blue button-down shirt, shiny shoes. His brown hair had streaks of gray along his hairline. His hands were in his pockets. If he was supposed to be their idea of non-intimidating, it didn't work; Luke Des Moines came across much the same and he'd been a wife-beater and a rapist. Shiny exteriors all too often hid rotten cores.

"Stop right there." Tanis aimed the Colt at his middle. "I pull the trigger, there's two ways this'll go. Worst case? A slow, painful bleed out. Best case, a lot of extra effort needed to eat and shit the rest of your life."

He stopped fifteen feet away, his hands sliding from his pockets so he could show her his bare palms.

Tanis spit out her smoke. "Got poison on you?"

"Yes," he said frankly, his Florida twang in full effect. "But I left it in the car. You sounded like you wanted to talk. We're listening."

She eyeballed him. He could have been a lawyer or a banker, or an insurance salesman. He had 'fine, upstanding citizen' written all over him, and if she had to venture a guess, that shiny black BMW parked across the way was absolutely his. She supposed they could have dressed up an average Joe and paraded him in front of her, but he walked the walk and talked the talk too well.

"What's a guy like you doing with a couple of Gorgons anyway?"

He smiled, showing off blindingly white, capped teeth. "They're magical, aren't they? Strong. Beautiful."

Buddy, your idea of beautiful and mine are way different. Rainbows are beautiful. Horses are beautiful. Women with snake hair and bronze hands and faces that look like they'd been vacuumed backward? Not so much.

"Look at what they can do," he said, reverently. "I've never seen such power. Love them, fear them, that's all they ask. They only harm those who mean them harm. They're peaceful. Loving."

"Unless you're a lamia. Or the poor bastards whose house they want."

He smiled, daring a step forward like he was going to evangelize her—or whatever the 'love my snake-bitch' equivalent was—and she shot the pavement beside his foot, sending him skittering back, gravel flying. The color drained from his face, but he tried to play cool despite the hammering pulse at the base of his throat.

"You stay right there," she said. "You got a way to talk to Stheno and Euryale? I'm listening. Hell, I'm negotiating." She hopped down off of the car and popped open the Honda's trunk. The remaining half of the heart was right there, in the salt, and she lifted it up to shake the container at him. "Here." She lobbed it his way. He barely had the wherewithal to catch it, but once he had it in hand, he lifted the lid and peered inside.

"What is it?"

"Ask your mommies. They'll know."

Sharp-Dressed Man pulled out a phone and dialed, his face screwed up in distaste at the body part in his possession. He backed away from Tanis, probably hoping to keep her out of his conversation, but she could hear most of it. Could hear him talking to someone with a shrill female voice who demanded to know why he dared to ask for his mistresses by name.

"The lamia wants to talk to them," he whispered.

It took three different people on the other end of the line, the request filtering up the ranks, for him to get a Gorgon on the phone. Euryale, by the sounds of it; Tanis had only heard her through the floor in the basement, but the tone of her voice was unmistakable—high pitched, oddly nasal and soft at the same time.

He walked forward to offer Tanis the phone, but she waved the gun at him again.

"Throw it. You stay over there," she said.

He did as he was told, and she snatched it midair and put it up to her ear.

"*You give us back that which you* stole? *In half measure? And then wish to bargain with us,*" Euryale said in greeting.

She sounded amused more than anything, which was good, because Tanis didn't have another round of crazy, bitchy, screaming snake woman in her.

"It's good faith. I want to cut a deal."

"Your life for the mother snake? Is that what you want?"

"Among other things."

"Other things, she says." Euryale's laughter was a wisp of a thing: light, airy, almost pleasant to listen to. *"I'll hear you, Lamia's child. I'll hear your offer."*

"Good. I'll come to you, then. I want to meet in person, you and Stheno, and I come alone. Know this: if you fuck me over, the Den will run and you'll spend another sixty years looking for them. Keep your priests away from me and I'll give you everything. *Everything.*" She paused to let that sink in. She'd been full of shit on the Lamia and Den running thing—she'd made no such arrangements—but they didn't need to know that. Lying on the phone was infinitely easier than doing it in person. Something she'd come to understand over time was that creatures who'd lived for thousands of years, like Lamia and the Gorgons, were exceptional at reading body language. Their bullshit meters were almost preternaturally good.

But over the phone? Not so much. And the humans would be too dumb to know any better.

Euryale clicked her tongue a few times, thoughtful, but then she burst into delighted laughter. *"You make this easy. Too easy. Come to me and we'll talk."*

"Keep the priests away from me or no deal," Tanis warned.

"As you like, lamia. Now come."

CHAPTER TWENTY-SEVEN

Tanis followed the BMW through the Glades, all the way to a tiny road that was impossible to find unless you knew exactly how and where to look for it among the cypress trees. Narrow, winding, two miles long—there was no hope of anyone stumbling across it, or the house at its end, unless you damn well knew where you wanted to get. Someone had built themselves a secluded little paradise in the wetlands. The Gorgons had promptly murdered them and claimed it for their own, but hey, at least someone got to benefit from the privacy.

The windows of the Honda were down, so she could smell for a rear ambush when she drove up to the house. No bodies near, but many ahead. All ahead, in fact. The Gorgons were centered on the porch steps, side by side, their sundresses rippling with the breeze. Their priests flanked them. Some were in street clothes, but most wore the white robes with the green sashes and billowy palazzo pants. There had to be a hundred of them altogether, all shapes and colors represented, all standing far back from the hissing snakes writhing atop their mistresses' heads. Karl, the man who'd doctored Cassandra, was there, as was the blind woman from Daphne's removal and the driver of the car at the gas station attack. Mr. Clean-Cut BMW and his never-before-seen partner, Mr. Obnoxious Combover and Pineapple Shorts, left the car to stand at the foot of the house steps with their brethren, Clean-Cut holding the Tupperware with the prophet's heart in his hand.

Tanis eyeballed them all from the safety of the Honda, then peered past them, looking for more zealots. She found none, but in the distance, to the sides of the house, were the statues of the Gorgons' victims. Standing among them was a half-snake girl with no breasts and no arms, her head lolling forward, her hair curls forever captured in stone.

At least she rests in the same garden as Daphne. Even if Daphne's statue is toppled and headless.

Tanis killed the engine and went to the trunk. Bernie's shotguns were there, and she selected a pair, looping one over her shoulder with a sling and carrying another. The Gorgons and their priests could poison her all they wanted, but she'd make a few of them into sprinklers before she went down. A straight petrification and she'd be fucked, but at least her statue would look badass in the garden.

She was about to close the trunk and its mini-arsenal away, but then she spied Maman's black feather resting atop one of the white, crinkly Walmart bags. She hadn't put it there—in fact, she was pretty sure she'd left it in the visor of the Caddy—but somehow it'd made the trip anyway.

"For luck," Maman had said.

Tanis slid it into her pocket. With what she was about to do? She needed all the luck in the goddamned world.

She shoved the trunk closed and circled around the car, nostrils flaring and searching for priests, but so far, the Gorgons were playing fair. The onslaught was ahead, not to the side or behind. Tanis held the shotgun to her chest, her teeth clenched around an unlit cigarette. Figuring that could be interpreted as rude, she tucked it behind her ear, standing thirty feet from the house with her legs braced apart.

Euryale was as unpleasant to look at as she'd been days ago:

human body, bronze hands, green fingernails and toenails, black, lidless eyes. Poison-crusted chin and mass of self-cannibalizing snakes atop her head. Stheno was somehow worse. From the neck down, she was dark and lithe, taller than her sister by some inches, long legs and nice hips. The problem was the boar's head attached to her neck, complete with tusks, a broad pig mouth, and a snout. She wasn't furred like a boar; human skin stretched over a porcine skull with whiskers bristling the chin. Her eyes were the same black, lidless orbs as her sister's, and atop her head, instead of brownish snakes, she had dark green and blue ones in an unruly tangle.

In fact one of her green snakes was snapping at one of Euryale's brown snakes. It was darkly fascinating. But Tanis was there to betray her mother, not watch serpent Olympics on a couple of Gorgon heads.

"I'll give you the Den," she announced as her opener, loudly, so everyone gathered could hear her. "They're getting ready to leave, but not yet. They can't go without me."

"Why not?" Stheno. She spoke in the home tongue, her voice crisp and deep and blasting from the porch with impressive volume.

"I'm my mother's consort. Or, well, she wants me to be." Tanis frowned.

"And you do not wish this thing?" Euryale this time, leaning into her sister's side. Stheno put an arm around her waist. Tanis tried to ignore how the snakes atop their heads intertwined, biting one another, tearing pieces away from one another, but it was hard not to watch.

She jerked her gaze down. "No. I have a mate. Which brings me to my first condition. I get out alive, my human girlfriend and her family are left alone. You'll swear on it. Swear on Dumballah." She lifted the statuette from her neck and wiggled it around. "The snake father."

The Gorgons turning on her was not such a farfetched notion. If they were after true genocide, identifying Bee as part-lamia put the baby at risk. Putting her under the umbrella of Naree's family, though—why would they care about humans?

It's not a lie. Not really.

Even if I don't get out, my kid does.

"Snake father? I do not know of this god. He is new?" Stheno demanded.

"No. He's a lwa."

Stheno snorted derisively. Euryale smiled, an ugly, awkward thing on her snake mouth and protruding fangs. "Yes, fine. We will swear on this... what did you call it? Lwa? Yes, that. Little god. I have not heard of him either."

Little god. Okay, sure, whatever. I guess immortality makes you arrogant?

Tanis relaxed her grip on the shotgun. She hadn't realized she'd been clenching it, but the moment she heard that they'd make the vow, her muscles unfurled and the gun tilted toward the ground. Anything else she got out of the negotiation, from that point on, was gravy.

"What else do you want? And how do you propose to do this?"

No question about whether or not it was a trap, but again, immortality and arrogance went hand in hand. There wasn't a lot to worry about when almost nothing could kill you. Hell, even Tanis's Styx plan wouldn't kill them. It might put them away awhile, but they'd end up as someone else's shitty problem down the line.

If all goes well.

And Papa didn't lie to me.

...shit. Why didn't that occur to me sooner?

She frowned.

"I want time to get the little kids out," she said, trying to shove her misgivings aside. "Lamia's yours; the lamias that fight you, yours; but the kids deserve a chance. They're not immortal. We'll die off, be out of your hair sooner rather than later, with Lamia gone. None of them can breed and Lamia treated them—all of us, really—like shit. I can see—"

Tanis flinched, because she didn't want to praise them, what with Bernie's pained end, but an agreeable pair of Gorgons made it easier. "—I can see your people are happy, devoted.

The lamias don't have that. We never did. We were victims of circumstance. Any daughter you spare is a mercy. Maybe they'll get a life worth living after our mother is gone."

"Ooor..." Stheno disengaged from Euryale's side, one of her green snakes struggling to swallow a brown snake torn off Euryale's head. She navigated the porch steps, through the throng, her priests parting as much to avoid her spitting, gnashing head of serpent death as to let her pass. "Maybe putting them out of their misery and sending them to Tartarus is a kindness?"

"If that's your call, so be it. All I'll say is I understand hating our mother, but the rest of us aren't your problem. We're all just sad sacks looking for a better day."

Tanis should have felt guiltier about the prospect of handing over the Den and her sisters. Another person—a better person— would have, she knew. But she couldn't muster it. The people she'd truly known, even remotely cared about, were gone. Bernie, Fi. Barbara would get out with the children, but the rest? Pitiable, yes, but pitiable strangers. Tanis had to worry about herself, her girlfriend, and her daughter. She'd do what she could to warn the others before the Gorgons came, but she couldn't start a mass exodus or her mother would be clued in.

You can't make an omelet...

Stheno stopped ten feet in front of Tanis. Tanis could smell her strange body chemistry, the weirdness of her sweat and that signature scent that was vaguely reptilian but also Other. Euryale drifted to her side, the two of them joining hands. They looked nothing alike, and yet the way they peered at Tanis, the tilts of their heads, the dead blackness of their eyes, gave Tanis a come-play-with-us-Danny vibe.

"And how do you propose to get us in?" Euryale asked.

"Give me one of your followers' cell phones. I'll text you from it once the kids are out. We'll use a tracker through GPS."

"And why not your own device?"

"Because I don't want you finding me later," she said simply. "One of your followers' phones works better. They can have it back when you bring the party."

The Gorgons shared a look, one of Stheno's longest snakes inching across Euryale's shoulder and questing lazily down the front of her dress like a docile pet. Euryale stroked its head as she gazed into her sister's eyes.

"Fine," they said at the same time, turning their heads to look at Tanis, doing nothing to dispel the creepiness.

"Jefferson!" Stheno barked. Mr. BMW stepped forward, but didn't get too near, his attention fixed on the nest of snakes stretching to reach him with gaping maws.

"Yes, ma'ams?"

"Give the lamia your phone."

He cut the Gorgons and their hair a wide berth so he could do as he was told. Seeing it was password protected, she tapped the screen. "Code?" He provided it, she committed it to memory, and promptly pulled up his contacts list. "Who on here can I text once I'm in the Den?"

"Muriel," he said. "She's our head priestess." He motioned behind him, to the blind woman at the top of the stairs. Tanis nodded and turned off his GPS before sliding the phone into her back pocket, right beside Maman's feather.

"Then we have a deal," Euryale said. "We will be waiting for you."

Tanis caught Jefferson/BMW's eye and handed him the statue. She motioned at Stheno. "Take it over."

He did, his upper half bent away from the Gorgons, one of the green snakes dangerously close to his face and snapping. Eventually he dropped to his knees, crawling across the ground and through the dirt to bring the statue to his mistresses. It looked wrong, such a finely-tailored man so obsequious before them. Worse, Euryale put her hand on his head, careful with her toxic nails so she didn't prick him as she stroked over his forehead and along the shell of his ear.

He's like a labradoodle in Dockers. Maybe if she scritches, his foot will start thumping.

It wasn't an ideal time to crack jokes, but chalk it up to gallows humor.

He lifted the statue. Neither Gorgon looked particularly

interested in the bottle, which was good, because opening it and smelling the water inside would tip them off. Both sisters looked at Tanis expectantly.

"What do you want us to do?" Stheno asked.

Papa didn't actually say, so...

"Both of you touch it, say, 'I swear no harm will come to you, your girlfriend, or her family.' That should suffice." She pulled the cigarette from behind her ear and tucked it into her mouth. With her focus elsewhere, she might not betray exactly how tense she was to see them with her water in their possession. She watched the flame pop up from the lighter, the tip of the cigarette go red, the first puff of smoke erupt. From the corner of her eye she spied two hands, one human-looking, the other bronze with green nails, encircling the statue.

Both made the oath, verbatim, giggling all the while. That part didn't bother her—she knew it was a ridiculous request, she knew she'd react similarly in their position. No, what bothered her was when Stheno tugged the statue from BMW's hand and let it swing on its cord before her boar snout. She tossed her head, her tusks gleaming, and with a snort, threw the fetish to the ground and shattered it, the water inside pooling on the ground. An ant, poorly placed, poorly timed, walked through it before the dusty ground swallowed it up and promptly dropped, legs twitching a few times before going still. Tanis stared, her nose assaulted by the putrid stench of decaying river, and she braced for the inevitable deluge of questions and accusations.

...but there were none. Not from the Gorgons, not from the human a few feet away.

They can't smell that?

Are their noses that bad? Or did Maman doctor it somehow?

"Silly snake god." Stheno turned her back on Tanis and headed for the porch, her followers bowing their heads as she ascended the stairs to reclaim her place by the front door.

Euryale toed one of the shards on the ground, her snake mouth tilting into a frown. At least, Tanis thought it was a frown; it was hard to tell.

"You put your faith in false gods, lamia, when there are real gods before you."

And then she, too, drifted away, leaving Tanis gawking at the broken Dumballah in their driveway.

CHAPTER TWENTY-EIGHT

DOES IT MATTER if the water spilled? And how do I know if it worked in the first place? Were there special words they were supposed to say?

Hell, does it really matter so long as they can't find Naree? I didn't mention Bee, but if they scry for her...

Fuck. Fuck, fuck, fuck.

She drove to Adder's Den, thoughts spiralling, hands sweaty on the steering wheel. Naree, for the time being, was safe. They had no reason to go after her so long as they didn't know the baby was Tanis's. They likely assumed Tanis was sterile, like the rest of the lamia, which worked in Bee's favor. It was possible they'd scried Tanis and Naree's conversations about the baby's parentage, but there was no way to know for sure, and the Gorgons certainly wouldn't be forthcoming with that information, no matter how civil they'd been during negotiation.

Tanis parked a quarter mile from Adder's Den and pulled out her phone, eyeballing Naree's name on her contacts list before typing. It was far too long of a message at first, with details about the deal she'd struck, why she'd struck it, the vow Stheno and Euryale had made, and every other thing that had set her on her suicidal course, but before she pressed Send, she erased all of it.

The less Naree knew, the better. Tanis hated lying to her by omission—hated that she didn't have any sure way to protect Naree and Bee—but neither of them could be held responsible for information they didn't have.

But if she could help them at all...

> Hey sweetheart. If you don't hear from me by tomorrow, call Poul Mwen in New Orleans. Ask for Renaud and tell him I sent you. Say you want to hide from a scrying. They'll tell you what to do. I love you. Kiss Bee for me.

And, before Naree stabbed her in the gut with a monsoon of texted feelings, Tanis turned off the phone and pocketed it. She looked through the windshield at the overgrowth before her. The world was a wash of green until the trees met blue sky, the fat, white clouds on the horizon edged with gray and promising later rains. She breathed in deeply, inviting calm, but there was no calm to be found in the face of the decay.

Pungent. Cloyingly sweet rot laced with smoke and charred meat, like a barbecue where all the raw hamburgers had been left out on the counter for a week.

She climbed from the car, her shotguns at the ready, the Colt and the Glock tucked into her jeans. Her head tilted back, nose leading her toward the rankness, over familiar paths, her boots crunching sticks and twigs, the tall grass hissing and rustling as she walked through it. Soon, she saw the shorts on the flagpole that told her she was home, by some vague, awful definition of 'home.' The smell was stronger there, wafting from the entry shed, thick and sour and terrible and making her wish she didn't have such a sensitive nose.

Did the Gorgons get here first? Is this some fucked-up trap?

Tanis approached the shack right as Kallie and another sister Tanis only somewhat knew walked out. They carried corpses of humanoid daughters over their shoulders, the dead wrapped in sheets, the sheets drenched red. An arm had fallen out of one of the make-do shrouds, revealing a bloodied stump with no hand attached.

Kallie's lip curled.

"She took your leaving poorly," she snapped. "Too many gone because of you. Too many for her to eat, so we're building a pyre. Maybe next time you'll think about someone else before you abandon us."

"Is that what I smell?"

Tanis looked to the wetlands beyond the Den's borders. An oily pillar of smoke twisted in the eastern sky. She'd missed it walking in; the trees had shielded it from view.

"We're gathering the last of the bodies now." Kallie's hand clenched around the corpse on her shoulder. "We're almost done. You should be doing this. It's your fau—"

"No, it's not." Tanis swung the shotgun up and away from them, so it was pointed at the sky. She didn't want to look threatening, though she supposed approaching with that much ammo slung over her body didn't exactly speak to a warm and fuzzy homecoming. "It's Lamia's fault, taking out her shit on people who don't deserve it. I had my reasons to run. Good ones, too. I'm not shouldering her anymore. And if you're smart, you won't either. Go, run. Get out of here. How's she going to send sisters after you to drag you home if they're all too dead or gone to come get you?"

Kallie looked horrified; the sister with her, confused. Tanis hadn't outright warned them of what was to come, not in so many words, but she'd said her piece and offered them an escape. If they didn't take it, that wasn't her problem.

Is that true? You're about to call down the fury. Every death will be your doing. Every one.

Lamia has to go. But the rest of them?

Kallie shoved by her, purposefully knocking her back with the rank, bloodied remains on her shoulder, the cold legs thwacking Tanis in the chest. Tanis stumbled to stay upright, watching her sister lamias disappear behind bushes along their border. For a moment, she reconsidered her plan. What she'd said to the Gorgons wasn't inaccurate—the lamias' lives were horrible. Too horrible, in most cases. Broken and battered and never knowing kindness. They were indentured to their Mother because they were too afraid not to be, or too ignorant to know there was anything else out there for them. Was sending them to Tartarus on top of it all fair?

No. No it's not.

But life isn't fair and anyone who says it should be is living in a Mickey Mouse dream.

She pulled out BMW's phone and turned on the GPS, allowing it to triangulate in the middle of nowhere. Somehow, it got a signal, and she used that signal to telegraph the Den's whereabouts to Muriel. If they were still at the manor house, they were twenty minutes away, thirty minutes tops. Tanis headed for the shack, striding past the chairs where Bernie and Fi had played cards together just a week ago. They were empty now, which was unusual, but if Mother had cleaned house as much as Kallie claimed, it was possible they were low on manpower.

She jumped down into the tunnel and immediately started breathing through her mouth, less to block the corpse stench and more to buffer needless distractions, like the True Daughters' pheromones. None of it was ideal, not for Tanis or the people who had to live with the stink, but at least Lamia wouldn't smell Tanis's arrival and come for her with so much meatiness polluting the air.

Tanis looked around. Darkness ruled supreme; few of the lights had survived Mother's tantrum. Golden eyes peered out at her from the shadows, her sisters hiding, too afraid to leave their makeshift hovels to confront her for her betrayal. She said nothing as she walked, not toward Lamia's chambers, but to the other end, where Barbara kept the hatchlings and youngest children in cribs and on soiled mattresses. She practiced what she'd say in her head all the way, outlining a plan to send Barbara and some trusted sisters to the Percy's Pass lamia in the apartments until something more permanent could be set up for them.

Except.

Barbara sat on the edge of a mattress, a piece of broken wood clasped in her hands, a print dress hugging her thick curves all the way to her calves. The backs of her hands were the same silvery green as the scales that covered her head, her face, her neck. Her forehead, sloped like a snake, was furrowed, causing the scales to rise above her brow. Tears ran from her gold-and-black slitted eyes, making her greenness gleam all the brighter in the dim light.

There were no children.

Tanis surveyed the damage. The shattered cribs. The upended toy boxes. The changing table that had been thrown across the room and broken apart into four pieces. "What happened?"

Why bother asking? I know. It's written all over the place.

How could you, Mother? They were babies. They'd done nothing. How could you?

"Her," Barbara said simply. The shape of her head made her words sound different from most of the other daughters. Her voice was quieter and softer, sweeter in a way. Or maybe that was Tanis's fondness for the nanny who'd brought her up.

Tanis eyed Barbara a while, searching for signs of resentment or anger at her, but there was none. Barbara was lost to sadness. Tanis sat beside her on the old mattresses that probably hadn't been changed since Tanis had slept there ten years ago.

"She said they'd slow us down when we made our escape. Said she could make more. 'True bloods,' she called them. I don't understand why she'd say that." Tanis did, though, and when Barbara's shoulders trembled, Tanis moved her shotgun sling aside to wrap her arm across Barbara's shoulders. She held her close while Barbara quietly wept for Lamia's most pathetic victims.

The pyres saw our smallest bodies today.

No wonder Kallie hates me.

"Was Zoe lost with them?" Tanis asked quietly. "I made a promise to Priska."

Barbara sniffled. "No, as it happens. She's been in with the True Daughters. They like her—the leg like a tail. They think it's cute. I think it saved her life." Barbara dashed at her eyes with the back of her hand and sniffled before blowing her nose into a paper towel that had seen better days.

"Bernie shot Priska," Tanis said simply. "But on the right side. Rhea was getting her help. She'll be back for her."

Again Barbara said nothing, not judging, not doing anything other than sitting among the debris of the nursery and mourning those she'd cared for most. Tanis looked at her. "I'm going to go get Zoe, and then you need to get her out of here, for when Priska comes back."

"What? Out of where?"

Tanis looked at her, hard, and repeated herself. Slower. Each word heavy. "Go to my apartment. Take my keys." She fished them out of her pockets and forced them into Barbara's palm. "Do you know how to drive?"

"...yes, I learned years ago, but I don't understand. You know I don't go out there."

"I know you don't, but this needs to be the exception. Please. I lost Bernie, I lost Fi. I don't want to lose you, too. The kids are gone. You've got no reason to stay. I'll write down my— here." Tanis rummaged through the debris until she found something to write on. It was a *Frozen* coloring book, half full of crayon scribbles, and her breath caught in her throat seeing the marks left by little ones who'd never get the chance to finish their pictures. She scribbled her address with a broken blue crayon and a grimace, and—realizing Barbara might not know how to get to the apartment anyway—she pulled out her phone. "Fifty-five twenty-two. The code on the phone. Use the GPS. I probably won't need this anymore. Just... please? Please."

Barbara looked from the phone to the scrap of paper in her hand. "I don't like to go out there. They'll see me."

"It's worth the risk this time. Wear a hat. Shit, there's at least three hats in the trunk of the Honda. You can hide after you get to the apartment. Gaia is in Percy's Pass, at the apartments I moved into early on. She's in my contacts list. Call her and tell her you need to hide. She'll help you and Zoe both."

"What'd you do, Tanis?" Barbara asked quietly. "What'd you do that I should go hide with Zoe?"

Tanis didn't answer her. She put the shotguns aside and walked away.

OF ALL THE True Daughters, Mariam most looked and behaved like their mother. Large, pale, pendulous udders with purple nipples that rested on a thick midsection, a slab for a mouth, tangled dark hair and brown scales from the waist down. She wasn't quite as awful as Lamia, but she held rank in the Den and wasn't afraid to use it. One time, at three o'clock in the morning after Tanis had dropped off a boyfriend-du-month for their mother, Mariam had thrown a tantrum until Tanis had agreed to get her two Quarter Pounders with Cheese, making for an extra hour of work after a twenty-six-hour stretch of hunting. All Tanis had wanted to do was go home and sleep on Naree. What she'd ended up doing was popping three 5-hour Energies, dancing with a heart attack, and producing the hamburgers so Lamia didn't bash in her skull for upsetting one of her favored babies.

Of course of all the True Daughters, it was Mariam lazing about with Zoe clasped to her jelly chest. Zoe looked content enough, her dark hair in a French braid, her cheeks flushed with blush and her lips rouged red. Her snake-tail leg lashed against Mariam's thick, scaled trunk, and all Tanis could think of was an annoyed cat. The little girl didn't appear to be upset, though, as she voraciously pawed through a well-loved copy of *Harry Potter and the Sorcerer's Stone*.

Tanis passed the two guards by the door. Both eyed her warily, but she ignored them, sweeping aside diaphanous drapes to stand on a pair of overlapping Oriental rugs with colorful medallions. The big chamber was home to real beds with headboards and footboards and soft, jewel-toned comforters. Hanging drapes separated each 'room' to afford some illusion of privacy. Mariam was among five other True Daughters, all of them in repose. One had an e-reader in hand. One watched old movies on her television. One napped. One skimmed a magazine while she shoveled chocolates into her face.

Mariam lifted her head from her pillows. Her thick fingers toyed with Zoe's hair as she regarded Tanis coolly, eyes hooded, her extra lid blinking every few seconds.

"Consort."

Tanis frowned.

Wait, does Mother expect me to service all of these bitches, too?

Oh, no. No, no, no.

"I need Zoe for a few minutes," Tanis growled.

"Why?"

"I'm going to see Barbara." Mariam didn't look convinced that was a good enough reason to do anything she didn't want to do, so Tanis embellished. "She's upset. Ma"—she didn't want to scare the kid with the horrific reality of their mother murdering other children, so she chose her words carefully— "She left Barbara all alone. She could use a kid's company for a bit. Plus I saw Priska. I wanted to tell Zoe about our visit."

"Priska?" Zoe perked up, hearing her name. "Where is she? Is she coming home soon?'

"You bet. I talked to her just the other day. She's with Rhea."

Recovering from a shotgun blast. Because she dared come for me.

We'll leave that part out.

Zoe wriggled away from Mariam and loped over. The one leg, one snake tail combination meant she canted left, but she moved fast all the same, the prehensile limb as strong if not stronger than its mate. She paused midway through the chamber to eye Mariam.

"Can I borrow your book, Miss Mariam?"

"Of course you can. Just bring it back to me when you're done. Kisses."

"Kisses!" Zoe dashed back to hug Mariam, her face disappearing into folds of soft flesh, her arms wrapping around Mariam's arm because they weren't going to be able to get around her middle girth. Most of the True Daughters slanted fat, both because Lamia didn't let them out to move and because they were expected to breed whenever they were in season.

Which apparently Mariam was, because as Tanis led Zoe out by the hand, she called to Tanis's back. "Consort!" When Tanis refused to answer to the title, she switched to her real name. "Tanis. Stop."

Tanis's shoulder's tensed.

This won't be good.

Can't be good.

"I'll need servicing later. Would you like me to bathe? I will, out of consideration. I know you live among the humans and have, perhaps, acquired some of their ridiculous sensibilities."

Tanis rolled her eyes up to the ceiling, glad her back was turned so Mariam couldn't see the abject loathing screwing up her features. She could feel it—the pinch of her brow, the frown, the strain behind her eyes that made her squint. The idea of the thing, of being used, of being handed back and forth between Lamia and the True Daughters, made her skin crawl and her cocks shrivel inside her shorts.

It makes it so easy to hate them. The presumptuousness...

"No," she managed, guiding Zoe along.

Because you'll be too dead to matter soon.

CHAPTER TWENTY-NINE

No one asked questions as Barbara led Zoe outside. Seeing the denmother walking with a kid wasn't unusual, and despite Barbara's preference for down-below, she would often take children out to play, to air them out and get them some exercise so they wouldn't tear down the walls with their exuberance. That she walked a little beyond the circle wasn't noteworthy.

That the Honda was parked just out of sight was convenient.

Barbara looked self-conscious, exposed as she was to the world beyond her tunnels. She ran her hands over her scales, her dress. She shuffled her feet. She looked skittish and nervous despite Tanis and Zoe being her only companions. Tanis went to the trunk of the car and produced one of the promised hats, handing it over and, when it didn't quite fit on her skull, adjusting the band in the back so it wouldn't fly off with the first breeze.

"Do I look silly?" Barbara whispered.

"Nah, you look great. Let's get you out of here." Tanis piled Barbara and the child into the car. A part of her wanted to climb in, too, to go with them and make a great escape, but until she knew Lamia was gone for good, until she could be sure that the Gorgons upheld their part of the deal, she couldn't risk it.

Naree and Bee are out there, vulnerable.

They're my responsibilities. They're counting on me even if they don't know it.

"Tell Gaia you have Zoe. She'll know how to get in touch with Priska," Tanis said, leaning into the driver's window.

Barbara nodded, fussing with the GPS, so Tanis reclaimed her phone and set the address for her. A crisp British accent informed Barbara she had to drive a half-mile south and take a left.

Naree liked the British voice better than the American one. She called her Brittany.

"Is Priska there, where we're going?" Zoe demanded, holding the Harry Potter book in her lap, her fingers rustling through the pages.

"Not yet, but she will be, I promise. She asked me to come get you. But it's time for you two to get going, okay? Take care of yourselves."

Tanis pulled herself from the car and turned to go, but Barbara snatched her hand, squeezing her around the wrist. "Best of luck?" she offered, blinking slowly beneath the hat brim.

"I'll be fine," Tanis lied, stepping back. She waved at Zoe. "Be good for Barbara. Say 'hi' to Priska for me."

She watched the Honda pull away, the finality of their departure settling in and leaving her cold. She was probably scared on some level, but there were too many things to think about, too many what-ifs and worries about other people, she didn't have time to entertain it. There was probably some guilt, too, but it couldn't roost because the Gorgons were due soon. She didn't have a clock anymore, not after giving her phone to Barbara, but it had to be closing in.

If they show up. But why wouldn't they?

She headed back to the Den, again passing Kallie and her helper as they brought out yet another pair of bodies from the pile they'd amassed below. Tanis couldn't fathom a guess as to how many their mother brutalized, but it was at least thirty or forty if it included the children.

Kallie was almost at the edge of the town when Tanis called her name. She paused without looking back, tossing her head, droplets of sweat flying in every direction.

"What?" she snapped.

"When are we leaving?"

"Tomorrow night or the morning after. Bethesda and Lois are getting U-Hauls for Mother and the True Daughters. We have a car convoy planned, too. How many can your car take?"

"Four," Tanis replied, not mentioning she'd just given it away.

Kallie didn't waste another word on her, trudging through the woods with her gruesome load. Tanis headed back into the tunnels and recovered her guns from Barbara's broken nursery. They wouldn't do her a whole heck of a lot of good anymore, but how did the saying go? Better to have it and not need it than to need it and not have it?

She was picking her way around the nursery debris when her mother's voice rumbled down the pipe, a loud, ugly squawk that filled all available space, bouncing off of the pipe walls and rippling onward and outward forever. Every instinct Tanis had told her to flee, but she couldn't do that, not so close to the end of all things, and so she walked toward it, hoping beyond hope that the Gorgons would come before her mother tortured her or worse, raped her.

Her steps were heavy. All eyes were on her.

Past the tent town. Past the ladder exit. Past the entryways of the True Daughters' chambers, where the daughters lined up, some curious, some hungry, some disgusted. Past the guards at her mother's door, watching her and eyeing her guns warily. Her boots splashed down the waterline, steps heavy, legs leaden. She stepped into the birthing chamber with its distant twin lights suspended over the stacked mattresses. She looked around, she listened. She didn't dare sniff. Her grip on the gun tightened.

She came.

Lamia was damned fast, careening in from the right side of the room with a snarl. That huge body went from far to near in a heartbeat, coils circling Tanis's legs and wrapping her up, all the way to her chest and tearing her feet from the floor. Tanis dropped the gun she was holding, to clatter and bounce off the wall. The other shotgun was plucked away from her, snapping the sling and tossed like so much garbage, which left her only with the pistols, digging into her ass in her mother's death grip. She was hostage to a beast, to the corpulent, blue, veiny she-beast that loomed over her, her nipples pressed against Tanis's chest and leaking milk, her maw opened and revealing yellow stubby teeth and two enormous fangs.

Tanis jerked her gaze away from her mother only to see, in the corner, Lamia's last clutch—Luke's clutch—that had been born while she was gone. The eggs were shattered into pieces, the yolky insides leaking across the floor, no doubt adding to the abysmal stench of the place.

I'm so glad I didn't have to smell that.

"Look at me. Look at me, Consort."

Tanis set her jaw and did as she was told, staring into her mother's wide, monstrous face. A gob of something had congealed on Lamia's upper left cheek, crusted rivers running down to her chin.

"I should rip you apart for your disobedience." Lamia tightened her coils until Tanis thought her legs might break. Lamia reached up to grab her hair, jerking Tanis's head back and leaning in to press their noses together. Tanis could feel her hot, moist breath on her chin, on her throat, and she shuddered in revulsion.

"Did you think to kill me? With your guns? With your silly human toys? Is that what you thought?" Lamia screeched. She shook Tanis like a ragdoll, Tanis's neck jerking back and forth. She'd hurt the next day, assuming she got to *see* the next day.

The way things were going, that wasn't likely to be a concern. Especially not when she said, "Nah. If it was that easy, I'd have shot you years ago."

Lamia's fury was immediate and absolute. Her hands clasped around Tanis's neck, thumbs digging into the soft flesh beneath Tanis's jaw like she'd pop off her head, and squeezed. Tanis's world shrank, blackness encroaching upon the edges of her vision, her bones grinding together inside of Lamia's coils.

"I loathe you. I loathe everything about your pink skin. I may need you, but I hate you. Do you understand? *I hate you.* You are the means to an end. We are not equals, you and I, and we never will be." Her coils dropped from Tanis's shoulders to loop around her waist. Her hands let go of Tanis's neck. Tanis gulped air, grateful for the reprieve, but it was short-lived. Lamia's hands went to Tanis's biceps, fingers biting into the muscle hidden beneath her snake tattoos, and jerked. She didn't rip Tanis's arms off—that would make Tanis bleed out, denying her a proper baby daddy—but she did pull both arms from the sockets, the muscles stretching like taffy before they shredded inside their skin prison, the ligaments snapping like cords on a collapsing suspension bridge.

Tanis screamed. Her head tilted back, mouth gaped open, and she wailed her agony, her cries filling the Den, telling all who heard it that Mother had begun meting out her punishment. *This* was the cost of overstepping yourself in Lamia's world. *This* was how disloyalty was rewarded.

She couldn't move her arms properly, and she didn't want to. Any attempt felt like someone hammering nails into her flesh. She went limp, jaw grinding, cheeks wet with tears she loathed shedding. She bit back a snivel, even as Lamia lifted a hand and pressed a thumb to her right eye socket, rolling it around threateningly.

"Do you think you need this? Both of them, really? Perhaps I'll leave you one. I'll sew it open so you always have to look at me when I breed you. So you can't think of that girl of yours, that swine you like to fuck. What say you, Tanis? Do you want to shoot me with your guns now? How will you lift them?"

She pressed on the eye, slowly increasing the pressure until Tanis thought it'd pop like a grape. Lamia's talon dug into the skin beside her brow, the flesh splitting like a peach, blood streaking down Tanis's cheek and over her nose to splash down onto her T-shirt. She shuddered in her mother's grasp, the pain in her eye somehow managing to pull her attention away from her ruined arms. Lamia shoved again, the squishy orb close to bursting, white flares dotting Tanis's vision as the tension mounted.

Push. Push. Push.

Maybe she'll go too far. Accidentally kill me.

Please. Please.

Tanis groaned through the pain, trembled inside her mother's grip, when the first panicked screams echoed through the Den. Lamia's hand dropped from her face, her coils loosing and unceremoniously spilling Tanis onto the hard floor. Tanis's shoulder made first contact, the impact knocking the wind from her. She cried in agony, rolling onto her stomach, her arms useless meat to either side of her body as she inched forward, reduced to more worm than woman.

Lamia hissed and eased toward the chamber's entrance, her giant scales whispering as they coursed over the rock.

"KALLIE!" Her voice thundered out as she cocked her head to the side, listening, her nostrils flaring as she tried to smell the threat soiling her snake hole.

Tanis closed her eyes. She hurt in ways she'd never thought possible, her arms useless weights, her eye throbbing and birthing a blinding headache, but somehow, she found a smile.

They're heeere.

"What? What is this. KALLIE!" Lamia bellowed again. "ATTEND ME."

Kallie did not attend her. Lamia's guards, however, did, running down the pipe as fast as their legs would carry them.

"Men in white," one said. "Everywhere."

"What do you mean, men in white? Pig flesh? Tear them apart. Asunder. Asunder."

She slithered down the pipe after her daughters, abandoning Tanis in a heap. Tanis didn't move at first, too pained to do anything other than lie prone, but listening to the chaos just beyond Lamia's den, to the shouts and crashes and cacophony of invasion, she pulled her knees under her body, her chin perched on the ground to help keep her balance. It wasn't easy to gain her feet without her arms, but she managed it, and just in time, too. A terrified yell echoed into Lamia's chamber, telling Tanis to get out of the way or risk being run over. Her mother raced back into her room, eyes wide, face screwed up in terror as she whipped around, looking up at the thick slabs of rock forming her roof.

"Help me," she hissed at Tanis, climbing onto her stacked mattresses and straining to move the slabs that had taken a dozen daughters to place. "ATTEND ME, TANIS! *The Gorgons come for us*. We'll go... we'll make a new den. Together. Rebuild the lamias."

It wasn't funny. There was nothing funny about the situation at all. Except... well, there was, wasn't there? Lamia was in a total dither, terrified by the coming Gorgons, and—after nearly tearing Tanis's arms off—she needed help *lifting* something.

Tanis started to laugh. In some part, out of crazed acceptance that the end was *very fucking nigh* and there was nothing she could do about it. The other part, though, was utter astonishment at the suggestion that she could, should, or *would* help Lamia do anything after she'd threatened to sew her good remaining eye open and rape her.

"I wouldn't give you the steam off my shit, Ma," Tanis quipped. The blood on her face had dried, and she felt it tug at her skin when she grinned. "What am I supposed to do, anyway? Headbutt the rocks to death? You crippled me, you stupid bitch."

"Call for them. Your sisters. Make them help me. Save us. They're coming. Don't you understand, THEY'RE COMING FOR US ALL!" It was impressive that Lamia made as much progress with the stone slabs as she did, shoving them up enough to allow a foot-wide sliver of sunlight to shine down into her birthing chamber. She poked her face up at it, blinking against the brightness of the light and clawing at the stone, trying to get a better grip to shove it aside.

Tanis watched with morbid fascination.

Footsteps neared.

She would have smelled newcomers had she been breathing through her nose. She craned her head in time to see Euryale and Stheno marching up, side by side, a gaggle of their priests behind them in a wide arc, all wearing formal robes and belts. Muriel was among them, her walking stick striking the sides of the tunnel as she trudged along, Karl-the-makeshift-doctor clasping the priestess's elbow to guide her.

"Hey, ladies!' Tanis said cheerfully. She might have felt like shit, but at least this part of things was going as planned.

The Gorgons cast her a shared glance, but there was no smile to be found, only grim determination as they closed in on the frantic Lamia trying to cram her truck-sized body through a hole the size of a breadbox.

Stheno stepped forward, porcine face twisting into what must have been a smile, but it was hard to tell with the tusks and stubby teeth. "No escaping again, Lamia. Justice is here."

"Justice," her loyalists echoed, fanning out behind the Gorgon.

Stheno advanced. Lamia screeched in terror, whipping her tail around and sending the smaller god sailing into the den wall, sprawling out among the broken eggs. Euryale rushed forward with an enraged shriek, lunging for the back of Lamia's neck, her fangs sinking into the jiggling meat of Lamia's shoulder. The priests followed her lead, ants on a picnic lunch, save for blind Muriel, who stood back and waited, patiently, listening to the chaos. The priests' white robes billowed as they climbed the thrashing Lamia, weapons thrusting down over and over into her soft, blue flesh. Tanis watched dispassionately as Lamia's shoulder, breast, side, and flank all split wide, spilling blood over her sagging flesh, over her scales and onto the floor. It stained her mattresses and splashed the wall behind her. It wound around her arms in sanguine rivers that drizzled to her armpits and breasts.

"TANIS! ATTEND ME!" she howled, plucking a priest from her back and thrusting her hand into his stomach to tear out his guts. The hot, squishing mess spilled over her ham fist like ropes of sausage before he was thrown aside, insides leaking and staining his robe. Only when he lifted his head to scream did Tanis realize that it was Karl slapping at his ruined stomach, attempting to tuck his parts back into their fleshy cavern.

Cassandra's voice plucked at the strings of her memory:

"I see your death, with guts and gore. Your insides spilled across the floor. Goodbye, Karl. Goodbye, goodbye, goodbye!"

Stheno picked herself up, her dress covered in the gooey vestiges of Lamia and Luke's decimated clutch. Her eyes glowed an unearthly green as she approached Tanis's thrashing mother, her hands spreading wide, voice booming through the chamber.

"Enough of you! Enough running. Enough escaping. *Enough.* For our sister. For MEDUSA!"

Tanis stood behind the Gorgon, which is likely how she avoided the petrification stare. She felt the power, though; there was a drop in air pressure, like the calm just before a storm, followed by a coldness that blasted out in an arc from the front of Stheno's body. The magic conjured silence, silencing Lamia's shrieks, casting her in gray from her hair to her arms and breasts and all the way to the thick snake coils below. But it wasn't a complete freeze—there were hints of color at the tips of her extremities, in particular her fingers and the very tip of her tail.

Perhaps a god can't be petrified, or at least not for long.

Such was not the case for the priests who'd been climbing her, though. They were forever frozen, arms raised, faces contorted with zealous rage. They'd knowingly put themselves in harm's way without hesitation, doing the Gorgons' savage bidding with bloodthirsty glee.

The true power of the Gorgons was, perhaps, not in their magic, but in the control they held over their devotees.

Euryale slid down Lamia's stone back to find the floor. She went to her sister and took her hand, the two gazing upon their macabre work. Karl groaned behind them, but they paid him no mind. Petrification would have been a mercy in the wake of vivisection, but they did not spare him a thought.

"Call the others," Stheno said to Muriel. "Disassemble her into pieces and spread the pieces far. As far as we can take them. She will live, and eventually, she will purge the poison from her flesh, but with no legs to walk, no arms to hold, no tongue to speak, she will be a prisoner in her immortal flesh. Tell them I wish to keep her eyes, so she can look upon me and know her oppressor. Suffer long, and suffer well, Lamia. I've waited for this day."

Well. That's efficient.

Horrible, but efficient.

Good.

Tanis didn't say as much, though. The less attention she called to herself, the better.

Muriel turned and tapped her stick upon the floor, slowly making her way back to the main tunnel and out beyond. Her voice traveled through the Den, calling to the other priests, which explained the eerie quiet outside. Very soon a dozen priests appeared, all looking bruised, battered, or bloody.

Lamias aren't easy to kill.

"How many fled?" Euryale asked the frontmost priest, a lithe, Nordic-looking woman with a jagged cut in her cheek.

"Many. They are fast, but we killed the breeders, as you said."

"Good. The rest will die out without their queen. They are no matter."

The True Daughters are gone, but most of the others survived? That's better than I could have hoped.

Fuck you, Mariam.

Tanis slunk back into the shadows of the chamber, squatting to make herself as small as possible. It was, as it happened, the best seat in the house. The deconstruction started. Sledges, hammers, chainsaws—the priests came equipped. Most of the body parts snapped off clean, like stone, though some had already started to turn back to flesh, the innermost cores bleeding true. The lumps of Lamia were handed off chain gang style, down a line of worshippers that extended out through the tunnel door.

The breakdown took minutes—twenty, tops, if Tanis had to guess. Lamia's eyes were taken last, carved from her head with chisels and handed over to Stheno, who rolled them around in her palm like dice. Tanis could hear them clicking against one another despite the distance between them.

The Gorgon sisters stood shoulder to shoulder, fingers entwined, the snakes atop their heads calm for once. Euryale hummed a song Tanis had never heard before, and Stheno joined in with a harmony. It was a funeral dirge, best Tanis could tell, the melody haunting and full of despair, and they sung it through to completion, bowing their heads at the end as if they offered prayer to the dust and debris before them.

Perhaps it's a prayer for their fallen sister.

Perhaps it's a prayer to Tartarus.

They turned to walk out, together. Tanis had the fleeting hope that she'd be forgotten after Lamia's destruction, but then Karl wriggled on the floor, his bloodied hand reaching for Euryale's skirt and tugging.

"Please, my ladies. Grant me a final mercy," he gurgled, a crimson bubble spilling past his lips to soil his chin and the robe below. He was an island in a lake of blood, desperately trying to hold his intestines together. "Send me to the Elysian Fields."

Euryale smiled down at him, gently shaking him off like he was a pesky, wayward child wheedling for a snack. "Soon. Tartarus calls," she said. "Have faith."

"Finish me, please," he pleaded.

"No."

Another plea, another deflection, Euryale walking away from him. That was almost the end of it, except as Euryale went to take her sister's hand, her eye skipped over Tanis huddling in the corner. The Gorgon stared, and Tanis had the distinct impression that it was not pity for Tanis's condition, so much as curiosity and surprise that she'd lingered to see things through.

"Stheno. The betrayer is here still," Euryale said. "In the corner."

Stheno followed her sister's gaze. Tanis struggled to her feet and walked into the dim light of the ceiling lamps, her arms limp at her sides. "My mother injured me," she explained. "I didn't want to go into the fray outside useless. Guns aren't so good when you can't lift them."

Also, I wanted to see what you'd do to my mother.

Not worth dying for, but still satisfying.

The Gorgons approached. Tanis took a step back, but where would she go? Stheno could simply do to her what had been done to Lamia. And so she braced, even as the sisters drew near enough that their longest snakes could snap at her. One of Euryale's tried, looming before the Gorgon's face, but she batted it aside and it slithered back to rejoin its brethren.

"What to do with you?" Stheno said, circling around behind Tanis's back, and the hairs on Tanis's neck stood on end. A hand dipped down into Tanis's waistband and pulled out first the Glock and then the Colt. The guns were assessed and promptly dismissed. Stheno next pulled the black feather from her jeans pocket, and after a thorough examination, handed it over Tanis's shoulder to her sister. One of Stheno's snakes glided over Tanis's other shoulder at the same time, not snarling, but lazing there like Tanis had become a perch.

Euryale plucked the feather from Stheno's grasp, twisting it between her green-tinged fingers. "What is this?"

"A rooster feather," Tanis managed, but the fear was so thick in her throat, it strangled the words. She didn't know if the Gorgons' snakes afflicted the same poison as their mistresses, but with a second snake winding around her upper arm, things were not looking good.

"Why?" Euryale demanded. "Why carry it?"

"For luck."

"Ah, ah. Lesser gods again, lamia? What did I tell you about such foolishness?"

"Figured I could use every bit of luck I could get, all things considered."

Please. Please just go.

"...you would have made a good supplicant, I think. Given other circumstances."

Would have?

Oh, shit. Shit, shit, shit.

Euryale leaned in, pressing her snake face to Tanis's own, their cheeks aligned, heat to heat. "You will live on with our eternal gratitude," she whispered with her soft, sibilant voice. "You brought us justice. We honor you." The feather coursed over Tanis's neck and along her jaw. Down the column of her throat and over her upper chest to dance over the tops of her tattoos.

"If that's the case, why don't you let m—"

Euryale's claws pricked Tanis's flesh, and then they dug deep.

CHAPTER THIRTY

UNLIKE BERNIE, WHO'D gotten a diluted, minimal dose of poison, Tanis got a full hit direct from the source, which meant no lingering decay. It wasn't instant like Stheno's stare, but it didn't tarry either. First came the cold numbness settling into her feet. It coursed up to her knees. It deadened her waist and abdominal muscles and breasts and—almost mercifully—her shoulders and head. Next came the fire, the burning of fire ants biting the inside of her veins. It stung all over, needling, the sensation tearing through Tanis's body from one nerve to the next and making her twitch. Last came the drowsiness, a sleepy, leaden fog that drooped her eyelids, slowed her pulse, and made her muscles go slack.

Breathing grew laborious. Blinking was a chore.

This isn't as bad as I thought it'd be.

I'm tired. So tired.

Euryale's hand stroked Tanis's hair like she'd stroked Jefferson BMW's hair back at the manor house.

"Know your gods, little snake. Know who to fear, who to revere."

260

"No, you," Tanis rasped, her throat so dusty a thousand lakes couldn't wet it.

Tanis breathed deep, welcoming the tonnage settling into her bones and willing it to *take her away, Calgon,* but she couldn't go yet because a wretched smell rose from the floor, assaulting her nose and commanding attention. It wasn't the Den itself, though that was beyond unpleasant with the rot of broken eggs and Lamia's deplorable housekeeping. No, it was thousands of years of concentrated death; a bog of stench that hit her in the face, the likes of which she'd only encountered once before, so *of course* she laughed, which didn't sound like a laugh at all as her lungs seized up but more like a backed-up garbage disposal.

The Styx.

It's real. It was all real.

Euryale's face screwed up first in confusion and then in disbelief. It was difficult to follow her gaze—Tanis's spine had gone to rock—but she managed it over the course of a few seconds, forcing her head to dip despite an unnerving cracking sound and the sensation of dust crumbling off her skin. Shadows slinked around her's and Euryale's ankles like cats, weaving in and out, back and forth in lazy, rhythmic curves.

Stheno came to stand by her sister's side, similarly gawking at the floor and the death magic undulating below her knees.

"What is this?" she demanded.

"You promised," Tanis whispered. "You vowed..."

"Vowed to what? This is no Snake Father. What did you do, lamia?!"

Stheno reached out to clasp Tanis around the neck, squeezing, but the flesh had mostly gone to stone, so the strangulation fell short. The Gorgon yelped as the shadows grew bolder and hands—dark hands, a thousand hands made of blackness and the cold of the grave—grabbed at her body and tore at her dress, scratching at her legs and shackling her arms. Euryale was similarly afflicted, a maelstrom of magic rising and washing her body in an oily cloak.

"The Styx," Tanis managed, her throat closing, hardening, no longer allowing for words.

The Styx.

Yes, that is the last of it, then. The last from me.

"In the bottle. In her wretched bottle!" Euryale screamed just before a fat, black tendril broke from the shivering shadows to shove itself into her mouth and stifle her screams. More hands, all over, gripping her snakes and tugging at them, covering her eyes and nose in a shroud. Stheno's tusks went from white to black as the Styx swallowed her, too, her boar snout disappearing beneath a rising tide of power that not once, despite churning all around, touched Tanis.

The blackness on the floor looked like a whirlpool, like someone had filled a bathtub with ink and opened the drain. Faster it spiraled, round and round, the magic sucked into a vacuum that pulled everything in its grasp into its current, including the Gorgons. Stheno's enraged shrieks were muffled first by the power encapsulating her and then by the floor itself as she was dragged *down, down down*, not beneath Lamia's den but beneath the world, Tartarus seizing her and Euryale both.

Gone. They're gone.

Tanis wanted to relish her victory—she wanted the joy of knowing that Naree and Bee would be safe—but there was no place left inside of her for feeling. She was, as Bernie had been and countless others before them had been, stone.

And stone did not feel. It did not bleed. It did not breathe or think.

It sank. Stone sank, as Bernie had sunk.

Stillness crept over her mind. Her lungs filled but didn't drain. Her heart beat one last time. There was a fleeting image of Naree holding Bee and then the blackness came, pouring over her and spiriting her away to her ever after.

Just as a rooster crowed.

"BAH, STUPID KOULÈV. Getting yourself killed. Such a waste."

No one told her that Maman Brigitte would be in the afterlife scolding her, but then, death was the greatest mystery of them all, so who was Tanis to say if it was strange or not?

She floated in darkness, a buoy on a sea that wasn't at all cold. There was no stench of death, no River Styx or rotting bodies. No mongooses or never-ending fields of dead grass. It was a cozy little nest, her body swaddled in softness, the air smelling strangely floral with a dash of...

Tide?

Death smells like Tide?

She sniffed again, which was strange because wasn't she supposed to be non-corporeal and have no nose t—?

Yep, Tide. Tide detergent.

"Why?" Tanis managed with the mouth she didn't think she ought to have. Her voice was dry, but not like it had been after the petrification. This was plain old been-in-bed-too-long cottonmouth, not been-sucking-on-a-desert-for-six-years dry.

Someone slapped her face.

"Open your eyes, lazy. I've had enough waiting on you. Look at me."

I can't open my eyes. I—

Hey, I have eyes.

She sucked in a breath and tasted salty, coastal air. She smiled. Then she smiled more, because she had lungs, and a face, and in discovering she had a face, she could force open her eyes, blinking at the rude light stabbing at her retinas. The world was too bright for someone who'd been bathed in darkness, and she lifted her arm to her shield herself, understanding, as the back of her hand collided with her cheek, that she had arms—and better than that, those arms *worked*.

I'm not dead.

I'm not dead.

I'm not dead.

I'M NOT FUCKING DEAD!

"How?" she asked, rolling her head toward Maman's voice. There, a foot away, seated on a stool beside an antique end-table, was the lwa herself. Her braids were tucked back into a kerchief at the nape of her neck. Big gold hoop earrings, a big gold necklace with a fat amethyst wrapped at the end. She'd lined her eyes with canary yellow and painted her lips red. Her dress was green and yellow gingham check, the belt at her waist...

Distended. Hugely distended.

Tanis stared.

"There you are. You see now, koulèv, why I help you, yes? Maman gives you her feather and tells Papa he can't have you yet." Maman stretched out to run a wet cloth over Tanis's face and hair. That Tanis was in a bed, a blanket tucked around her waist, in a room with white wallpaper printed with baby pink roses, registered at about the same time as the baby in Maman's gut registered.

"Is it mine?" she demanded.

"My old man, he does not make the babies so easy. Death is not good at creating life. But strong koulèvs? They got twice the cock and twice the spunk. And here it is, three days? So fast. He's thriving already!" Maman cackled and leaned back in her chair, wringing out her washcloth in the basin beside the bed.

"*He.*"

I have a son.

She used me as stud.

She also saved my life.

Tanis frowned, but Maman didn't appear to care.

"So the good news first. You will recover. Stiff a while, but that will pass. Papa nearly had you to the gates before I laid my claim. He's sour I stole you, but I promised him a favor to make it up to him. Consider this the last time I can deny him, ya? Don't be stupid with the life have left." Maman reached out to pinch Tanis's bicep. Tanis winced, and Maman snickered. "Good sign that you can feel pain. When you first got here, I kept stabbing your toes with pins but you never flinched. I knew you'd pull through when you kicked me for it yesterday. Now this. It's good, it's all good."

All good.

Yes.

Sure it is.

"What's the bad news?" Tanis asked, unsure of how to feel. Relieved that she was alive, certainly, and grateful that

Maman had wrestled her away from her husband's clutches, yes. But she'd been used and she'd been tricked and now there were two mothers of her children instead of one and that was confusing, especially when you'd just nearly died thanks to a Gorgon curse.

This week is balls.

"Ah, the bad. I am lwa. You are not. Our boy will be mine and mine alone. This is probably not kind, but no one said lwa were kind. Perhaps saving your life sapped the last of my good will." Maman drizzled herself across her chair and tilted her head back, luxuriating in the cold air spewed out by the air conditioner in the window. "I forgot how hot women get while carrying. This is agony."

And then she said something in a language Tanis didn't understand.

"Am I in New Orleans?" Tanis asked, trying to sit up and discovering that was beyond her capabilities at the moment. Her back felt stiff, her legs like lead. She settled for rolling onto her side and resting her weight on her elbow.

"Yes."

"How did I get here?"

"That is for Maman to know and the little koulèv to wonder." Maman had her eyes closed, but she smiled all the same, her hand moving to her middle to rub. "He is kicking. Legs, not snake. This is good."

Yeah, that's great.

"And I've been here for how long?"

"Three days. Four? Renaud will be glad you are gone soon. Double the cocks means double the piss and his grandmother was born in this bed." That likely should have embarrassed Tanis more than it did, but her mind was too busy racing. If Barbara had Tanis's phone and Naree called it, she might have told Naree Tanis had died, or that she didn't know what had happened to her, inside the Den. And with Tanis plucked from death's door and relocated three states away from her last known location...

"Relax. My goodness, you are wound tight. You would think

it is the petrification, but you are just like this, aren't you?" Maman grunted and pushed herself to standing, waddling her way to the door with her arms pressed to the small of her back. "Renaud!" she called out, her voice booming through the house. "Send them! Koulèv is finally awake. Warn the girl that the koulèv's breath is like alligator farts."

Tanis frowned and cupped her hand around her mouth, blowing into it. It was, indeed, rank, and alligator farts didn't seem that far off the mark.

"Send who?" She reached for a glass of water beside the bed, not caring who it belonged to, and downed the contents, immediately feeling better.

"Them." Maman winked. "You told her to call Poul Mwen, ya? She called. When she heard you were here, she came the next morning. She is a good girl. I did not tell her our little secret." Her voice dropped to a conspiratorial whisper as she stroked her swollen stomach. "That is for us to know."

And with that, Maman lumbered down the hall, taking Tanis's second baby with her.

Tanis ran her hands down her face, grinding the heels of her palms into her eyes. The right eye was still tender from Lamia's abuse, but it was bearable, and she slumped back into her pillows and watched the door, waiting. Her nostrils flared, looking for scent and catching it—that sweet, familiar signature, laced with Skittles and Coca Cola. She swallowed a sob.

Naree wasn't so restrained. She cried as she climbed the house stairs and cried all the way to the spare room. She stopped in the doorway and stared at Tanis, tears running down her face, the baby awake and alert in her arms. Naree's glasses were on, her hair up on top of her head, her brow and neck dotted with sweat. She wore her purple NOLA T-shirt and a pair of teeny, tiny cut-off shorts; Tanis was surprised her labia weren't hanging out.

"Baby. You okay? You were gray. You were so gray." Naree rushed over to her bedside, smooshing herself against Tanis's chest as she blubbered, Bee sandwiched between their bodies. Tanis stroked her best girl's hair and whispered into her ear, reassuring her best she could because that was infinitely better than joining her in weep-fest. The baby let out an aggrieved squawk, and Tanis scooped her up and adjusted her, making sure her delicate neck was supported as she laid Bee out across her chest, the round little face pushed up against the side of her breast.

"Boob pillow," she said quietly, and Naree giggled, leaning in to place a string of kisses across Tanis's brow.

"You stink," she announced, and Tanis swatted her hip, her hand sliding around to her back and under her shirt to stroke her spine.

So soft. So familiar.

So mine.

"Yeah, I do. Like alligator farts, Maman said."

"I like her."

"I knew you would."

Naree pulled the chair as close to the bed as it would go and sat, her fingers clasping Tanis's. "They thought you'd die. You were practically black when I got here. I called the next day, like you said, and Renaud told me what had happened and to come right away. I flew down that night. There were people here—I don't know, like a coven or something—and they were taking shifts watching you. There was chanting and candles and... it was beautiful. I didn't understand any of it, but it was beautiful."

"That's vodou. It *is* beautiful." Tanis smiled and nuzzled at Bee's dark head. "How pissed were your parents that you left again so soon?"

"Furious," Naree admitted, her free hand stroking Bee's back and then rising to tangle itself in Tanis's hair. Her fingers massaged circles across Tanis's scalp. "But they'll get over it. I did promise we'd go home for Christmas, though." She paused. "All three of us. And I told them if they couldn't deal with me being a big fat dyke, they won't get to see their grandkid. Funny how quick that changed their song."

"Maybe they'll try to send us to one of those queer people reform jails." Tanis settled back into her pillow and let herself be soothed by the weight of her daughter on her chest and Naree's gentle stroking. She hadn't realized exactly how tired she was, but the little energy she'd expended had already taken its toll.

Being petrified is ass.

"You look exhausted," Naree said quietly.

"I am. It's been... it's sucked."

"Your mother?"

"Dead."

"I figured as much." Tanis cracked an eye to peer at Naree, and Naree shrugged. "Maman's got a set of eyeballs in a jar that watch you when you walk into the room. It's totally creepy. She said they were Lamia's, so I figured that was a good sign you'd won."

Maman took Ma's eyes.

...she took them when she came to get me.

Tanis cracked a grin and she laughed, her chest aching, but it was worth it, oh, it was worth it. She squeezed her hand around Naree's, careful not to press too hard, and Naree rewarded her by leaning in to kiss her on the mouth.

She crinkled her nose as her face hovered above Tanis's. "I hate to say it, but she's right. It's totally alligator farts."

Tanis smiled and pressed her lips to her nose. "Totally."

ACKNOWLEDGEMENTS

PUTTING A BOOK together is rarely a solo effort. I'm lost without friends, family, and a solid publishing team steering my ship into port. *Snake Eyes* is no different in that regard; it was adrift until a bunch of greater, more normal people anchored me so I could get it done.

David, Becky, Lauren, Greg, Eric—you're my lifelines and make getting out of bed every day worth it. I love you.

Mom and Drew—thank you for the love and support through all my ups and downs. Maybe one day I'll write a not-weird book. Probably not? But maybe. Hold onto hope.

Mike Condon—I love you. You're a fun, smart, awesome dude and a great dad. I wouldn't be as okay with who I am today if I hadn't looked to your example. This book is, truly, for you.

TS—twinsie. I adore you. You got me started down the right path in publishing and a little part of you is in every story.

Miriam—you're my favorite person a lot more than you realize. You're some parts agent, some parts therapist, some parts rock star and I appreciate you.

Dave Moore—thanks for giving me this opportunity. You, Jon, and Rebellion are an awesome team to work with. I had so much fun putting this together.

Evie Nelson—you make my words so much prettier, girl. You're like a walking, talking tube of lipstick. Like Revlon, only for words. That's meant to be flattering, I promise.

My LGBTQ+ Community—this is the first book I started and finished, front to back, after I'd stopped waffling at the closet door and walked out completely. You're friends and inspirations. You're brave and wonderful and so many of you make the world a better place. Live, love, laugh when you can. Stay strong. Stay proud.

I know I'm missing folks—beta readers of yore, vidya game friends, author friends, my social media buddies— but to name you all would take pages I don't have. Know that if I love you, talk to you, if I interact with you, if you ever made me smile, you make my books possible.

Much love and peace.

H

ABOUT THE AUTHOR

HILLARY MONAHAN IS a *New York Times* bestselling author creeping around south shore Massachusetts with her trusty basset hound sidekick. She writes scary stuff and funny stuff and kissing stuff, for adults and teens alike. Her pseudonym, Eva Darrows, is responsible for the critically-acclaimed *The Awesome* from Ravenstone, and the forthcoming *Dead Little Mean Girl* from Harlequin Teen in spring of 2017. She often spews opinions on Twitter under the handle @HillaryMonahan.